Pay Off

Pay Off

Stephen Leather

LARGE PRINT
Oxford

First published in Great Britain 1987
by
Fontana

Published in Large Print 2007 by ISIS Publishing Ltd.,
7 Centremead, Osney Mead, Oxford OX2 0ES
by arrangement with
Hodder & Stoughton, a division of Hodder Headline

British Library Cataloguing in Publication Data
Leather, Stephen
 Pay off. – Large print ed.
 1. Drug traffic – Fiction
 2. Revenge – Fiction
 3. Suspense fiction
 4. Large type books
 I. Title
 823.9'14 [F]

ISBN 978–0–7531–7962–8 (hb)
ISBN 978–0–7531–7963–5 (pb)

Printed and bound in Great Britain by
T. J. International Ltd., Padstow, Cornwall

For Zita

PART ONE

Only a mother could have loved the bearded, brooding face of Get-Up McKinley. Only someone with vast amounts of maternal instinct to draw on, who'd changed his nappy and breastfed him through countless sleepless nights, could have seen him as anything other than a nasty piece of work, mean, moody and malevolent. But even McKinley's own mother would have been wary of this glowering man-mountain whose face matched the grainy picture in the newspaper cutting I'd folded and unfolded time and time again in a succession of East End pubs, until the newsprint was grimy and smeared and I'd had to repair its tattered edges with Sellotape.

I'd watched him over the top of my chipped glass, studied his reflection in the mirror behind the crowded gantry, and walked close by him to the toilet. I was sure it was him long before I heard the acne-ridden young barman call him by name.

McKinley was standing in the professional drinker's pose, his feet shoulder width apart, his knees locked, his left hand resting on the beer-stained bar while the right held his glass, elbow crooked and parallel to the ground, the whisky emptied down the throat with a flick of the wrist, an economy of movement that a conjuror would have envied.

How do you describe six feet four inches of grizzly bear in a green corduroy jacket? I guess that's a good start, but you'd also need to throw in a few simple adjectives like big and ugly, and try to get across the barely-suppressed aggression of the man. McKinley was angry, very angry, and I couldn't take my eyes off the hand on the bar which was clenching and unclenching like a rattlesnake about to strike.

I'd spent three long weeks sniffing at McKinley's trail, but I was in no position to speak to him, not yet. Give me an asbestos suit and a couple of SAS-trained bodyguards and maybe I'd have been brave enough to approach him. Maybe, but don't hold your breath. McKinley wasn't in a particularly receptive frame of mind just then.

The source of his displeasure was a couple of young drunks, neither good-hearted nor bad, just boisterous and rowdy, leather-jacketed, flush with drink and youth. The taller of the two had twice knocked McKinley's drinking arm, the second time hard enough to spill his drink. Not deliberate, you understand, but that wasn't the point, not as far as McKinley was concerned, anyway.

There's an elaborate procedure to be followed when you spill somebody's drink, and it depends on the sort of pub you're in. If it happens in one of the trendy Fulham wine bars you smile politely and say how awfully sorry you are, OK yah? And you joke and it's forgotten. In your average suburban pub you apologize and offer to buy another, an offer which is always refused, and it's relaxed and friendly. If it happens in an inner-city drinking den, the sort of men-only places you find in Glasgow, Birmingham, Liverpool and the East End of London, anywhere the unemployment rate is high and the black economy booming, then the politeness is exaggerated, the apologies ritualistic, just in case the drunk you're dealing with is a dangerous drunk.

"Are you all right?"

"Aye."

"Are you sure?"

"Aye."

"Can I get you another?"

"Aye."

We were in Kelly's Bar in Leyton, and it's fair to say that it isn't my normal sort of London drinking establishment; no ice or lemon to go in my G and T, overflowing ashtrays, one underworked barman paid for by the YTS who was doing nothing to quieten the two rowdies as he gave a few half-washed pint mugs a casual wipe with a grubby cloth and placed a full bottle of lemonade on the bar, just out of McKinley's reach. No, my sort of place was about six miles or so due west, in the City or the West End, where they know the difference between a Wallbanger and a Sloe Comfortable Screw, where you need a collar and tie to get in and a full wallet to enjoy yourself, where noisy drunks don't bump into dangerous drunks and trouble is nipped in the bud.

Everyone called McKinley Get-Up because of an unfortunate incident that happened almost seven years ago, seven years which he'd spent in Wormwood Scrubs cooped up with prisoners who went to a lot of trouble to be nice to him.

At the age of twenty-nine he'd found his vocation as a bodyguard-cum-thug protecting a wholesale drugs dealer who arranged for heroin and cocaine to be brought in from Amsterdam, Ireland, or America, anywhere he could get it, and mixed it with talc or sugar or whatever white powder was floating about before selling it on to smaller dealers.

It was cash and carry and the seventy-five per cent profit margin was more than enough to pay McKinley a decent wage. His downfall came when the drugs dealer decided to branch out and put up the money for an armed robbery.

Three up and coming young villains had made him an offer he hadn't wanted to refuse. If he put up two thousand pounds for the shotguns, the getaway car and other expenses, he would be in for half of whatever they got from the superstore in Hackney they'd been casing for the best part of two weeks, and they reckoned the take could be as high as £65,000.

The three geniuses behind the plan were Alvin Miller, Dick Wallace and Charlie Leonard, three ne'er-do-wells whose combined IQ was less than the tube fare from Clapham Common to Clapham South.

They'd already done over a couple of filling stations and a post office with flick knives and hatchets, but the money had been frittered away. Now they reckoned they were ready for the Big Time, but for that they needed a stake. Ronnie Laing, McKinley's boss, was just the man to help three youngsters along the path to riches. For a price.

Laing slipped them the cash in used notes in a brown envelope and waited. Three days later Miller phoned to say that the job was off. Leonard had all but lost his leg slipping off a ladder while decorating his mum's front room. He was in hospital, in pain and no way was the job going ahead with just the two of them. A hundred and eighty pounds was left in the kitty and Ronnie was welcome to that and the three sawn-off shotguns.

No chance, said Laing. Get someone else or all three of you will have broken legs. Like who? asked Miller. Like McKinley, said Laing, and now I'm in for sixty per cent of the action.

Twenty-four hours later McKinley, Miller and Wallace were sitting in a four-year-old Rover with Miller's brother Tommy acting as driver, going over the plan for the last time. All three would go in carrying holdalls, put a few things in wire baskets, use three separate check-outs and then pull out the shooters. Miller would fire his, they'd get the girls to empty their cash registers while Wallace got the manager to empty his safe in the office. Simple. They'd already gone through it three times for McKinley as he sat in the back seat, his shotgun dwarfed by the fingernail-bitten hands in his lap.

They moved. Miller went in first, Wallace second. McKinley counted to fifty and followed. All the blue-handled wire baskets had gone so he grabbed a trolley and pushed. One of the rear wheels was sticking and it squeaked sideways along the tiled floor as he wandered down past the cereals picking up packets of Cornflakes and Frosties. He threw in a tin of dog food — he'd always wanted a dog — and by the time he got to the check-out Miller and Wallace were waiting, fuming silently. McKinley frowned an apology and Miller nodded twice. All three threw off their woolly caps, pulled down their stocking masks and brought out the guns. Miller pointed his at the ceiling and pulled the trigger. The noise was deafening, bits of the plasterboard ceiling fell around him in a cloud, sticking to his stocking like pieces of tissue paper to a cut chin.

"Right, get down on the floor. Now!" he yelled, but nobody moved. One of the young girls sitting in front of a cash register started to cry quietly. The manager came out of his office, stopped and raised his hands above his head. Still nobody moved. The fire sprinklers came on, a shower of cold water washed the pieces of plasterboard from Miller's stocking mask and a trickle ran down the back of his neck. A couple of the girls held plastic bags over their heads and watched him anxiously.

"Down on the floor. Everybody down on the floor. Now," he screamed and fired the gun again. This time everyone moved. "Oh Jesus, no. Get up, McKinley! Get up!"

They were all caught five minutes later in the carpark by a passing plain clothes police car packed with armed Flying Squad detectives just about to go off duty.

McKinley didn't fare too badly in court. His gun hadn't been loaded; Miller and Wallace reckoned he'd have sawn the wrong end off his shotgun given the chance and there was no way they were going to let him loose with a loaded gun. That, coupled with a surprising lack of previous convictions, kept the sentence down and he was out in seven years with a criminal record and a nickname that stuck.

A bit thinner now than he looked in the newspaper photograph, taken as he had left the Old Bailey handcuffed between two beefy police officers, McKinley was scowling in much the same way.

Eventually his patience snapped and he turned to his right, banging his glass down hard on the bar.

"Why don't you two twats just piss off?" he thundered, but he didn't wait for an answer, just drew back his massive fist and smacked the shorter one in the mouth, sending him spinning and staggering across the bar, blood streaming from his splattered lips.

His friend took a step back and put his hand inside his leather jacket, bringing out what looked to be a butcher's knife wrapped in cardboard which he stripped off to reveal a polished steel blade. McKinley seemed not to notice and pulled back his fist again.

I thought the sound of the lemonade bottle in the barman's hand would have made much more noise when it connected with the back of McKinley's head, but it didn't smash or even crack, it just went "thunk" and McKinley's legs folded up like a collapsing deck-chair and he slumped to the floor. The two lads decided that discretion was the better part of valour and made for the door.

"Are you going to bar him?" I asked the barman as together we helped the unconscious McKinley to an empty seat by the gents.

"Are you joking?" he replied. "Would you try to stop him coming in? Besides, he was provoked. McKinley's OK so long as he's left alone."

The sleeping giant began growling and I didn't want to be around when he woke up with a sore head, so I said I'd be back and walked out into the cold night air. One down, three to go.

Killers come in many forms. The old man going too fast in a car and mowing down a child on a zebra crossing. The thug with a knife who wants your wallet and doesn't care what he does to get it. The pensioner who can't stand to see his wife suffering from incurable arthritis any more and pushes a pillow against her face. The soldier firing his gun in the heat of battle.

The poisoner, the strangler, the axe murderer. There are men you can hire to kill, men who'll beat in a man's skull for a few hundred pounds. There are men whom you'll never meet, who will kill for a six-figure sum paid into a Swiss bank account, half in advance, half on completion. The world is full of killers, and so are the prisons.

Me, I could never take a life. My father took me when I was twelve years old to his brother's grouse moor near Inverness and helped me to fire his favourite twelve bore, rubbing my shoulder better when it hurt, kidding me for missing, not knowing that I didn't want to hurt the birds or his feelings and pretending to be in pain was the only way to save both.

I guess he understood because the next time he tried was when I was fifteen, but I hadn't changed and this time I was old enough to tell him so, to tell him that blasting birds with shotguns wasn't my idea of fun and what was the point of raising birds just to shoot them out of the air and honest, father, I'd really rather not. It did hurt him, I know, but he didn't say anything and the guns went back to his study and he never took them out of the guncase other than to clean them from that day on.

He was of the old school, my father, huntin', shootin' and fishin', until a riding accident put paid to all but the fishing. Even that pleasure caused him pain, standing thigh high in fast flowing freezing water flicking flies at salmon, and his orthopaedic surgeon told him more than once that it was doing him no good. Humbug, my father told him, fishing and work are the only pleasures I've got left and I'm damned if you're going to take either away from me. He reckoned that the only good advice the surgeon ever gave him was to lie on the floor if the pain got too bad. It seemed to work and I'd often go into his study and find him lying on his back with his ebony stick by his side, reading one of his leather-bound books or going over a balance sheet, Bach playing on the stereo.

I'd sit by him and he would explain things like share-holders' funds, liabilities and provisions, loan capital; and by the time I was fourteen I could read a balance sheet and profit and loss account like a comic, understanding how a company operated just by looking at the figures. I was hooked faster than a careless salmon, which is exactly what he'd intended, because he had my career mapped out from the time I was born and there was no way on God's earth that I wasn't going to end up in my uncle's merchant bank.

He was a gentle man, and a gentleman, and other than where foxes, grouse and salmon were concerned he lacked the killer instinct. I was the same. I might not have inherited his passion for country pursuits but he had taught me to be honourable in business, never to cheat or lie, and to feel guilty if I broke any of his rules and now that was holding me back, and I had to find a killer because I knew I wouldn't be able to do the job myself.

Killers come in many forms but I wanted a professional, a mercenary. I'd arranged for a newsagent near my flat in Earl's Court to get me a copy of *Professional Soldier* magazine. It took him two weeks to get hold of it, and by the time he gave it to me it was a month out of date. It's one of the few places where mercenaries actually advertise their services between pages devoted to a thousand and one ways of killing silently and what's new in portable rocket launchers. You can buy everything you need to start or fight a war through the adverts in *Professional Soldier*, from jungle clothing and survival rations to the latest military hardware. You can also buy men. I picked out three possibilities and circled them in blue Biro.

SAS-trained small-arms expert requires work, distance no object. Experience in explosives, anti-tank combat and hand-to-hand. Box No. 156.

Have gun, will travel. Does anyone out there need a combat vet who wants a piece of the action? London based. Box No. 324

Ex-para needs work. Anything considered. Box No. 512

I wrote the same letter to all three, telling them that I had an interesting proposition to put to them, that I'd pay well and that they were to phone me at the flat if they were interested. I stuck the envelopes down, put on first-class stamps and walked down the two flights of stairs to the street and put them in the nearest post box. The first call came two weeks later from mercenary number one, the SAS expert.

"You the man with an interesting proposition?" asked a rough Liverpool accent. "This is Box 156."

"You've got the right number," I said. "Who are you?"

"First things first. What's the job, where is it and how much are you paying?"

"I'd rather meet you first, then we can go over the details."

"When and where?"

"The American Bar at the Savoy Hotel, Wednesday lunchtime, say half past one. How will I recognize you?"

"You won't. I'll find you. Carry a copy of *The Times*."

"I imagine most of the people in the Savoy would be reading *The Times*. Make it the *Mirror*. I'll be wearing a dark blue suit and a red tie and I'll be sitting at the bar."

"I'll be there."

Wednesday at one o'clock, I got out of a taxi on the Strand and walked past the Savoy Taylors Guild to the huge canopy that marks the entrance to the Savoy. Across the road stonecleaners were scouring the dirt off the National Westminster Bank, and a thin film of white dust settled on my shoes. Porters in the Savoy's green and yellow livery were loading calfskin suitcases into a blue Daimler, while a suntanned executive sorted through his wallet. All were covered in white flecks of dust.

The foyer was almost deserted, so at least my friend Box 156 wouldn't have any trouble recognizing me. I dropped the *Mirror* onto the bar and asked for a Tamdhu as I slipped onto the stool. Caricatures of Liza Minelli, Lauren Bacall, Ginger Rogers, Fred Astaire and Greta Garbo, all by Almud Bonhorst, glared down at me from the walls and I raised my glass to them. I was proud to be performing in front of Hollywood's finest.

I spotted him as soon as he walked into the bar. He was impossible to miss: close cropped hair, a camouflage combat jacket and scruffy jeans. The boots were cherry red. He walked with his feet splayed outward, hands thrust deep into the pockets of his jacket as his head jerked left and right like a startled rabbit. Somehow I'd managed to lumber myself with a twenty-four carat headbanger, and if the only thing identifying me had been a copy of *The Times* I could have got rid of it and played innocent, but I was labelled as clearly as a jar of Nescafé at Sainsburys. Not only was I the only man in the Savoy carrying a copy of the *Mirror* and wearing a blue suit and red tie, but I was also the only person in the bar. All that was missing was a large neon sign above my head flashing the word "sucker". Hell, hell, hell.

"You the man with the mission?" he asked from six feet away. No, son, I'm the Avon lady. The barman's eyebrows shot up like clay pigeons, his chin dropped and my stomach turned over. Hell, hell, hell, should I bluff or run?

"Could be," I said. "What can I get you?"

"Guinness, a pint. And a packet of crisps. Salt and vinegar." The drink he got, the crisps were off. I took him over to a table by the baby grand piano where he could nibble at the stuffed olives and not be within earshot of the barman.

"So what are you up to?" he asked, a piece of olive stuck firmly in the gap between his front teeth. I leant back in the decidedly uncomfortable chair, crossed my legs and narrowed my eyes. Bluff or run? No question about it. I might as well enjoy myself.

"First things first," I said. "Have you been in action before?" He looked uncomfortable, shifting in his seat and rubbing his boots together.

"Not as such, no, but I spent four years with an SAS territorial regiment, trained with them in Wales, live firing, explosives, the works."

"Parachuting?"

"Some."

"Freefall?"

"No, but I made four static line jumps."

"That'll be a problem, the job I'm setting up requires a HALO from twenty thousand feet with full kit, at night. And there could be enemy fire."

"Jesus, what are you planning?"

"I'm not planning anything, the planning has already been done. I'm just handling the recruitment. Two hundred men, hand-picked, for the Sultan of a small but very rich country out in the Middle East. Or more accurately the brother of the Sultan who wants to take over. There's a lot of money at stake because the country is swimming in oil. Our team will be freefalling in from a couple of Hercules and splitting into three sections, taking out the palace, the oil fields and the communication systems.

"The whole mission should take less than twelve hours, and we'll be taking no prisoners, on either side. In fact that's one of the stipulations of the job. A suicide pill will be placed inside a fake tooth. The Sultan's brother can't afford to have anything go wrong with the attack, and if it does he wants to make sure there's nobody around to tell tales. And the sort of money he's paying he's entitled to expect that."

By now the young "SAS expert" was sweating and his cheeks were flushed. It was difficult to tell if it was

16

the thought of having a dentist's drill in his mouth or swallowing poison or the Savoy's chair which was causing him the most distress. Hell, if he swallowed this story he'd swallow anything, the tooth, the poison, even the chair.

"We're going in with bazookas, mobile missile launchers, grenades, the works. It should be one hell of a war. And if, I mean when, we take over there's a good chance we'll be kept on as the new Sultan's bodyguard, unless the cunning old bastard tries some sort of double cross.

"He'll also be looking for help on the interrogation side afterwards. It seems the present Sultan has been tucking away hundreds of millions of dollars in bank accounts all around the world and our employer would obviously like to know where the money is. I hope you've got a strong stomach, it's liable to get a bit messy."

I don't know what the guy was looking for, cheap thrills, hard experience to beef up his part-time toy soldiering or what, but my Arabian tales had put the wind up him and no mistake. He'd stopped chewing on the stuffed olives and most of his pint was untouched.

"Well, I'm your man," he said, and neither of us believed him for a moment. I took a few details from him, told him I'd be in touch and off he went into the wide blue yonder, a first-class prat and a second-class time-waster. I wanted a killer and I'd turned up a pussycat.

I never did hear from the *Have gun, will travel* vet. Maybe it was a joke, maybe he was lying bleeding to death on some far-off battlefield I couldn't pronounce in a month of Remembrance Sundays, or crouching in ambush high in the hills of Afghanistan, maybe I've just got an overactive imagination, who knows? I never found out, anyway.

The ex-para got in touch two days after the headbanger. Quiet, confident, no messing about. His name was Jim Iwanek, he'd left the Paras eighteen months ago and had been working as a bodyguard for a casino operator until recently. Where could we meet? I wasn't superstitious so the Savoy seemed as good a place as any. He agreed. "I'm about five-eleven, short black curly hair and I'll have on a brown check sports jacket," he said, like a policeman giving evidence from his notebook. "I look forward to meeting you."

He was bang on time and just as he'd described. OK, he missed out the brown cord trousers, the brown brogues, the crisp white shirt and the light brown tie, but who's counting? I went over and introduced myself, bought him a double Teachers and took him to the table by the piano.

There was another thing he hadn't mentioned, his eyes. They were blue, a cold blue, difficult to read until maybe it was too late. Eyes that looked me over, measuring me up, calculating distances and angles, eyes that could just as easily work out twenty-four different ways of killing me bare-handed as they could spot a lie before it left my lips. You can tell a lot from a man's eyes: if he's lying, how he'll react to stress, sometimes even what he's thinking. Iwanek's eyes were as cold and hard as ice daggers and he hardly blinked as he crossed

18

his legs, smoothed out the creases in his trousers and asked me what it was I was offering.

I took a sip of my whisky. He hadn't touched his. "I'm thirty-two years old and I am what's called a corporate financier, a sort of merchant banker without a bank. I help arrange bank loans, company takeovers, share flotations, that sort of thing. Sometimes I act as a company doctor, find out where a firm is going wrong, why it's losing money, suggest a remedy. I make a lot of money doing what I do because I do it well, very well. I'm an expert and in the City I'm a survivor. More than that, I'm a winner. But I have a problem, a big problem, and it's one that I can't cope with on my own."

Iwanek hadn't moved while I talked, but I knew I was being measured up, assessed, and labelled as either truthful or not to be trusted.

He leant back in his chair and steepled his fingers under his broad chin. His hands were smooth with long, delicate fingers and perfect, well-manicured nails. A stainless steel watch peeped out of his left sleeve as he gently tapped his two index fingers against his upper lip and looked into my soul.

"I've been wronged, badly wronged, and I'm out for revenge. Two men have done me a grave injustice, just how bad I can't tell you and maybe I never will but they deserve what's coming to them. You'll have to trust me on that score.

"One is a drugs dealer and property developer with very nasty criminal connections and a stack of dangerous friends. The other is one of his associates, a

19

business man of sorts, a whizz kid who's acting as a front for the other guy's money.

"If these guys had crossed me in the City, if it had been business, then I could have coped on my own, I could have fought back. If they'd broken the law I could have gone to the police, or sued, but they were far too clever for that."

"What did they do?" he asked.

"I can't tell you that. I just need your help, and I'm prepared to pay for it. And to pay well."

"You want them killed," he said, and it was a statement, not a question.

"I want them dead, or put away for a long time. And I don't want to be directly involved. I have a conscience, Jim, a set of values that was drilled into me from a very early age so no, I couldn't point a gun at either of them and pull the trigger."

"You want someone else to do your dirty work." Another statement.

"Yes, but not in the way you think. Sure, I could go into any of a dozen pubs in the East End, spend a little money and have their legs broken, maybe even killed. What would it cost me, a few hundred pounds? I could do that, but I couldn't live with myself afterwards. All my time working in the City I've been honest, I've never doublecrossed anybody or deliberately hurt them. My word is my bond might sound corny in this day and age but that's what my father taught me and those are the values that I've stuck to. I can't betray him or myself, and I won't even try."

"It's not corny, but it puts you in a very difficult position. Maybe an impossible position. You want two men dead yet you're going around saying 'thou shalt not kill' like some pious prophet. Either put up or shut up, you can't have it both ways. And if it's an assassin you want then you've got the wrong man. I've killed, but in battle and that's a whole different ball game. It's one thing to run down a Falklands hill firing at men trying to kill you, it's another to sneak up and shoot someone in the back of the neck. Soldiers have standards, too, and backshooting isn't one of them." He started to get up, but I held out my hand and motioned him to sit down.

"You don't understand, just hear me out." He settled back in the chair but there was a tenseness about him, an unease that was making both of us uncomfortable.

"One of the things I do best is to lay down strategies, to calculate how people will react in certain situations. To gauge the reactions of directors and shareholders, to anticipate the actions and reactions of others and to plan accordingly.

"I have a plan, a set of actions which, if I put them into effect, will give me the result I'm looking for. I think I can get my revenge without pulling the trigger or paying someone to do it for me."

"A set up," he said. "You're going to set them up." He was smiling now.

"Yes, and for that I'm going to need help, people with skills I don't have. It's the same in business. You need advice, you bring in a consultant, you pay him to provide the services and knowledge you don't have

21

yourself. It works with computers, marketing, public relations, so why shouldn't it work for me? I need expertise which you have and I'm willing to pay for it."

I leant forward and looked into the ice blue eyes. "I'm not going to lie to you and say that I'm putting all my cards on the table. You're smart enough to know that I'll be keeping a couple of aces up my sleeve and probably a joker, too.

"I'm going to set these two creeps up to be knocked down, and I need your help. At some point I'm going to get involved with drugs dealers and I need someone who can handle a gun, someone who is obviously prepared to use it. I'm virtually certain that you won't have to fire it and I'm damn sure you won't have to kill anyone, but I have to have someone who looks the part. And of course it'll be useful to have someone who isn't afraid to shoot just in case anything goes wrong. Are you in?"

"I'm in," he said.

"I don't know when I'll be going ahead but from start to finish the whole operation should take less than a month. I think I'll need you for two days, and I'm willing to pay you five thousand pounds. What I propose to do is to give you a retainer of a thousand, a show of good faith on my part. When I know I'm ready I'll give you a further thousand and the balance on completion. When I ring I'll need you right away, so if you're taking on anything else make sure you can leave at short notice, like immediately." I took out a brown envelope from my inside jacket pocket and handed it to him. He didn't even bother to count the twenty pound notes inside. I passed him a card and asked him to write down a number where he could be contacted, any hour day or night.

"You're forgetting something," he said. I raised my eyebrows. "The gun," he said.

"I assumed you could provide that."

"You assumed right, but we have to decide what we're going to use and you're going to have to pay for it."

"What do you suggest, something small?"

"No. You want to show we mean business so you want something impressive. If you're going to kill it doesn't matter what it looks like so long as it does the job. If you mean what you say about not wanting to kill then you want something threatening. That's why so many villains use sawn-off shotguns. OK, I know you can get them without individual licences and the shot can't be identified, but at the end of the day they're used because they look so bloody big and menacing.

"Look down the barrels of a sawn-off twelve bore and you're guaranteed to piss yourself. Yet when you actually fire one they do little serious damage unless you're right up close. The shot spreads out all over the place, painful and uncomfortable but usually they don't do too much damage beyond a range of twenty feet."

"That sounds fine by me — can you get one?"

"Sure — but it'll cost you — another four hundred pounds."

I handed him the cash from my wallet. "Look after it until I call you."

"I'll be ready — and waiting. And don't forget, the retainer only holds me for one month." He stood up to go, holding out his hand. I shook it firmly.

"Jim, it's been a pleasure doing business with you." Two down, two to go.

Highway robbery they used to call it, when a guy dressed in black astride a huge sweaty horse pointed a blunderbuss at stagecoach drivers and yelled "stand and deliver". It was easy money in days of yore, no police, no street lights, no problem. The only thing that could go wrong was the coach driver plucking up enough courage to draw a weapon and fight back. It didn't happen much. Even Get-Up McKinley could have made a go of it way back then. Things have changed, though.

Nowadays there is a much more profitable form of highway robbery, stealing cars. McKinley wasn't bright enough to break into a car and get the engine started without a key — hell's bells, he'd taken his driving test eight times — but there are hundreds of men and women around who make a nice living stealing cars.

Best profits are made at the luxury end of the market, the same as selling them legally. To make a profit selling Ford Escorts you need a high turnover, with Jaguars and Rolls-Royces you only have to get rid of a few a week to live well. Car thieves know that, so it's only the joyriders and youngsters who steal anything worth less than £10,000. The professionals stick to the classier models.

It's easy money, too. Step one, take an advance order from South Africa, Hong Kong, Australia, anywhere where they drive on the left is best. It's not too vital, though. If some Saudi prince wants to jump the queue for a Rolls it will be his chauffeur who'll be driving, so he's not going to be too bothered about which side the steering wheel is on. Step two, select your car. In London that's no great problem: stand in the Strand with your eyes shut and throw a spanner — chances are that it will bounce off a Porsche or a Rolls or a BMW. Find the car you want and break in, then drive it to the sort of garage where nobody is going to ask any awkward questions. That's the difficult part over.

The next step is to open the bonnet and get the chassis, frame and vehicle identification numbers and stroll along to any main Post Office and fill in Form V62 — it'll set you back all of two pounds. You'll have to sign a declaration that the original registration document hasn't been passed on by the previous owner or been lost, destroyed, mutilated or accidentally defaced. OK, so strictly speaking you are telling a lie but then you did steal the car in the first place so that shouldn't keep you awake at night.

Two weeks later, three at the most, your new registration documents arrive from DVLC Swansea — isn't new technology wonderful? They handle more than a thousand of the V62 forms every week and they don't bother checking — they haven't the time or the resources.

You, sir, are now the proud owner of a luxury car complete with relevant documents. Drive it into a crate or container and deliver it to the nearest docks. Simple. It's big business — in Britain alone a car is stolen every six minutes and never recovered. Right now Scotland Yard's C10 Stolen Vehicle Investigation Branch is looking internationally for more than twelve hundred Mercedes, a thousand Jaguars, two hundred and fifty Porsches and a hundred Rolls-Royces. They've more chance of finding Lord Lucan than of turning them up.

The hardest part of the whole operation is actually getting inside the car, and for that you need a professional. I don't know how to do it, you probably don't, you need someone with experience, someone who can deal with central locking systems, and who won't panic when a policeman taps him on the shoulder and says, "Having trouble getting into your car, sir? Can I be of help?"

The trouble is car thieves don't advertise, you only hear about the amateurs who get caught and appear in the magistrates' courts, and I wasn't after an amateur.

I'd rented a lock-up garage a couple of hundred yards from my flat, and the morning after I'd met Iwanek in the Savoy I picked up the keys off the lounge table and walked down the two flights of stairs and into the early sun. It was a short walk to the garage and I unlocked the up-and-over door and went inside, pulling it closed behind me.

I switched on the light and it gleamed off a brand new red Porsche 911, well, almost brand new, anyway. I'd bought it nine months ago as a present to myself after handling the flotation of a local radio station. The fee I earned for placing the shares on the Unlisted

Securities Market was more than enough to pay for the Porsche, and what the hell, you only live once. That was before my mother died in a car accident, though; that had taken most of the pleasure out of driving.

In the corner was a second-hand blue and white Honda 70cc that I'd picked up for £120 through an advert in the London *Standard*, and a full set of mechanics' tools that had set me back five times that figure. I took off my pullover and jeans and slipped on a pair of brand new green overalls and got down to what I knew was going to be several days of hard work.

It took me a full day to get the head off the engine, and two hours to mangle the insides of the cylinders and give it the sort of treatment it wouldn't have had with twenty-five years of constant use — Mr Porsche would have cried his eyes out, and to be honest I felt pretty bad at ruining one of the best cars I'd ever driven.

A Porsche mechanic could have done the job a lot quicker but that would have been like asking a plastic surgeon to amputate a leg, and besides, no mechanic in his right mind would cripple a car without wondering why. It took me another day and a half to put the bits back together again; I only went back to the flat to eat and sleep and I eventually emerged from the garage with an aching back, my skin and hair dirty and oily and my hands covered in cuts and bruises, but the Porsche was well and truly knackered.

Back in the flat, after showering and throwing away the stained overalls, I rang up a Porsche dealer and asked for the price of a new engine. Ouch. I spent the next week driving around as many backstreet garages as I could find, tucked away in unfashionable mews, hidden under railway arches and behind blocks of rundown flats in areas which were in no danger of ever becoming gentrified.

Most of the mechanics just sucked their teeth and said they couldn't even begin to tackle a masterpiece of Teutonic engineering that was obviously on its last legs, several suggested I tried a Porsche dealer and a couple quoted a price which wasn't far off the official cost and told me it would take weeks, if not months, to get a new engine.

Eventually I struck gold. His name was Bert Cook and his lock-up garage in Camden wasn't much bigger than mine. He was bent over a yellow Jag which had seen better times when I drove up, and he waited until the Porsche juddered to a halt before he came over, rubbing greasy hands on a piece of grey cloth hanging out of his overall pocket.

"Sounds rough," he said, rubbing his pencil-thin moustache below a mottled, bulbous nose. "Very rough. Cylinders are definitely on their way out, you're kicking out a lot of smoke." He wiped his nose on the greasy cloth.

"Performance is right down, too," I said. "It used to kick you in the pants when you put your foot down, but now it's worse than a twelve-year-old Cortina. Haven't had it that long either."

"Should still be under warranty, then?" he said, putting the cloth back in his pocket, grease smeared over his nose.

I tried to look sheepish, a guilty schoolboy caught with his pockets full of stolen apples. "I'd rather get it done on the QT, actually."

"Ah," he sighed, and winked. "I get your drift. Well, I might be able to help. Hang on while I make a call."

He busied off to the back of his lock-up, keen to help now that he reckoned he knew the score. When somebody wants to pay good money to fix a car that's still under warranty that can mean only one thing. And if he thought my pride and joy was stolen, who was I to put him right?

He came back after five minutes, a grin on his oil-stained face. Bert just happened to have a friend who had a friend who could get me a complete Porsche engine for half the price the dealer had wanted, including fitting, no questions asked.

"Have to be a cash deal, though," he said. "You bring her in Saturday morning and she'll be back with you by Sunday night." I tried to look relieved and grateful, shook Bert by the greasy hand and drove back to Earl's Court and parked my battered Porsche.

An hour later I was back in Camden, this time on the Honda in a massive black anorak, red crash helmet and yellow plastic trousers, a clipboard pinned to the handle-bars, just one of the hundreds of would-be cabbies doing the Knowledge in London.

It was four o'clock, Thursday afternoon, and if Bert wanted my Porsche in on Saturday morning the chances were that he'd be going off for the engine tonight or tomorrow. I felt lucky, and an hour after I arrived back at his garage he locked up and walked over to a battered red pick-up. I was about a hundred yards down the road so he didn't hear me start up the bike. He pulled out from the pavement, grey smoke belching from the exhaust, and I followed as he turned into Camden High Street and down past Euston Station and its throngs of home-going commuters.

There was no problem at all in keeping up with him, in the rush hour traffic the Honda was much faster than his truck and it was so distinctive I could hang well back.

He drove through Bloomsbury, and before long we were over the Thames and heading for Battersea. I felt luckier and fifteen minutes later he pulled up in front of another lock-up garage, much the same as his own except this one had the legend "Kleen Karparts" above the brown-painted twin doors.

Bert wiped his nose again on the dirty cloth and sounded his horn three times. A door opened and he disappeared inside. Kleen Karparts was in the middle of a row of small businesses, a bathroom shop with suites for £199, a bookmakers, three or four shops with shutters down and "For Sale" signs up and a couple which were open for business but with nothing in the windows to give a clue as to what they sold.

At the end of the road was a narrow passage which led to a muddy track behind the backyards of the shops. Karparts was fourth from the end and set into the wall there was a weatherbeaten door painted the same dirty brown as the front entrance. The door had warped badly and by pressing against it I could get a pretty clear view of what was going on inside.

A man wearing dark blue overalls and a welding visor was cutting away at what appeared to be a brand new Mercedes, and as I watched he pulled away the rear wing in a clatter of metal. At the front of the car a young lad, sixteen or seventeen at the most, was using a winch to take out the engine. There were two or three other cars in the back yard in various stages of being stripped, and one of them looked like a Porsche, but as there was virtually just a chassis left it was difficult to tell. Lying around were piles of electric wiring, headlamps, carbs, bumpers, enough parts to build yourself several complete cars if only you could work out how to put them back together again.

Another youth came into view, small and dark and wearing a black leather motorcycle jacket, laughing with Bert who was wiping his nose yet again. They walked up to the man in the welding visor who had now moved over to the driver's side. He noticed the two of them, switched off his cylinders and pulled away his visor revealing a crop of purple hair and three gold earrings in one ear.

"Dinah," said Bert. "How's it going?"

"Triffic," replied Dinah as he pulled at his virgin ear. "Should have these done by tonight and then I'll start cutting up the chassis for scrap. I can't strip them fast enough, we've done two Mercs this week and I've got a backlog of orders for Jags, BMWs, the lot. I might even have to go legit."

"I bet," said Bert. "The Porsche ready?"

"It's inside. Can I do you for anything else, body panels, lights, windows?"

"No thanks, Dinah, just the engine, that's all I need for this job. I'll tell you what, though. I'm going to be needing a rear axle for a Merc 500 SL some time in the next couple of weeks, maybe a gearbox too. I'll give you a bell."

"Consider it done, there's always a market for Merc parts. Not the easiest cars to get hold of, though, but I'm working on it."

"Yes, well, you know what they say, Dinah, practice makes perfect, and when it comes to getting hold of cars there's no one getting more practice than you."

"Nice of you to say so, Bert, but I'm still not going to give you a discount. Harry, give Bert a hand with the Porsche engine and for God's sake count the money first." He reached up and pulled the visor down and turned back to the Mercedes, laughing as the two men walked back towards the garage.

I crept back down the passage and waited at the entrance to the road until the two men came into view, pushing a mobile winch which they used to load what seemed to be a brand new engine onto Bert's pick-up. He pulled himself into the driver's cab, started it with a shudder and drove off, smoke still pouring from the rusty exhaust.

There was a pub opposite Karparts, a run-down drinking man's den, the varnish on the windows cracking with age and the rough-cast stained where rainwater had flooded down from a blocked gutter. I stripped off my waterproof gear and pushed it into the carrier on the back of the bike and walked inside the gloomy bar.

The ex-boxer of a barman asked, "What can I get you, chief?" and I paid for a whisky and sat at a creaky circular table circa 1950 in the corner facing the door. Twenty minutes later Dinah came in, his overalls swapped for jeans and a grubby green sweater which clashed perfectly with his purple hair. With him were the two youngsters from Karparts, and Dinah brought out a wad of five-pound notes from his back pocket to pay for a round. At the back of the pub was a pool table and after a few minutes Dinah's companions walked over, pushed in two ten-pence pieces and started to play. I picked up my glass and went over to Dinah, sitting alone at the bar.

"How's it going, Dinah?" I asked.

He turned from his glass and looked me up and down. "Do I know you?" he asked.

"Not yet, Dinah, but you will, you will. I need a car and I think you're just the chap to help me get it."

He shook his head. "Try a garage, mate — I deal in parts and spares."

"Second-hand parts by the look of it, and most of them hot enough to cook sausages on."

"What are you getting at? You the law?"

"Do I look like the police?"

"As a matter of fact you do. Sod off and leave me alone."

"Look, Dinah, the fact that I'm here talking to you in the pub and not bursting into your yard with a search warrant should prove to you that I'm not a cop, but if you want I could give them a ring. I think they'd be fascinated to hear about the operation you're running over there. Pays well does it?"

"What operation? What do you think I am, a surgeon?"

"Of sorts, Dinah, of sorts. How did you get a name like Dinah in the first place? Parents expecting a girl, were they?"

The change of subject took him by surprise and his mouth hung open in amazement. "My name's Maurice, Maurice Dancer —"

"I don't believe it," I said interrupting. "Maurice Dancer? Somebody in your family must have had a sense of humour. Had a tough time at school did you?"

He shrugged. "Yeah, I guess so. For a while, anyway, then Maurice was shortened to Mo and then I got the car bug and got stuck with the nickname Dyna-Mo and that got shortened to Dinah. What's it to you, anyway?"

"I just want a chat, Dinah, that's all. Let me get you another. What are you having?"

"Bitter, a pint."

"OK."

"And a double whisky."

"Expensive tastes, Dinah, can you afford them?"

"If you're paying, I don't have to. Get us a meat pie as well, hey? I haven't eaten today."

I bought Dinah his supper, and we went over to the corner table where I watched his two mates scuffing the pool table and spilling lager down the pockets as Dinah attacked his pie and drank his whisky in two swallows.

"What's your game?" he asked finally, brushing crumbs onto the floor and picking up his beer.

"As I said, Dinah, I need a car, and I think you're just the man to get it for me."

"But I've already told you that selling cars isn't my game."

"Dinah, I'm not stupid. I know exactly what your game is. And it's not Subbuteo."

"What are you getting at?" he asked, and started tearing a soggy beermat into tiny pieces, flicking them into a dirty ashtray.

"Dinah, it's simple. You're a car thief, and I presume you're a good one. Your yard over the road is packed with parts you've taken from almost new cars, you steal them and strip anything of value. The chassis and any other identifiable bits you probably sell for scrap. Am I right?"

He said nothing, his eyes fixed on the table, fingers busy destroying the wet cardboard.

He obviously wasn't going to reply, so I continued. Maurice Dancer, this is your life. "It's virtually the perfect crime. The only risk is when you actually take the car away, and the way you look you'd probably be able to claim it was a first offence and that all you were doing was taking it for a joyride, officer, and you're very sorry but it won't happen again, your honour, because you're the product of a broken home and an uncaring Government and you'll get nothing worse than a few months' probation.

"But underneath that ludicrous purple hair I reckon there's a brain a bit too smart to be caught red-handed. Am I right?"

He looked up and smiled, showing crooked teeth. "Maybe. Maybe you are. But I still don't know what you want from me."

"You asked me what your operation is, Dinah. Well, I think you're making a nice living selling bits of cars that would cost an arm and a leg if you bought them honestly. Luxury cars, the Rollers, the Mercs, the Porsches, cars where you're talking three figures for a spare wheel and four for an engine.

"You supply a need, Dinah, like all good entrepreneurs. You sell parts, no questions asked, to cut-price mechanics. They get the spares they need, you get a roll of fivers in your back pocket. Everyone's happy, the only loser is the guy whose car you've knicked and he'll be able to claim on his insurance.

"The beauty of the scheme is that once you've taken the cars apart all the evidence is gone, it's virtually impossible to trace things like axles, body panels, windscreens and lights. And once you've changed the numbers, selling an engine is no problem. I like it, Dinah, I like it a lot. If a business like yours qualified for the Business Expansion Scheme, you'd have investors queuing up halfway round the block."

"I haven't stolen a car from you, have I?" asked Dinah, realization breaking across his face like an early dawn.

"No, Dinah, you haven't."

"Thank God for that. That's been a nightmare of mine for years, that one day somebody will tap me on the shoulder and ask for their motor back before plastering me all over the wall. There's some very dodgy people driving Rollers, you know?"

"You don't have to tell me, Dinah. Now listen. I want you to steal a car for me. Two cars to be precise, a Merc and a Rolls."

"No sooner done than said. Any particular colour?"

"Not just a particular colour, I want two particular cars. And I don't want to keep them." His eyes brightened. "And I don't want you to strip them, either, so you can forget any thoughts you had on that score. I want to borrow them and return them so that no one is any the wiser."

"You planning a robbery or something? If you are you can count me out. I'll steal cars, sure, but that's as far as I go."

Villains are like that, each to their own. They specialize and are usually reluctant to operate in territory they're unfamiliar with. They might progress upwards through the criminal hierarchy, acquiring new skills, but at no point would a safeblower get involved with a fraudster, or vice versa. Dinah would no more consider taking part in a robbery, no matter how far removed he was, than a solicitor would think about extracting a tooth.

"No, Dinah, I'm not planning a robbery, but I'm not prepared to tell you why I need the motors. What I am prepared to do is to offer you a thousand a car, half in advance. Then, when I'm ready, I want you to break into the Rolls and wire it so that I can drive it. I'll use it for a couple of days and then I want it put back in perfect condition. The Merc's a different matter. All I want you to do there is to open the boot and relock it. That's all you have to do, Dinah, and I'll pay you two grand."

"Mine's a pint, and you're on."

I got Dinah his pint from the bar and stood it in front of him along with the half-inch thick brown envelope I'd been carrying in my inside pocket.

"One other thing, Dinah. This buys your silence as well. Don't let your two pals in on the act, no subcontracting. I'm paying for you. And I want a telephone number where I can reach you. The job will be at short notice, very short notice. It could be any time within the next three or four weeks. Just be ready."

He wrote a telephone number on a scrap of paper and raised his glass. "To a long and profitable partnership," he said.

"No, Dinah, to a short and profitable one. Make no mistake, this is a one-off job, there'll be no repeat fees. I'll be in touch."

Back outside, I pulled on the waterproofs and crash helmet and drove back to Earl's Court where I dumped them with the bike behind a busy service station and walked to the flat. Three down, one to go.

I'd gone to a lot of trouble to find Dinah but it had been worth it, and now I had three in the bag and all I needed to complete the set was a woman. Not just any woman but one who would sleep with a man for money, and do a few other extra little tasks for me. Got it in one, I was after a prostitute, but the last thing I wanted was a woman who looked like a whore. That would have been a dead giveaway, like using a plastic maggot to catch a wily old pike. No, what I needed was something luscious, a tasty morsel that the old predator would fall for hook, line and sinker.

Bleached hair, heavily rouged cheeks and thick eyeliner were out, she'd have to be young, intelligent and enthusiastic, but a professional. The sort of girl you'd be happy to see marry your brother, if you had a brother and if he was the marrying kind. My brother, David, isn't. And he never will be.

So, step one, find your whore. That didn't appear to be a major problem, they're not hard to find in a big city. Or in a small town come to that. In Glasgow you'll find them around Blythswood Square, huddling on street corners waiting for a lift to the nearest multi-storey carpark where lusts are satisfied, almost, for as little as ten pounds. Birmingham, Manchester, Bristol, they've all got their red light areas, and what the hell I was in London which has more whores per head of population than anywhere else in Britain. One of the growth industries, servicing the foreign tourists and visiting businessmen.

There was no way I was going to go kerb crawling around St Pancras or walking through Soho on the off chance that I'd bump into the perfect pro to complete my gang of four. The only thing I'd pick up that way was an infectious disease. Doctor, doctor, I think I've got Hermes. Don't you mean Herpes? No, I think I'm a carrier. I'd been lucky getting Iwanek so I was pretty impressed with the power of advertising. At a local newsagent, not the one who'd got me *Professional*

Soldier, I picked up a couple of guides to what's on in London and also managed to find a contact magazine, "Middle-aged executive with own house and understanding wife seeks young blonde with big breasts for friendship with a view to unnatural sex", you know the sort of thing.

The contact magazine was worse than useless and went straight in the bin. One of the London guides had a series of adverts for massage parlours and private masseurs that looked more promising, some of them offering a rub down in private apartments, discipline in your own home, a few were even in Arabic.

Five seemed hopeful, three in the West End, one in the City and another south of the Thames. I rang them all and the Kennington number was answered by a man so that was a definite non starter. The other four sounded like the same girl, a treacly deep voice, stroking the back of my neck and tickling me under the chin, all could fit me in, when did I want to come round, what was my name, they looked forward to seeing me.

Despite the personal nature of the adverts the three in the West End were all massage parlours, the only privacy was in the form of tiny cubicles and a production line of girls in bikinis and sweat, cold eyes and warm hands. I didn't bother revealing I was a reporter, I just left.

The girl in the City turned out to be five feet four, long blonde hair and blue eyes and living on the tenth floor of one of the tower blocks in the Barbican complex. She was in her late thirties with a good figure that was starting to go and small lines around her eyes that crinkled as she smiled but threatened to become deep ravines within a few years. But she was bright and warm and fun despite being ten years older than I needed so I stayed for an hour and left her flat feeling a lot better than when I'd arrived. I'd paid her fifty pounds in advance, but as I went I gave her another ten pounds and I couldn't help smiling and nodding when she asked if she'd see me again. I was getting soft, but then I hadn't been too hard to start with. I decided to go up to Pitlochry to see David.

Shona picked me up at Edinburgh Airport and drove me the seventy miles to Shankland Hall in her Rover, or rather our Rover as it was leased to our company, Scottish Corporate Advisors. Shona and I had met at St Andrew's University, but while I cut my financial teeth in my uncle's merchant bank after getting a lower second-class degree, she pocketed a first with no trouble at all and went off to work for the stockbrokers Wood Mackenzie in Edinburgh in their research department, specializing in the retail sector, followed by a spell examining the inner workings of the gilt-edged market. When I decided to set up on my own she leapt at the chance of joining me. I was lucky to get her and now we were partners, equal partners.

As she settled back in the driving seat of the Rover she looked more like an aerobics instructor in one of the plusher dance studios, bright pink tracksuit, white tennis shoes and her long dark hair tied back in a pony tail with a pink ribbon. She looked about seventeen.

But put her in a dark two-piece suit and she'd more than hold her own in any boardroom, big brown bedroom eyes or not. One very, very clever lady and she wasn't spoiled one iota by the fact that she knew it. I just wished she wouldn't keep teasing me about her superior degree, but that was a small price to pay.

She powered us past a removals lorry before turning and asking, "How's the Big Smoke?"

"Big," I said. "And smokey. How's business?"

"How do you think? You've been away for almost a month and the cracks are starting to show."

"You're a big girl, you can handle it." She could, too, and the little girl lost act wasn't fooling anyone. She relished the opportunity of showing what she could do on her own.

"Do you want a rundown on what's happening?" She asked.

"No, Shona, not just now. Later."

"Damn you, when are you coming back to work?"

I rested my hand on her knee but she jerked it away angrily. "Soon," I said. "I only need a few more weeks, maybe a month."

"It's been almost three months and that's time enough for grieving. Getting back into harness would be the best thing for you."

"Yes, doctor."

"I mean it."

"I know you do. I'll be back soon, I promise. How's David?"

"Missing you. Wants to know when he can live with you again. He keeps asking if you're dead, too. Don't leave him there too long — he panics. So do I." Then she smiled to herself and pressed the accelerator hard to the floor. Little girl lost, indeed.

"They're looking after him all right?"

"Of course they are," she replied with a toss of her pony tail. "They're professionals, and the sort of money you're paying reflects that. The food's better than I'm getting. I'm thinking of taking a few of our clients there instead of to the North British. The service is probably better, too."

She spent the rest of the drive filling me in on business, whether or not I wanted to hear. I had other things on my mind but I listened with half an ear, nodded when she asked if I agreed with the way she was handling things and offered her a few words of advice. She was doing fine.

We pulled into the gravelled drive which curved in front of the grey stone building that was Shankland Hall only two hours after I'd landed at Edinburgh. Originally built as the private residence of a wealthy tobacco baron who decided to devote his retirement to the pursuit of country pastimes, it had been sold to pay off death duties just after the Second World War and was now one of the best, and most expensive, private nursing homes north of the border. Tucked away in a sheltered valley to the east of Pitlochry it's a case of out of sight, out of mind for many of the residents, dumped there by uncaring relatives with money to spare. In David's case, though, it was a temporary home, he wouldn't be there long. I hoped.

He was waiting at the top of the stone steps leading to the large oak double doors, holding the arm of a nurse in a dazzlingly white starched uniform. He was jumping up and down with excitement and waving with his free hand. My daft brother.

As I got out of the car he left the nurse and ran down the steps to grab me around the neck, and he squeezed me so tight that I couldn't breathe. "Missed you, missed you, missed you, missed you," he whispered into my ear. "Don't go, don't go, don't go."

"It's all right," I gasped, and reached behind my neck to unclasp his hands. I held them in front of me and looked into his brown eyes which were starting to fill with tears. "It's all right, I'm here."

A tear rolled down his plump cheek, dripped off his round chin and onto his blue linen trousers. David's my younger brother, my only brother, and he's nineteen years old. The only difference between David and you, me and the Duke of Edinburgh is that David was born with one extra chromosome in each of his cells, a tiny amount of genetic material that's enough to throw his whole body out of kilter and produce a baby that will never, ever, grow up to be "normal".

It happens in something like one out of every 660 births and they used to call them Mongols and now they call it Down's Syndrome but David is David and that's all there is to it. The doctors keep measuring his IQ and coming up with numbers between sixty and seventy which is bright for a Down's Syndrome adult but so low as to deny him a life on his own, not that he'd want one.

44

He is happy, most of the time, and fun and affectionate and occasionally flashes of intuition would come shining through like a lighthouse beam slicing through fog.

Then he'd spoil it by trying to eat his soup with a fork and laugh because he knew full well what he was doing — teasing me. He'd hug me and ask me to promise never to leave him and I'd say I wouldn't ever leave him for good and that he was safe with me. My daft brother.

"Go and say hello to Shona," I said and pushed him away.

He rushed over to Shona and grabbed her from behind as she locked up the Rover, picked her off the ground and gave her a bear hug that made her gasp.

"Put me down, David," she laughed. "You're hurting." But he wasn't, he knew his own strength and he knew by the way Shona was laughing that she was enjoying it. He giggled and put her down, seized her hand and then pulled her over to me and caught mine, linking the three of us together.

"All for one," he shouted.

"And one for all," we chorused. It was his favourite joke, but it was more than that, it bound us together and he knew that he could depend on us both.

Now he was laughing and giggling and squeezing my hand tight, swinging it back and forth. He'd been at Shankland Hall for about three months now, since the day after the funeral, and it wasn't doing him any good, I could see that.

His eyes flicked nervously from face to face, eager to please and anxious not to offend. Even Shona's visits weren't enough and she was getting to see him every couple of days, but he wouldn't be right until he was back in a house with me, knowing that I'd be home every night and there to read to him before he fell asleep.

"Come on, David," I said. "Let's go for a walk. Shona has to see the sister."

"Man talk," he giggled and released Shona's hand. As we walked down the drive and over the close-cropped lawn he kept turning back to look at her like a spaniel being taken away from his owner, but the tight grip on my hand showed that he was glad to be with me.

The lawns sloped down to a string of trees, an oak, a sprinkling of silver birch and a line of conifers marking the path of a stream that meandered across the estate.

David sat with his back against the oak, scratching like a cat while I lay on the ground beside him, picking tufts of grass and shredding them, staining my fingers bright green. It was a fresh, clean day, the sort of day for a picnic, a day for playing football or for just lying by a stream tickling trout. "Shoes off," I yelled and helped him pull off his big black boots and roll up his trouser legs. I followed suit and we were soon up to our knees in the cold, sparkling water.

David stomped and splashed and got us both so wet we were in line for a row from the sister when we got back. He soon tired me out and I dragged him over to a large, dry rock in the middle of the stream and we sat there with our feet dangling in the water.

He draped his arm across my shoulders and rested the top of his head against my neck, breathing deeply as if he were fast asleep. His legs were swinging gently, making slow whirlpools in the stream and he was humming quietly to himself, a tuneless tune with no structure, no pattern. I began talking, he loved to be talked to, following the rhythm of speech even when he couldn't always grasp the meaning. Empathy rather than understanding.

"I've run into a problem, David," I said. "I found Get-Up McKinley easily enough — I told you I would. It took me a couple of weeks to track him down and make friends with him but now he's on the payroll part-time. Sometimes he drives me about and sometimes I use him as a minder. It's his first steady job in a long time. Oh, and I found out why he's called Get-Up."

I told him the story of how the unfortunate McKinley got lumbered with his nickname and he giggled, kicking water over me.

"I've found a good man with a gun, too. His name's Iwanek and he's one of the paratroopers who fought in the Falklands but now he's out of the army and he's been working as a bodyguard. I'm going to have to be very careful with him, he's very clever and very fit, if he decides to turn against me or to go it alone then I really will have problems."

David looked worried and his grip tightened so I added quickly, "Don't worry, I know what I'm doing, you know how carefully I've planned all this. Nothing can or will go wrong." He relaxed again. "Iwanek is providing his own gun and I'm going to give him a call when everything's set up.

"The car thief was easy, too. His name's Dinah, that's short for Dyna-Mo, and he's the strangest looking young man you could imagine. Remember those punks we saw when we went shopping in Princess Street before Christmas?" He nodded excitedly. "Well, he wears clothes like them, a black leather jacket with shiny chains and scruffy jeans with holes and tears. And his hair is purple and spikey and he's got three gold earrings in one ear, like a pirate. But he's bright and there's nothing he doesn't know about cars and let's face it, who'd believe that a purple-haired punk was a top car thief?"

"Not me," he laughed. "He sounds fun."

"Funny he is, but I'm not so sure about him being fun. He takes his work seriously and he's made a lot of money without ever getting caught. He's the least of our worries because we only have to use him twice and he has no way of knowing what he's getting involved in. And I know enough about him to make sure that he won't talk to anyone else about the deal.

"So I'm three-quarters of the way there, David, but I'm having trouble getting hold of a suitable girl."

"Like Shona," he said, suddenly serious and frowning slightly, forehead furrowed as he looked into my eyes, almost nose to nose, his hot breath on my lips. "She's nice."

"Shona's too nice, you daft brush. We want a woman of easy virtue, a high class lady of the night who'll charm her way into Ronnie Laing's pants and lead him astray. She's got to be pretty, witty and fun but hard enough to cope with a villain like Laing. And we've got to be able to trust her completely. She's a vital part of the plan, David, but I can't find her. The sort of girl we're after doesn't walk the streets and she doesn't have to advertise. What am I going to do?"

The question was rhetorical but David took it seriously, he shrugged and tilted his head from side to side like a budgie gazing at its reflection in a mirror. He was biting his lower lip with his uneven teeth, his face pained with concentration as he tried to help, feet now unmoving in the rushing water.

"Don't look so serious," I chided, and ruffled his hair. "I'll think of something. It's going to be all right. Trust me."

Eventually he spoke, slowly and with a great deal of concentration. "Tony like girls, you told me," he said, eyes wide open, head tilted back, proud because maybe he'd found the solution.

Tony had come to stay with us three months ago, before I'd gone down south, and he'd delighted David with his stories of life in London and his visits to the Middle East and suddenly I realized what he was getting at. "Sometimes you amaze me!" I yelled and dragged him to his feet and hugged him hard.

"Come on, back to the house, last one there's a cissy — and whatever you do don't blame me for your wet clothes."

I scooped up our shoes and socks as he rushed off and I held back to let him win. We were both out of breath and panting when we reached Shona who was leaning against the Rover, smiling and waving. "Having fun?" she shouted.

"Yes, yes, yes, yes," chanted David. She helped him on with his shoes and socks and we went in for tea. Afterwards, as Shona and I drove away from Shankland Hall, I watched him waving goodbye from the top of the steps, still holding hands with the nurse, and even from the end of the drive I could see he was saying "Don't go" over and over again.

"Sometimes he amazes me," I said to no one in particular.

"Who?" she asked.

"David," I said. "My daft brother."

She drove in silence, handling the car expertly in and out of the twisting bends back towards Edinburgh.

"I have to go back to London. Tonight," I said and winced inwardly as her face fell.

"No, you don't," she answered and flicked her pony tail in annoyance. "I meant what I said about the cracks starting to show. I've got a couple of big headaches and I need your help."

"Tell me," I said, prepared to be convinced.

"The main one concerns Crest Electronics. I'm having trouble convincing them that they should go ahead with their employee share ownership scheme. They know they can afford it, they know the benefits it'll bring, and I've trotted out all the old arguments until I'm blue in the face. They've got one foot poised over the edge, they just have to be persuaded to take the plunge. I think you'd swing the balance. Will you stay?"

I couldn't help but smile. "Yes, I'll stay. You knew I would."

"I hoped."

"One day," I said. "One day is all I can spare. Then I have to get back to London." Tony could wait twenty-four hours.

"Agreed," she said, and drove me to her Edinburgh flat where we spent the night, together but apart.

Shona and I had made the unspoken decision years ago not to get involved. Friends yes, lovers no. People who knew us as a pair found it hard to believe that it was possible for us to work so closely together and to perform as well as we did as a team without going to bed.

We'd never talked about it but it came to a head a couple of months after we'd set up Scottish Corporate Advisors, and were spending the night in a hotel in Aberdeen after helping an up-and-coming diving firm negotiate a six-figure loan from the Clydesdale Bank.

We'd booked separate rooms but we were so high on the adrenaline of a job well done that we spent most of the evening at Gerards, a top class restaurant, not just for the food and drink but for the sheer pleasure of each other's company, basking in the glow of mutual success. We were talking and laughing and touching as the waiters waited patiently to close up for the night, and then we reached the point where our eyes met and the air was thick and time stopped and we either had to take it further or kill it.

I can still remember the moment as we both silently came to the same conclusion, and we smiled and Shona shook her head slowly. What we had was too important, too special, too precious, to risk spoiling. It would follow a pattern that could end with us losing everything. I read it in a book once, one of Stephen King's I think, but I can't remember which one. "First it was love," he wrote, "then it was like love, and then it was over." Becoming lovers would have given it a beginning, a middle and an end, and I didn't want ever not to know Shona.

I guess what we had now was love without being lovers. And we had the business. We knew we were heading for the top, together but apart.

We were in the office bright and early going through the newspapers.

It's surprising just how much business you can pick up that way, from profiles of businessmen on the way up, recruitment advertisements pointing to a firm expanding and maybe in need of new capital, rumours of multinationals moving into Scotland to take advantage of Scottish Development Agency incentives and the twenty per cent unemployment rate, all were opportunities waiting to be grasped.

I ploughed through the *Glasgow Herald* while Shona read the *Scotsman*. Glasgow and Edinburgh are separated by a forty-minute train ride but they're poles apart, and nowhere is that more reflected than in their newspapers. Neither is a true national newspaper, they are far too parochial for that. There's hardly any overlap in circulation, which has led to both becoming complacent in their newsgathering, each maintaining only a token presence in the other's camp. There's no competition because a Glaswegian would no more think of buying the *Scotsman* than he would of giving up his seat to a lady on the bus. Equally, if you see a copy of the *Herald* in the capital then it was probably brought over by a passenger on the early morning train, and he was almost certainly riding in the first-class compartment. But any Scottish businessman worth his salt reads both.

My sortie down south had cut me off from much of the Scottish news, which always gets a poor showing in the English papers and London-based television. It's a different country, no doubt about it.

The people from Crest arrived at ten, there were three of them carrying identical black briefcases, middle-aged men starting to thicken around the waist after too many expense account lunches and too many hours at their desks.

Normally Shona and I tried to meet our clients on their home ground, it puts them at ease, but they'd wanted to get away from their factory for a few hours.

It was a doddle. Shona had been right; the three of them, the managing director, his deputy, and the financial director, all knew what they wanted, their minds were already made up. All they wanted was to be told what clever chaps they were and to have their egos massaged. By both of us.

I'm in two minds about employee share schemes. Its supporters will tell you that it gives the workforce an interest in their company as well as an incentive to keep the firm on a healthy profits curve. It's supposed to cut down absenteeism, reduce strikes, slash wastage and probably cure the common cold.

I suppose I'd better explain how it works. A company agrees to set aside a proportion of its profits, usually above a certain limit which it sets itself, and it converts the cash into shares which it then divides among the workforce according to salary, length of service and so on. Some of the country's biggest firms do it — ICI has one of the longest running and they reckon it's a great success. Me, I'm a cynic. I reckon most employees prefer a cash bonus to the shares and anyway it usually ends up getting pissed against a wall. And there's a lot to be said for working for one company and holding shares in a competitor — that way if your employer goes bust you don't lose your savings as well. Still, we were getting a very healthy fee from Crest for setting up their scheme, so who am I to knock it?

Crest Electronics is one of the Scottish new wave companies, non-union, full of earnest young men and women grateful to have a job and keen to work long and hard for the good of the firm. They'd have been right at home in Japan, in fact it was the land of the rising yen that had saved many of them from the dole queue. The Japanese had set up a few assembly plants in Scotland along with their American counterparts, and before long they'd created the so-called Silicon Glen, and anybody who was anybody, Motorola, IBM,

National Semiconductor, had to be represented north of the border. Soon the big boys were investing millions in wafer fabrication facilities to churn out tailor-made silicon chips, and there was a golden opportunity for local entrepreneurs to get in on the act, supplying services and components.

But unlike Aberdeen, where the locals were quick to make a killing by ripping off the oil industry, the Scots were slow to exploit the sunrise industries, with one or two notable exceptions.

Crest is one of those exceptions, manufacturing things like circuit boards and electronic bits and bobs that I couldn't begin to understand. Profits had risen through the roof and they'd be going public before long, assuming the bubble didn't burst.

They wanted to share their good fortune with the work-force and Scottish Corporate Advisors was more than pleased to help.

There were a few minor creases to be ironed out, and they'd wanted to redo their profit forecasts in the light of a pick-up in advance orders, but they left after an hour and a half eager to tell the workers the good news at the next daily industrial liaison discussion circle, or maybe they'd interrupt the lunchtime aerobics class. Whatever, our five-figure fee would be in the post.

"You didn't really need me today," I told Shona as she drove me to the airport.

"Don't you believe it," she said. "They aren't the only clients who are getting edgy because you're not around. We're not a one-man band, we're a team. When we bill them it's on the basis that they're getting both of us, our combined experience and skills, not just mine. Your presence convinces them that they're getting their money's worth." The voice hardened, it had an edge that I didn't like, I'd heard her use it on bolshy carpark attendants and unhelpful shop assistants. On a good day she could use it to slice cheese. "Let's be honest, you're not pulling your weight. For the moment I can handle it, but not for much longer."

Message received, Shona, loud and clear, don't rub it in. "I'll be back soon, I promise. Three weeks maximum. Cross my heart."

She nodded curtly and didn't say another word until she dropped me at the airport and kissed me on the cheek. "Be careful," was all she said before driving off. At least she didn't say "Don't go."

The first time I met Tony Walker was more of a head-on collision than a meeting. We were both after a small meat processing firm in Paisley, outside Glasgow. It did little more than take in carcases at one end and throw out plastic-packaged joints and chops at the other. It had been a family-run business for years but the directors were a far cry from the nineteenth-century founders.

They all drew very high salaries, ridiculously high in view of the dwindling sales and non-existent profits. They drove around in brand new BMWs, except for the old man of the firm who kept the chairman's title, salary and Rolls.

In its heyday Young's Meat Processing plc was a gold mine, and during the sixties it had gone public with investors desperate to buy shares. Things started to go wrong some fifteen years later, and by the time Tony and I were interested it was on the slippery slope to liquidation while the family swanned around in their flash cars and spent more time on the golf course than they did in the office.

The main factory was run-down and nothing short of demolition would put it right, and customers were vanishing as the big supermarket chains pushed north of the border. Young's once had a healthy stack of gilts and for a long time the interest from them had boosted profits, but they had gradually been sold to pay off borrowings and the firm was now sinking deeper and deeper into debt.

It did have one worthwhile asset, though, and it was more than enough to keep the vultures hovering. Young's had a Stock Exchange listing, and I was approached by an up-and-coming grocery chain which wanted to go public but which didn't want the expense or the trouble of going to the market on its own.

My brief was to arrange a mutually beneficial takeover, an agreed bid that would give my client the prestige of a public company — and access to City fund raising — and give the Young's family the chance of taking the money and running. Or more likely driving away in the BMWs. Easy enough, you'd think, and normally it would have been but in this case I'd reckoned without Tony Walker.

He'd spotted the potential of Young's as a shell company all the way from London and had managed to buy up about three per cent of the shares in the market for £72,000. He'd then persuaded one of the older directors to sell him his stake for cash and that took Tony's holding to twelve per cent, and then he started putting pressure on for a seat on the board.

Tony had started professional life as an accountant, but soon realized he could do a lot better by running companies himself instead of just looking after their books. He'd borrowed something like a quarter of a million pounds from his father, a retired farmer, and started buying strategic stakes in companies ripe for takeover.

It was a bit like betting on racehorses, but more often than not the favourite romped home and the winnings piled up. Then he came to the conclusion that he could do even better if he took part in the race himself, buying shares in companies and then negotiating for them to be taken over, more often than not from a position of authority within the firm. He usually made a double profit, a healthy management fee from the company and a boost to the value of his shareholding, which he would sell soon after the bid went through.

He was doing the same at Young's and had just got his seat on the board and had a West Midlands electronics company all ready to reverse into it when I came onto the scene. By then the share price was already on the way up, partly because the market was well aware of Walker's reputation and also because you can't do anything in this business without making ripples and the brokers knew there was a battle in the offing. My only chance was to put together an agreed bid, a package that all the directors would accept and recommend to the rest of the shareholders.

My tack was to appeal to their chauvinism and play on the Scottish roots of my client, "Wouldn't it be a terrible shame to let this proud Scottish name be taken over by a crowd of heathen Sassenachs, remember Culloden", and so on. My pleas fell on deaf ears and glazed eyes while Tony was out wining and dining the sixty-eight-year-old matriarch of the Young's clan and playing golf with the rest of the board at a level well below his seven handicap.

I was fighting an uphill battle and the City watchers of the *Glasgow Herald and Scotsman* had just about given up on me when I decided to take Shona for a meal in one of Edinburgh's plusher restaurants.

We'd planned to overhaul our strategy in a bid to snatch victory from the jaws of this wide-mouthed London predator, but as it turned out we saw Tony Walker shoving smoked salmon and shrimps into his mouth in a secluded booth with the chairman who had hired me to spearhead his offer for Young's. Shona and I turned on the spot and drove back to our office in Charlotte Square without speaking.

Not until we had walked through the door did she say, "Bastard, bastard, bastard" with a venom that was not completely out of character. She flung herself into her dark green leather chair and put her feet on her desk, knocking the blotter to one side. "Bastard, bastard, bastard."

There were any number of reasons why Tony could be having a quiet tête-à-tête with our client: a shared interest in good food was one, a chance meeting was another, but they were both about as likely as scoring a hole in one on the Old Course at St Andrews by teeing off at Bearsden Golf Club.

If it had been above board and Tony was offering to sell his stake or switch his allegiance then Shona and I would be involved, so what was going on was obviously not the sort of behaviour likely to win Brownie points from the Takeover Panel.

The reason why the two so-called adversaries were dining together had flashed into our minds at the same moment — our bid was nothing more than a red herring to boost the share price so that Tony and the directors could make an even bigger profit on the deal when his electronics company eventually gained control, a profit which would no doubt be shared by our client.

Which was great news for everybody except the West Midlands firm, which would be paying over the odds, and Shona and me. A failed takeover bid wouldn't do much for our reputations — or our fees.

We spent the rest of that evening putting away the best part of a bottle of Tamdhu and planning what we'd do to Mr Tony Walker. He'd booked himself a suite on the fifth floor of the North British Hotel and the following day I went to see him.

To this day I'm not sure how it happened but I walked into his room fuming and ready to take a swing at him but within half an hour we were the best of friends. It just happened. It wasn't personal with Tony, it was always business, just business, and when it came to making money there wasn't a stroke he wouldn't pull. He admitted that quite openly, he didn't apologize, he just smiled and said I wasn't to take it personally and that if it would make me feel any better then OK, I could take a swing at him but wouldn't I really prefer that he bought me a good lunch?

To make myself feel better I ordered the most expensive items on the menu, but by the end of lunch we were laughing and joking and the prospect of Scottish Corporate Advisors losing a takeover battle didn't seem like the end of the world. He became a firm friend, I'd trust him with my life if not my money, David loved him, and after Shona he was the first person I rang when my father died. He was on the first Shuttle up to Edinburgh, I cried on his shoulder and he helped organize the funeral and sat by me at the inquest.

As it turned out Scottish Corporate Advisors didn't win or lose the fight for Young's. The West Midlands company suddenly lost interest and I wasn't altogether surprised when our client decided to drop out, too. Tony got his fingers burnt to the tune of £30,000, though he managed to cut his losses by selling his shares at a much lower price to an Edinburgh life office which saw Young's as a possible recovery situation.

It was only much later that I discovered Shona had phoned down to Birmingham and dropped a few hints about what Tony was up to. She's a lot harder underneath than I am, and she bears grudges, but now even she'd warmed to Tony. There was still a vague wariness about her whenever he was near, though.

Eventually word got round and Tony found it harder and harder to play the takeover game, and some eighteen months ago he'd joined up with a friend from his old university and now worked as an armaments middleman, selling mainly to the Middle East and doing a fair amount of juggling with end-user certificates. It was far from being a clean business, Tony had to make up most of the rules as he went along, and that often meant shunting money into Swiss bank accounts and encouraging buyers with wine, women and cocaine. With Tony it was just business, nothing personal.

As soon as I arrived back in London I phoned Tony and offered to take him for a drink that evening in a wine bar down the road from his Mayfair office. He was already sitting at a brass and glass table nursing a white wine and soda when I arrived.

"Doctor's orders, sport," he said after he'd jumped to his feet, and shook my hand and slapped my back and rattled my teeth. "Told me to lay off the hard stuff, liver trouble and all that. Can't say I like this muck, though. And it's about twice the price of a half-decent whisky."

"You can afford it, Tony, stop complaining," I laughed. "I've seen you collect enough receipts to know the sort of expenses you get. Just to make you feel bad I'll have a double Glenmorangie, and you can pay for it."

He slouched over to the bar, tall and fair in a dark blue business suit and highly polished shoes. He'd grown a moustache since the funeral and it added about fifteen years to his long, thin face. A thick rectangle of black hair, it half covered a thin scar that ran from the left side of his lip up to the middle of his cheek. The few times I'd asked him about the scar he'd laughed it off with jokes about jealous husbands, scorned lovers and frustrated business partners and after a while I'd stopped asking. There was a lot I didn't know about Tony Walker but I loved him like a brother.

He brought the tumbler of malt back to the table and sat opposite me, careful to cross his legs so that the sole of his shoe faced away from me, a hangover from dealing with Arabs. He caught my look and smiled, reaching for the peanuts on the table with his left hand, just to show me that he wasn't fully converted to Middle East customs.

"How's the lovely Shona?" he asked.

"She's fine. Sends her best." Not true, she didn't know I was going to see him.

"And David?"

"He's well. He's staying at a private nursing home for a few months just until I get myself straight. They look after him really well but he can't wait to get back with me."

"And when will that be?"

"Soon. Soon, I hope."

"I hear Shona is handling most of the business herself at the moment. And handling it well by all accounts. She's a capable girl, you should watch her. I should have paid more attention to her myself — I could have saved myself several thousand pounds."

"Now, now Tony, down boy. And what big ears you have."

"Word gets round, sport. You know how the grapevine works. Been down here long?"

"Just arrived off the Shuttle, the noo," I said, lapsing into a music hall Scottish accent that made him smile.

"Flying visit, or business, or social?" he asked, and it felt suddenly as if I were being interviewed by a high-powered headhunter, feeling my way through traps set for the unwary. Tony raised his thick eyebrows and looked me straight in the eyes through long, dark lashes, but unlike Iwanek's penetrating gaze Tony's was warm and friendly and caring.

"Business, Tony, but it's got more in common with your line of business than mine. I'm in the middle of setting up an export deal with a West African country, dictatorship to be more accurate, and I'm due to entertain one of their Trade Ministers in London next week."

"Entertain?"

"Exactly. And I'm afraid it's not the sort of business I'm au fait with."

"What's his predilection? Boys, girls, camels? Drugs?"

"Girls, or at least a particular type. He likes them classy, very classy, the ultimate Sloanes. He likes them pretty, well-groomed and intelligent. This guy was educated at Sandhurst, he's not out of the jungle. She'll have to be talkative, witty, charming . . ."

64

"And screw like a rabbit?"

"Exactly."

"Not quite your line of country, sport," he said, sipping his drink and grimacing.

"We're branching out."

"Are you sure you're being one hundred per cent honest with me?"

No, Tony, I'm lying through my teeth but if I told you the real reason I want the girl you'd try to stop me. "Hell, Tony, if I could go into details I would, but I can't. Now will you help?"

"Of course I will. You knew that or you wouldn't have come to me. I just want to make sure that you aren't getting in above your head. Is there anything I can do to help? Some of these tin-pot states can be murderous."

"Just give me a name, Tony. I know what I'm doing."

He took one of his gold embossed business cards from his wallet and scribbled a number on the back. "Her name is Carol Hammond-Chambers. You'll have to mention my name or you won't even get past her answering machine. Carol is very selective and very, very pricey. But by Christ she's worth it."

"You haven't?"

"Of course I have. You wouldn't buy a car without test driving it first, would you? There you are, then. I've introduced some very important clients to her and it was vital that I knew what they were getting into — if you get my drift."

"And how is she?"

"The best, the absolute best. Worth every pound. Sexy, but very bright with it. You can't go wrong with Carol. She lives with another girl, Sammy. She works for me from time to time as well. A nice pair." Freudian slip? Probably not, knowing Tony.

"Why do they do it?" I asked.

He sipped his wine before answering. "Different reasons," he said. "Carol has an expensive habit to fund and working for me means she gets well paid and moves in the sort of circles where the coke flows freely and is as pure as the driven snow. Best of both worlds."

"I tried sniffing coke once but the bubbles got up my nose," I said and Tony laughed.

"What about the other girl, this Sammy?" I asked.

"Sammy's more of a mystery. You'll understand what I mean if you meet her. She's very smart, very sociable. She enjoys the company of stimulating men, men with power, men I can introduce her to. She's more than able to handle the physical side, too, and I think she enjoys that as well. To be honest I've never been able to work her out. Sometimes she'll turn a job down simply because she doesn't like the man's politics or his sense of humour. Strange girl. And I know for a fact the money's not important, she comes from a wealthy family, father's a Surrey landowner and farmer. Look, sport, are you sure I can't help?"

"If you could you'd be the first person I'd come to, believe me. You've done more than enough giving me Carol's name."

"Good. I mean it, if things get tough call me. And take care. You can give me your number in London before you go, too. Now, have you heard what happened to Ferguson over at Kleinwort Benson?"

Then he was off, gossiping and joking like the Tony I knew, but he was worried about me now and perhaps it had been a mistake going to him.

The voice on the answering machine was smooth and soothing, the sort of voice that relaxed you but at the same time gave you a hint of pleasures to come, illicit pleasures, pleasures to make your toes curl.

It was the sort of voice that usually belongs to fifty-year-old telephonists with spots and halitosis who flirt outrageously with men they'll never meet, but in this case Tony had promised me it belonged to a body that would more than live up to my expectations. I left my name and number and said that Tony had suggested I give her a ring.

My phone rang ten minutes later, which meant she'd just got in, had been in the shower, or more likely that she'd been in all the time and had rung Tony first to check up on me. Whatever, her warm sultry voice seemed to float out of the receiver, wash down my neck and tickle my back and I could feel my toes pressing against the top of my shoes. It wasn't Carol, it was Sammy. Tony's first choice was all set to fly to Oman for an extended "holiday with friends" but she was sure she'd be able to help. It was Sammy's voice on the answering machine. If ever I get knocked down by a bus and go into a coma, play me tapes of Sammy's voice. I'll either wake up or die happy.

I asked her if she'd like to go for a drink and she said why didn't I just go round because she had more than enough drink for two, and I couldn't help wondering what Tony had told her as my toes fought and slashed to cut their way out of my shoes.

An hour after the call I was at the door of her Kensington flat, one floor up in one of those white buildings that used to hold one very rich family but are now home to several very, very rich families. To the side of the building were parking spaces for three cars and standing next to each other were a Rolls, a Mercedes and a Jeep — Dinah would have loved it. McKinley waited outside in our rented Granada. I was still waiting for my Porsche to be repaired, and even when it was I doubted that I'd ever let him take the wheel.

The names above the entryphone at the main door had said S. Darvell and C. Hammond-Chambers but there was no label on the shining white door to the flat itself, just a brass knocker in the shape of a diving dolphin.

She opened the door and I saw a flash of red hair cascading down to sun-browned shoulders, a wide mouth with teeth every bit as white and sparkling as the front door, then my eyes drifted down to breasts thrusting to get out of a backless white dress which stuck to her waist and hips and ended above the most perfect calves I'd ever seen.

Sammy was a cracker, an absolute angel who'd turn heads and necks and even whole bodies in order to get a better look. My eyes returned to her face, eventually, and the slightly mocking smile told me that she was getting the sort of attention she was used to and which she expected.

"Come in," she breathed and I walked into a room which looked like a soap powder commercial. Everything — walls, carpet, settee, coffee table — everything was white, even the blue-eyed cat which lay on a sheepskin rug and purred and stretched and sounded every bit as sexy as its mistress was a dazzling white.

Another girl walked into the whiteness from a bedroom, toting a green fabric suitcase and a matching holdall. Carol? Couldn't have been anyone else. I thought of Tony's test drive and I grinned.

"You must be Carol," I said, and held out my hand to a curly-haired brunette with big brown almond eyes, lips that formed a permanent pout and a figure that matched Sammy's inch for inch, though she was a hand shorter. The leather jacket was white and so was the blouse, but the skirt was black and slit to the thigh and the legs were brown and sleek and long.

"Must I?" she asked, dropping the suitcase with a dull thud and taking my hand. She glanced at Sammy and smiled. "Yes, I suppose I must."

The voice was pure Cockney, belying the name and the body, and I mentally cursed Tony and his twisted sense of humour. Ultimate Sloane, indeed.

"I love the flat," I said, looking round and releasing the cool, scarlet-fingernailed hand. "How on earth do you keep it clean?"

"Why should it ever get dirty?" asked Carol. "Sit down, I'll get you a drink."

"It's OK, I'll get it," said Sammy. "Anyway, I thought you had to go."

"Shit, yes, what's the time? Oh no. Was there a cab outside?" she asked me, her eyes widening.

"No," I said, but just then we heard a horn sound in the street below and she picked up the case and headed for the door.

"I must dash," she said. "I'm sorry I can't stay, but I'm sure you'll get on with Sammy. Oh, and when you see Tony next, give him my love. Tell him I'll phone when I get back and he can check my tan."

"I'll tell him," I laughed, and then the door slammed and she was gone.

"Hectic," I said to Sammy.

"Yes," she nodded, shaking her head so that the waterfall of red hair swung back and forth. "She got a call from a friend in Oman. Here today, gone tomorrow. That's the way it is with Carol. No ties, no commitments."

"The flat?"

"The flat's mine. Carol helps out with the rent but she'd never take on a mortgage in a million years. In the sixties they'd have called her a free spirit."

"And now?"

"Irresponsible, I suppose. No, that's not fair, Carol just has different priorities to me."

She walked past me and something smelled sweet and expensive, the sort of perfume that back-street chemists make cheap copies of and sell out of cardboard boxes in shopping precincts.

Walking over to the four-seater sofa was like wading through an uncut lawn, the thick lush pile came halfway up my shoes. I dropped onto the soft white upholstery and slowly sank into it until my backside was a good six inches below my knees.

The cat purred and rolled over, eyes fixed on my shoelaces. It was probably grateful to see something, anything, that wasn't white. Hell, I'm surprised the poor thing hadn't gone snow blind living with Sammy and Carol. I felt so sorry for it that I let it play with them, dangling my foot over its eager paws.

As the cat and I got acquainted Sammy came back from the drinks cabinet, which stood next to a large picture window overlooking a verdant garden square where sparrows fought and squabbled and a thrush sang its heart out. That's what the residents pay rates of £1.68 in the pound for, I guess.

I didn't think I could stand without an overhead winch so I was grateful when she walked over and handed the glass down to me. I was even more grateful when I discovered it wasn't white wine or white rum or white anything. It was a malt, a good one, and it came with a splash of water which is just the way I like it and that meant she had a severe case of woman's intuition, she'd made a lucky guess or she'd had a long chat with Tony and I wondered what he had told her and if he'd asked her to go ferreting for him. Or maybe she had just smelled the whisky I'd drunk for Dutch courage before I left my flat.

Our fingers touched as I took the crystal tumbler and I got a slight shock of static electricity, a combination of the carpet, her dress and the thin film of sweat that I could feel all over my skin. The girl made me nervous, she was almost too beautiful, too well-groomed. It was difficult being in the same room as her, I was like a schoolboy on his first date and it was all I could do to stop biting my nails.

She floated down into the settee next to me and pulled her knees up onto the cushions so that one brushed against the outside of my leg. I didn't jump but my heart soared and I just melted as she looked at me and ran her finger up and down the stem of her glass. I came to as the cat began scratching its claws down my socks and I cleared my throat and started the semblance of a conversation.

"Have you known Tony for long?" I asked and wished I'd bitten my tongue instead.

"About three years, on and off," she said. "I work for him every couple of months, usually Arabs, and usually they want something a little different." She raised her eyebrows, daring me to ask what was different, but I didn't rise to the bait, all I could think of was the warmth of her leg against mine.

"What is it you want me to do?" she asked. "Tony said you had something special in mind but he wouldn't tell me what."

"Tony was teasing you," I said. "I want you to do much the same as you do for him, only for a client of mine. Only he isn't a client of mine. I'm not explaining this very well, am I?" I was embarrassed, that's why, discussing sex with this beautiful girl that I fancied

72

something rotten as if I were talking about a secretarial job.

"No, you're not. Let me get you another." She uncurled and drifted up and off the settee, God knows how but I suppose the long suntanned legs had something to do with it. She returned with another whisky and I don't remember drinking that one either. She made me laugh, she told me stories about Tony that I would dredge up next time I saw him so long as my memory held out; she told me about her parents, her time at Oxford, we touched on everything but her profession though after a while it became clear that it was more of a hobby than a job. I told her about David and Shona and before long I told her everything.

I needed someone to talk to, and I knew that unless I gave her good reason she wouldn't help me and she was perfect for the job. It wasn't pillow talk, that would come later, this was just getting it all off my chest. Like a chat with an analyst, that's the way I looked at it. I was pissed, and when I'm pissed I talk too much.

If you've got a couple of thousand pounds to invest there are a number of things you can do. In fact a host of friendly advisors will beat a path to your door with a view to tucking away your nest egg in one of their many and varied schemes.

You can shove it into a building society or deposit account and forget about it, collecting the interest every few months. It's boring, to be honest, and you'll never make a fortune unless you start with half a fortune and wait ten years or so, but your capital is as safe as houses.

You can put the lot into Premium Bonds, and wait for Ernie to pick one of his electronic ping pong balls out of his electronic hat with your number on it. You've more chance of winning than you have of being struck by lightning but statistically you're better off putting your hard-earned loot in the care of Mr Bradford and Mr Bingley. If your luck's in you could cream off a fortune, but that could also be said of the football pools. I guess that's why so many people are glued to their TV sets on Saturday afternoons — dreaming of the big one, but if it doesn't come off, well, there's always next week, isn't there? It's a mug's game. You might as well toddle into a casino and plonk the lot on zero. Sometimes that comes up, too.

At the opposite end of the financial spectrum are the out and out gambles, the City equivalent of betting on a 250–1 outsider running in the Grand National. There are get-rich-quick schemes like buying those large containers used to ship antiques over to America, disgraced diplomats to Nigeria and stolen cars to the Middle East. You rent them out to export companies and pocket a healthy profit, in theory, but more likely they'll just lie rusting in some disused dockyard and your money will evaporate faster than goodwill at a creditors' meeting. Not to be recommended.

Anyway, back to Mr Average looking for a home for his two grand. He's probably heard about the stock market, the mystical exchange where fortunes are won and lost, and if he is a little curious he's maybe read about penny shares, buying them at 9p each and selling a few months later when they're worth £6.15. Mr Average, being average, is more than a little greedy and reckons that the stock market is the place for his hard-earned cash.

He might be right, but he'll be playing in one of the biggest casinos in the world, with rumours and counter-rumours sending share prices soaring and crashing, a bad set of results blighting a firm's shares for months, a takeover bid sending them through the roof.

Putting all your eggs in one basket is a doubtful way of investing, but Mr Average's £2,000 would have to go on one share to make any sense at all, dealing costs and stamp duty see to that, and picking that one share makes it a gamble. Back to the racecourse.

There is an alternative: a unit trust or an investment trust. Different animals but with a similar aim, the spreading of risk. Get together a group of investors, pool their capital and put their money into several shares, gilts, maybe even property. Then spread the rewards. There'll obviously be a few misses, but the many hits will more than cover them.

The main difference between unit and investment trusts is that investment trusts come in the form of shares listed on the stock exchange. To buy unit trusts you go to the firm which manages them. Both sorts of trusts specialize, in sectors like electronics or natural resources, or in parts of the world like the Far East or America.

Edinburgh has always been a major centre of investment trusts, going back to the days when canny Scots realized there was many a mickle to be made out of America, but they were also canny enough to realize that there was safety in numbers. Shareholders made small fortunes out of their investments, but even bigger fortunes were made by the men who managed the funds. That's still the case.

Take a gold sovereign and place it over a small scale map of Edinburgh centred on Charlotte Square, and you're probably covering more millionaires per square foot than anywhere outside the City of London. Many of them are fund managers, men who make their money by looking after other people's.

These days most of the Ivory & Simes and Martin Curries have branched out into other lucrative areas like pension fund management, but my father had always stuck to what he knew best, looking after an investment trust that was his pride and joy. He'd managed Scottish Commercial Overseas Trust, SCOT as it was called, since he was a young man fresh out of St Andrews University with a first in economics.

My grandfather got him the job by pulling a few well-greased strings. My family's always been like that: doors are opened and more strings pulled than at a campanologists' convention to make sure the next generation gets a head start on their peers. Don't knock it until you've benefited from it.

Father took to it like a duck to water, long expense-account lunches, meeting old friends from school and university, drinks with the G and T brigade, and free publicity in the quality Scottish press. All he had to do was to keep up with the FT Index, and he had the experience of a flock of Scottish stockbrokers' analysts to draw on. OK, I'm making it sound easy, but running an investment trust is a darn sight more fun than breaking rocks for a living.

It's just a matter of running with the pack, switching into sectors as they become popular and ditching them when sentiment goes against them. Japan this year, America next, making sure you sell at a profit wherever possible but never being afraid to cut loose a dead loss.

The really good guys, the ones that earn £100,000 a year and more, set trends rather than follow them. They know, based on instinct or research, where to invest and where to sell, but everyone knows who to watch and the sheep follow the wolves and everyone makes a good living, my father included.

For the whole of his working life my father ran the SCOT investment trust with John Read, another St Andrews graduate. But when Read died of a massive stroke two years ago my old man was left in sole charge, and the mantle didn't fit too well on his shoulders.

He should have taken on more staff right away, beefed up the research side, maybe even taken on a few more non-executive directors, but at fifty-nine years old it was the first time he'd had his hands on the reins and he was reluctant to give them up.

By then SCOT was doing fairly well, with investments worth a total of fifty-two million, though its performance lagged well behind the high-flyers. In fact

SCOT had under-performed the investment trust sector average for the past five years but it had still done better than many. It was just after Read's death that Ronnie Laing, drugs dealer, and Alan Kyle, property developer and self-styled City tycoon, crawled out of the woodwork.

There's another big difference between unit trusts and investment trusts. A unit trust is an open fund, the more money that comes in the more units are created. If investors withdraw their money then the number of units is reduced.

An investment trust is different, it's a closed fund, set up with a limited number of shares. The only way to increase the share capital is to issue more shares, which sometimes happens. You buy them through a stockbroker and it's the City that sets the price. A share that's in vogue or is doing particularly well will have more money chasing it than a dullard, and its price will rise.

Now, the fact that investment trust shares are sold on the stock market leads to an interesting phenomenon called the discount. The price you pay for a share is more often than not less than the actual value of its investments.

Say a fund's investments are worth a hundred million and there are fifty million shares, then the net asset value, the value of each share, is two pounds. But you'll be able to buy the shares for quite a bit less, perhaps for as little as £1.50. In that case you'll be getting the share for three-quarters of its value and the discount would be one quarter, or twenty-five per cent. That's not an unusual figure.

That's fine and dandy, it means that shareholders are actually getting a boost to their investment, every £1.50 they put in has two pounds working for them and producing dividends. But it wasn't too long before some wily investment trust managers realized that they could take over smaller trusts and take on ready-made portfolios at a bargain price. A hundred million pounds worth of investments might cost only seventy-five million on the stock exchange.

Well, it's not exactly as simple as that because once the City gets wind of what's happening the discount narrows pretty rapidly and the share price is soon the same as the net asset value. Timing is obviously crucial and the faster the takeover goes ahead the more money the predator makes. Tony dipped his toe into the investment trust pool and came out smiling once or twice.

It's a good deal for the predator, who gets investments on the cheap, and the shareholders are happy because they make a quick profit, though more often than not they're prepared to take shares in the predatory investment trust in place of cash. The only losers are the managers of the original trust who lose the goose that's been laying their golden eggs, but they can always go back to accountancy, or soliciting, or selling shoelaces on street corners, or whatever it was they used to do before climbing on the gravy train of fund management.

Once investment trusts started snapping each other up other interested parties began to take notice; private trusts and pension funds didn't need telling that they too could do a lot with cheap investments. They could keep the stocks and shares they liked and sell the rest through the market, a highly lucrative form of asset stripping, on a par with buying up cheap tenanted property, getting rid of the occupants and selling the freeholds. Nice work if you can get it.

She'd sat patiently by me on the virgin white settee and her eyes never left my face other than the two times when she'd refilled my glass. She hadn't yawned, she hadn't spoken. Sometimes she pushed her hair behind her left ear but it wouldn't stay put, and occasionally she reached over and touched my shoulder gently and listened, head slightly on one side, which is why her hair kept falling across her eye. The cat had long since become bored with my shoelaces and lay on the back of the settee, eyes closed and paws opening and closing as it tortured dream mice. I'd stopped feeling her leg against mine and I wasn't looking at her any more, I was looking at the window but not through it, just looking into the middle distance as I talked in a quiet voice that I barely recognized as my own, getting it out of my system like a fever that has to be sweated out.

Of course other people recognized a good thing when they saw it, and that's how Laing and Kyle came on the scene. Laing was a drugs dealer with a cash flow that would make a Swiss banker blush with pleasure, Kyle was a downmarket version of Tony Walker.

For Kyle it wasn't just business, it was a pleasure to grind people's faces into their misfortune, particularly if it was a misfortune he'd brought about. Kyle was a short, stocky man with a hard face and a harder heart and a reputation for losing his temper, if he'd ever managed to find it in the first place.

He always dressed immaculately; his silk tie matched by a handkerchief, he wore sharp suits with a gold-buckled leather belt and his shoes never cost less than the average weekly wage.

He'd started his career as a property developer, doing up run-down buildings and selling them at an inflated profit, breaking rules and legs and trampling over anybody he could to get a leg up the ladder. Sometimes he'd trample on people just for the hell of it, just for practice, just because he liked it. He graduated to the City, set up a company offering financial services, took over an office cleaning firm, a pool table business, a couple of minor hotels that were barely disguised brothels. He was still breaking heads and working an eighty-hour week in his office near Bishopsgate.

He'd met Ronnie Laing one night in a gambling club in Mayfair, tall, willowy Ronnie Laing with his pale blond hair and deep set blue eyes covered by green-rimmed glasses, a blonde on each arm and a wide gold band on his wedding finger. Kyle liked him immediately, and liked him even more when Laing split the pair of blondes right down the middle, one each. The following morning they got to talking and that's how the partnership was born. That's what I heard, anyway, but that was afterwards when I was looking for information and paying for it and howling at the moon for revenge.

I don't know how or why they picked on SCOT, maybe it was the twenty-eight per cent discount, maybe it was its size, maybe it was the fact that my father was in sole charge and less able to protect his baby than one of the larger investment houses, but they chose SCOT and went for it with all the subtlety of a Chieftain tank.

They attacked in two waves, each buying quietly in the market, softly softly until they reached just below the five per cent mark at which point they would have a notifiable stake. Then they pounced, lumped the two stakes together, snapping up another ten per cent in the market on the same day as the price started to take off. In all they bought one fifth of the £52 million trust for a little more than seven million, much of that the profits from Laing's drug operations though the shares were in the name of Kyle's company, Property and Financial Services. They'd been buying SCOT shares for about £1.18 compared with a net asset value of £1.51, and Kyle made a cash offer of £1.42 for the rest with the backing of a consortium of merchant banks who recognized a good thing when they saw it.

If the deal came off Kyle and Laing would get their hands on a £52 million portfolio for about £46 million, which meant a profit of six million once they'd liquidated it. Not bad for a couple of months' work, and it would be a hundred per cent legal and above board. Well, it would have been if they'd played it by the book, which of course they didn't. What Laing and

82

Kyle wanted was a quick settlement, they wanted the directors of the trust to agree the bid and recommend that shareholders accept the PAFS offer before another predator started sniffing around.

One of the second ranking merchant banks prepared the bid document. Their fee of £120,000 would come off PAFS's profits, but Laing and Kyle reckoned it was worth it, image was everything, but behind the scenes they played dirtier than anyone in the City had ever played before. They took the vicious techniques of Laing's world into the sedate Edinburgh financial sector and the effect was similar to dropping a piranha into a tank of goldfish.

In the space of just four days one of the directors found that his £15,000 chestnut hunter had gone lame, not surprising with a six-inch nail rammed up its hoof as far as it would go; another received black and white photographs of his twin daughters stepping off the school bus. They'd been taken with a long lens and were slightly fuzzy, and they didn't come with a message because one wasn't necessary. Another opened his front door to find a bottle of sulphuric acid standing next to the early morning milk delivery and a carton of raspberry yoghurt. All three received phone calls on the same evening and at a board meeting two days later they told my father they'd decided to accept the PAFS offer, had already agreed to sell their shares to Kyle and would be recommending that shareholders did the same.

My father told them not to be so soft, that he was looking for a higher offer which would mean a better deal for the shareholders. That night he got a phone call and the next day his wife, my mother, got into the family Volvo and drove down the hill to the local shops and smashed headlong into a lamp post when the brakes failed. It wouldn't have been so bad if she'd been wearing her seat belt but she wasn't, and she ripped through the windscreen in a shower of glass cubes and crumpled onto the pavement where she died of a ruptured spleen and pierced lung three minutes later, in the arms of a passing postman, bleeding heavily over his grey slacks.

The following week she was buried in the pretty local churchyard and control of SCOT passed to Kyle and Laing.

Two days after the funeral I drove to the office. It was a Sunday and I wanted to get my desk straight, I knew that I had to keep working, keep my mind occupied, to do something to blot out the memory of how she'd died, an ugly freakish accident in a two-year-old car that had just been serviced. I stayed until after dusk, then threw my briefcase into the passenger seat of my Porsche and drove slowly back to the family home on the outskirts of Edinburgh, indicating at every turn, stopping on amber, checking the mirror at every opportunity and keeping both hands firmly on the wheel. My mother had named the rambling stone house in three acres of well-tended gardens Stonehaven, and she'd stamped her personality on it like an adopted child.

The house was quiet as I unlocked the front door, stepped into the oak panelled hall and rested the case next to the umbrella stand. I headed for the kitchen, I wanted a coffee, but I heard Bach through the study door so I changed direction and went in to see my father.

He was lying on his back by the side of his huge Victorian desk, a wedding present from a distant cousin, a black walking stick by his side. The damp weather always gave him trouble with his back and it had been drizzling steadily all day. I heard a sniff and a sigh and I turned to see David sitting behind the door, back ramrod straight against the hand-printed wallpaper, chin up, tears streaming from unseeing eyes down sodden cheeks.

He shuddered and sighed again, his lips tight together and his nose running and mixing with the tears. His fists were clenched and his arms clutched across his chest and he started to rock backwards and forwards, banging himself against the wall and wailing, a mournful moan of pain that shocked me to the core.

"David, what's wrong? What's the matter?" I asked. I knelt beside him, one knee either side of his outstretched legs, and held him close, his chin on my shoulder as he cried and cried. "Stop crying," I said.

I turned my head towards where my father was lying. "What's the matter with David?" I asked, but my father hadn't moved and it wasn't a stick lying by his side, it was his favourite shotgun and the blue and white wallpaper behind the desk was speckled with red. As I stood and walked towards his feet I could see that the top of his head was missing, and fragments of brain and skin and blood and shot covered the top of the desk. I

85

noticed then the smell of cordite and shit in the room and I didn't have to kneel by the body to see that he was dead.

I took David by the hand and led him from the room, sitting him in an armchair next to the telephone table in the hall as I rang Shona, Tony and the police, in that order. Then I brought a thick blanket down from a bedroom and wrapped it around David and I went back into the study and picked up the letter lying on the desk, and I sat next to David and waited and read the letter again and again and then I folded it up and put it in the inside pocket of my jacket and waited.

By then I was into my fourth tumbler of whisky and Sammy had leant her cool unlined forehead on my shoulder, breathing gently while her hand rested on my arm, her drink on the coffee table untouched.

I continued. "The coroner was sympathetic, and without a suicide note he was willing to accept that my father had shot himself accidentally while cleaning his gun. There was the usual warning always to check that guns weren't loaded indoors but he wasn't fooling anybody."

"What was in the letter?" she asked, so quietly that at first I hadn't realized she'd spoken.

"It was rambling, the ramblings of a man who'd lost everything, almost everything, I don't know, maybe everything. His job, his wife, what else was there for him to live for? Two sons, maybe, and a big empty house that would always remind him of her. He felt he didn't belong in a world where gangsters like Kyle and Laing could get away with murder. The phone call he'd received before she died was from Laing, telling him to forget any ideas of master-minding a counter bid for SCOT, to let sleeping dogs lie, to keep out of it, old man, or you'll be even more of a cripple, old man, and wouldn't it be a pity if anyone else in your family had to use a stick to get around, old man.

"He said in the letter that he didn't want to live any more, not in a world where that could happen, he wanted to be with her and he said he was sorry, very sorry, and the notepaper was stained with tears and the handwriting shaky, the scrawl of an old, dying man. Christ, Sammy, he was only fifty-nine. He didn't have to die. Neither of them did."

"Hush," she said, and put her arm around my shoulder. "They couldn't have known what would happen. They couldn't have known that your mother would be in the car or that she wouldn't be wearing her seat belt. It was just a terrible, terrible mistake."

"No," I said, harshly enough to startle her and wake up the cat. "No. They might not have meant to kill my parents but they did. Maybe indirectly, but they were responsible. They were responsible."

She stood up and held out her hand to me, and I took it and she pulled me up and took me into the bedroom still carrying my glass. The bedroom wasn't white, it was blue, blue patterned wallpaper, a thick blue fur bedspread, blue velvet curtains half drawn, a wardrobe and dressing table of blue-stained wood. A picture above the double bed showed a sea scene, white-tipped waves whisked up by a strong wind.

She slipped the dress down over her shoulders, she was wearing nothing underneath, and she said nothing until she'd undressed me. "Tell me what you want me to do," she asked, so I made love to her under the waves and then I told her.

It was light when I left her flat, rubbing my chin because I needed a shave. McKinley was asleep in the car, head resting between the seat and the window, chest rising and falling as he snored loud enough to be heard a hundred yards away. I rapped on the window just behind his ear and he woke with a start.

"OK boss?" he asked.

"Sure, Get-Up. Let's go."

"To the flat?"

"To the flat. And don't spare the horses."

He started the car on the fourth attempt, which was good going for him, though to be fair we'd only had the Granada a week. He pulled away from the kerb, gently scraping a yellow VW and grinning sheepishly.

"Sorry, boss," he said and crashed into second gear.

"Forget it. Just get me home."

The courtship of McKinley had started the week after I'd seen him get knocked senseless in Kelly's Bar. I'd gone back to the pub and bought him a bottle of whisky in sixth of a gill measures, matching him drink for drink. I'd eaten a full plate of pasta and lined my stomach with milk and twice in the Gents I'd forced my fingers down my throat and thrown up as much of the whisky as I could. My head was swimming by the end of the evening but I was still on my feet. McKinley was impressed. So was I.

I told him I was a dealer, motors, stolen goods, drugs, anything I could make money from. I told him I needed extra muscle, I told him I could do with a driver. What about me? he asked, giving me a friendly nudge in the ribs and shooting me three feet along the bar, I've got muscle and I can drive. Like a lamb to the slaughter.

I told him I'd pay him £300 a week and he took my hand in his giant paw, looked me in the bloodshot eyes and thanked me from the bottom of his heart. I'd never regret it, he said, and apart from a few near misses in the Granada he'd been right. I had installed him in a cheap hotel around the corner from my flat and paid his bill one month in advance. Now he was a constant companion, though the main problem was finding him enough to do.

To back up my cover story I got him to drive me to various hotels (business meetings), casinos (poker games) and restaurants (can't tell you what's going on, Get-Up, but it's big), and more often than not I'd leave him outside in the car while I had a quiet drink or a meal alone.

Once I left him waiting outside the Hilton for four hours while I slipped out the back way and wandered around the shops in Oxford Street looking for a present for David. It was important for Get-Up to think that I was wheeling and dealing, though putting on an act was a hell of a lot more tiring than the real thing.

Gradually I spoke to him about his past, about the work he did for Laing, the people he'd met, the places he'd been to, teasing out the information I needed like a splinter from a septic thumb, careful not to arouse his suspicions, never pressing too hard, changing tack if it looked as if I was touching a sore place.

The information was obviously old, he'd been in prison for seven years after all. A few of the names he mentioned had passed on or gone inside, but most were still in business, one had recently been featured in one of the more sensational tabloids under the headline "Drugs King In Sex Bribe Shocker".

I told Get-Up that one of my major interests was dealing in drugs, particularly hard drugs, north of the border, but that I'd run into problems with a supplier up in Glasgow and was lying low in London until tempers had cooled.

The probing usually took place late at night in pubs or clubs after a great deal of drinking and several self-induced Technicolor yawns. I was starting to get anorexic, but Laing's involvement in the drugs world was falling into place. Background that I couldn't get from McKinley I managed to dig up in the Daily Express cuttings library.

British customs officers seize more than a hundred million pounds' worth of drugs each year — it breaks down into something like forty-six million pounds of cannabis, forty-eight million pounds of heroin and seven million pounds of cocaine, and that's just the tip of a mind-blowing iceberg. There are less than three

90

hundred Customs and Excise officers and about twelve hundred policemen working on drugs and their batting average is roughly one for one — one smuggler arrested for each officer per year. And that's with the help of CEDRIC, a £1.2 million computer based on a couple of Honeywell DPS 8/20s which is even more sophisticated than the hardware used by MI5. It's hidden away in a nondescript building in Shoeburyness, near Southend, and it replaced the old card index system which was scrapped in the spring of 1983.

Its top secret data base can cross-check all information collated by the various anti-drug agencies.

Suppose a one-eyed midget with a wooden leg gets caught trying to drive his Morris Minor off the Channel ferry with a boot full of cannabis. At the touch of a button CEDRIC will spill the beans on how many midgets are involved in smuggling, how many have only one eye, if any are dead ringers for Long John Silver and if any are to be found sitting on a pile of cushions at the wheel of a Morris Minor. You get the picture? But CEDRIC is a victim of the truism faced by all the miracles of silicon chip technology — garbage in, garbage out. The information that comes out is only as good as the facts that are fed into it. And nowhere within CEDRIC's memory banks was the name Laing, Ronnie, and there was no mention of a blue Rolls-Royce Corniche with a white soft top and personalized number plates. Tap in a description of a tall, willowy, middle-aged man with blond hair, deep set blue eyes, green-rimmed glasses, a wide gold band on his wedding finger, maybe include his passion for young girls, and CEDRIC might give you a handful of near misses but the one thing he wouldn't give you is Laing, Ronnie, because Laing, Ronnie, had never been caught with so much as an aspirin in his possession, in fact Laing, Ronnie, had never been caught period.

He arranged to bring drugs into the country, he financed drug deals, he sold drugs on to wholesalers, but he never came within sniffing distance of anything that would raise the eyebrows of a lab assistant in a police forensic laboratory. Most of the cash he made went straight into Channel Island banks and was then laundered through Kyle's expanding business empire, so he didn't even have to account for suitcasefuls of fifty-pound notes in his Hampstead home. Ronnie Laing was now way past the stage where he had to finance supermarket robberies to make a quick killing.

The chances of the long arm of the law grabbing Laing by the silk collar were slimmer than a turkey's of surviving Christmas. He was insulated at two levels: a courier brought the drugs in and a middle-man, either trusted or scared witless, would handle the arrangements, never ringing Laing, only speaking when spoken to. On the few occasions a deal had gone sour it was only the couriers who ended up getting caught, and they knew it was more than their lives were worth to talk.

Getting drugs into Britain is a lot easier than most people think. From the simple trick of using false-bottomed suitcases to swallowing condoms full of heroin, much of it simply walks through the green "nothing to declare" channel with throngs of sunburnt holidaymakers.

The customs can't and don't search everybody and a professional courier at work is harder to spot than a Herpes carrier. A sniffer dog is only good for fifteen minutes before getting bored, or stoned, or both. The West German police reckon they can train a wild boar to do the job all day long, but the British depend on the services of just twenty-nine dogs, which equals about seven hours concentrated sniffing a day. Not much of a deterrent.

Getting the drugs over on the Channel ferries is even easier, which is why undercover drugs police officers pose as passengers, hoping that couriers will relax their guard while in the ship's bars and restaurants. No, they don't catch many, which is hardly surprising. If your car's sills were packed with heroin you're hardly likely to offer the barman a few grams in exchange for a double vodka and tonic and a packet of pork scratchings.

There's always the possibility that a zealous customs officer might take it into his head to drill a hole in the sills, just on the off chance, so a better way is to dissolve the drug, especially cocaine, in warm alcohol and soak it into the carpets of the car, maybe into the upholstery and the car blanket as well for good measure. Dry them out, drive through customs and then extract the drug with more warm alcohol. Filter, evaporate off the alcohol and you're left with pretty pure cocaine. And for the non drivers, it works just as well soaking the clothes in your suitcase.

Some of the more inventive car couriers have come up with a nifty variation — before driving out of the country they take out an AA five star insurance policy. After picking up the drugs in Spain or Holland or wherever and packing them away in any one of a dozen hard to find places, they nobble the motor, call in the AA and fly home. A few days later the car, and the drugs, are delivered. And what customs officer is going to search a family car on an AA Relay truck? Well, they all do now, actually, after an undercover Customs officer overheard a husband and wife courier team discussing the scam while celebrating in advance on the ferry to Calais.

Ultra cautious smugglers can remove themselves even further from the dirty end of the business, by shipping drugs into the country in hollowed-out wooden elephants from India, inside drums from Africa, or even by impregnating postcards and airmail letters with LSD microdots.

But Ronnie Laing had progressed way beyond such ruses, and when he wanted a delivery he had heroin or cocaine or cannabis or any combination of the three shipped in from the Continent and collected at any of a thousand possible landing places scattered around Britain's 7,000 miles of coastline and driven back to London.

Customs and Excise have seven coastal cutters to patrol those 7,000 miles of beaches, coves and cliffs so a smuggler has more chance of winning the pools than he has of bumping into the boys in blue, and chances are that the drugs ship can outperform the cutter and its volunteer crew without breaking into a sweat.

Any captures are usually the result of intelligence work rather than diligent patrolling, so a professional team has few problems in getting through. And if the smugglers are unlucky enough to meet a cutter they can't run away from, then the consignment is simply pitched overboard and collected later. Ronnie Laing was sitting pretty, or at least he was until he was hit on two fronts, from North and South America.

The land of the brave and the home of the free has a drugs business worth some hundred billion dollars a year, about the same as the whole Federal budget. Cocaine is now a growth industry with twelve million men and women using it regularly and 5,000 new addicts created every day. Supplies were rushed into the country to meet the ever-increasing demand but, as usual, the free market system created a surplus.

If it were wheat, or oil, or Coke with a big "C", then it would probably have been sold off cheaply to the Russians, but they wouldn't touch capitalist drugs with a cattle prod. So with the North American market pretty well saturated, in fact stoned out of its twelve million tiny minds, and with street prices falling, it wasn't too long before the drugs bosses looked towards Europe, and to Britain in particular.

In America drugs mean Mafia, and in Britain Mafia means trouble and Ronnie Laing was gradually squeezed out. And just to prove that it's always darkest just before it goes pitch black, the villains who actually export the drug, the South American cocaine barons, mostly Colombians, decided they would deal directly with Britain and cut out the middle-men and they make the Mafia look like disorganized boy scouts. The Mafia might issue a contract for a killing, the Colombians don't even bother to write a memo. They just get the job done and worry about the paperwork later.

They're highly organized and, with the South American's disregard for human life other than his own, frantically vicious. Laing found himself with a smaller and smaller share of the London drugs cake and eventually he was left with the crumbs, which is about the time he met up with Kyle and decided to put his not inconsiderable fortune to a more, but only slightly more, legitimate use.

The phone call from Tony was short and to the point, the conversation of a man used to speaking on lines which are bugged. He told me where and when he wanted to meet, but gave no hint as to the why. "Just be there," he'd said. "And come alone."

The where was St James's Park, the when was five minutes after I climbed out of the Granada opposite Horse Guards Parade, the wind tugging at the coats of the two policemen stopping non-permit-holders from parking outside the barracks. The coming alone was no problem because I gave McKinley the rest of the day off and told him to meet me at the flat the following morning.

Big Ben chimed in the background as I walked along the path to the lake which bisects the park, past the concrete snack bar that's a scaled down version of Liverpool Cathedral, the modern one, not the pretty one. Pigeons, geese and ducks were taking bread from tame tourists, waddling from hand to hand, too gorged or too lazy to fly, waiting until positively the last minute before getting the hell out of my way.

Stand in the middle of the footbridge, Tony had said, and wait for me. He was late, walking from the direction of The Mall across the grass under the towering horse chestnuts, giving a wide berth to a game of football between white overalled painters and carpenters who were blasting a muddy ball at goalposts made of dropped pullovers.

We both leant on the faded blue-green railings, facing towards Buckingham Palace. The flag wasn't flying so the Queen wasn't at home, but if she had been, and if she'd been standing on the balcony with a pair of powerful binoculars, then maybe she'd have wondered what we were talking about, and if she'd had a supersensitive directional microphone and had been able to pick up what we were saying, maybe she'd have wondered why two grown men were verbally fencing like a couple of nervous interviewees.

"What's going on, sport? What are you up to?" he asked.

"What are you talking about, Tony?"

"Just listen to him," he said, more to himself than to me. "When I give you the word I want you to turn round very slowly and look at the fountain at the other end of the lake. Pretend you're deep in thought, listening to what I'm saying, then turn your head to two o'clock and tell me if you recognize the man sitting on the bench there. Do it now."

I followed his instructions, not sure what to expect but knowing something was wrong. It was Iwanek, dressed just the way he was when I met him in the Savoy, except that he'd added a dark brown raincoat with the collar turned up. Shit, shit, shit. Tony hadn't turned but I knew he was waiting for me to speak, to explain.

Two men, both with hands thrust deep into the pockets of dark overcoats, approached Iwanek, one from behind, one walking along the duck-strewn path, and simultaneously sat down on either side of him. It looked like something out of a George Raft movie and I smiled. Tony had always had a taste for the melodramatic. Iwanek got up to go, I could feel the tension from a hundred yards away, and one of the men laid a restraining hand on his arm and spoke to him. He settled back down, resigned but with the air of an animal that realizes it's trapped but is still looking for a way out.

"Well?" said Tony, and this time he turned and we both looked at Iwanek like a couple of used car dealers at an auction, assessing the merchandise.

"What makes you think I know him?" I said.

"Just listen to him," he whispered again. "Playing with fire, playing with the big boys." He sighed and looked at me, eyes hard and cold. Like his voice.

"Three reasons, sport. One, he was waiting for you outside the wine bar when we met two days ago. Two, he followed you here today. Three, he can't take his eyes off you. There's either something very wrong here or he's in love with you. Talk to me."

"I hired him."

"To do what? To follow you? Is that what he is, protection?"

"No, I guess he's checking me out, the equivalent of you or me asking for references or getting a credit check done. It's not a problem." A lie, that one. Iwanek was a problem, a real humdinger, and one that I wasn't sure how to deal with. Hell, hell, hell.

"What's going on?" he pressed. "What in God's name would you want to hire a man like that for?"

I suppose lying is like eating raw oysters, the first one is the hardest, you've got a psychological barrier to cross, but once it's done you never look back, it just gets easier and easier. I had no trouble with lie number two but if I'd had a life-size portrait of myself in the attic, done in oils and framed in gilt, then the face would have started to blemish, the skin to wrinkle and age.

"This client I wanted a girl for is going to need looking after while he's in London. That guy there was recommended to me, and I asked him to recruit another two. There's quite a bit of money involved, I suppose he just wants to confirm who he's working for." That sounded about as solid as a self-assembly kitchen unit, because if it was bodyguards I'd wanted then I would obviously have gone to Tony, but he let that pass.

"What do you want to do with him?" he asked.

"Let me talk to him. I'll point out the error of his ways."

"I could get my two friends there to give him the good news."

"No, I don't want him hurt, he was just a little overenthusiastic. Can I borrow them for a few minutes, though?"

"Sure. They won't break."

I walked over the bridge and down to the path where the three of them sat like a row of brass monkeys. I stood in front of Iwanek and he looked up at me, unsmiling.

"Satisfied?" I asked, and I knew I had to be careful because everything I said would be relayed back to Tony and I was in enough trouble already. He just kept looking at me, curious rather than afraid.

"Are you satisfied?" I repeated. I had to convince him that I was in control, a hard man who could cause him a lot of grief if I chose to. The two men sitting like a couple of bookends would go a long way to persuading him, and if the worst came to the worst I knew they could hurt him badly. But then I'd run the risk of losing him.

"You wouldn't have expected me to accept the sort of job you offered without knowing what I was getting into," he said, and the tone left me in no doubt that he was the hard man, not me.

"You've already accepted the job and you took my money. It's too late to be checking up on me. You're hired and there's no going back. You've given me a dilemma, Jim. I can't have you following me all over

London, now can I? You'll get in my way. But if I break your legs, correction, if I get these two to break your legs, then you'll be no use to me. What shall I do, Jim? Advise me."

"These two don't worry me," he said, and I believed him. "But I've got the message. I wanted to know who you are, what you do, and the sort of circles you move in. I still don't know what you're up to, but I've an idea now of the sort of business you're in. I won't bother you again. Give me a call when you're ready."

He got to his feet and walked off without a backward look, leaving me to escort the two heavies back to Tony.

"I don't suppose you'd tell me what you're up to even if I asked," he said. "So I won't."

"I'll be all right," I replied. "I know what I'm doing."

I didn't hear a cock crow and the sky didn't split open to unleash a bolt of lightning, but I knew I'd lied three times and that the third lie had slipped off my tongue like butter off a hot knife. I left Tony behind and went off in search of a cab, having added years to the hypothetical portrait in my hypothetical attic.

The evening sky was threatening rain as McKinley braked sharply in front of Sammy's flat, sharply enough to throw me forward but not sharply enough to snap the seat belt and send me tumbling over the bonnet. Not quite. The taxi driver who'd managed to slam on his brakes and squeal to a halt three inches from our rear bumper hit his horn angrily, reversed his cab and drove past glaring at McKinley who took not a blind bit of notice.

"I'll wait here, boss," he said.

"You're double parked, Get-Up, but we won't be long," I replied, but I was only halfway out of the Granada as she came through the front door and down the steps.

She'd curled her red hair and it bounced and shimmered as she walked, the ends stroking her bare shoulders. Her dress was long and black and could have been worn to a funeral if she'd wanted to be gang-raped by the pall bearers. It was slashed from the ground to just below her waist on both sides and her long brown legs flashed in and out as she clicked down the steps on high heels. Three things held the dress up, two thread-like silver chains across each shoulder and the swell of her breasts. Around her perfect neck was a single strand of pearls matched by a smaller group on her left wrist. It was all the jewellery she was wearing and Sammy didn't even need that.

"You look delicious," I said as I reached for her hand.

"Don't I just?" she laughed, and I helped her into the back seat and slid in beside her. "I hope you appreciate all the effort that went into creating this work of art."

"You'll be telling me next that bodies like yours don't grow on trees."

"They don't grow like this at all without a great deal of work. A lot of exercise, a lot of care and attention, and a lot of money."

"You make it sound like owning an expensive car, looking after the bodywork and keeping the engine in

102

good running order." She crossed her legs as I spoke and her slender foot brushed against my trouser leg.

"That's a fair comparison," she said, and already her hand had found its way to my knee, circling it thoughtfully. "But some collectors' cars are more than a hundred years old. I'll be lucky if I stay in concours condition for another five. And it's not as if I've only had one careful owner."

Now she was laughing, eyes sparkling as she tilted her head to one side and looked my face over. She reached up and stroked my right ear, nipping the lobe between finger and thumb. "Where are we going?" she asked.

We weren't going anywhere because McKinley was twisted round in the driver's seat, mouth agape, eyes eating up Sammy and what the hell, who could blame him? She'd turn more heads than a road accident dressed like this.

"Let's go, Get-Up," I said, and as he turned back in his seat his eyes were the last thing to move. He sighed, deeply and sorrowfully, like a poodle being asked to leave the bed of his mistress. He put the car into second gear and drove away from the kerb in jerks and jumps before switching the wrong indicator light on.

It took thirty minutes of McKinley's stop-start driving before he dropped us in front of the four-storey grey stone building in Berkeley Square which houses Spencers, a restaurant used mainly by advertising executives and media salesmen and anyone else on no-questions-asked expense accounts.

The square was clogged up with traffic and any nightingale brave or stupid enough to venture there to sing would be coughing up phlegm for a month. Several horns honked as McKinley leant over and asked what time he should pick us up.

"Just hang around, Get-Up. I won't be long," I told him. "Find a parking space nearby and keep your eyes on the front door."

I took Sammy by the arm and together we walked up the stone steps, past the twin bay trees standing guard duty either side of the door and through the bar.

The food in Spencers tended to be overcooked and overpriced and the decor completely over the top: vivid flock wallpaper, cheap paintings in expensive gilded frames, and huge ornate chandeliers with electric candles flickering annoyingly. But it did have one advantage over any of a dozen other places I would quite happily have taken Sammy to — Ronnie Laing could be found there three or four evenings a week, often dining alone. He used Spencers as his canteen, always had the same table, was treated like a long-lost relative every time he crossed the threshold and knew the menu by heart. He tipped well, usually took the maître d's advice on food and let the wine waiter choose his drink. They couldn't have loved him more if he'd rolled up his sleeves and pitched in with the washing up.

A phone call earlier in the evening had confirmed that Laing had booked a table, and as Sammy and I were shown to a booth I saw him sitting in a corner facing the entrance, on his own and halfway through a plate of mussels, either a large starter or a small main course.

"We'll sit here, if you don't mind," I said, as the waiter tried to steer us away from Laing, and I pointed to one of the small circular tables about twelve feet from where he was sitting. I recognized him from the photographs that had appeared at the time of the takeover but he wouldn't have known me from Adam. He didn't go to the funeral. He didn't go to either of them.

"Not at all, sir," said the waiter through clenched teeth, and the "sir" was very much an afterthought as he pulled out the chair for Sammy. Unfortunately it was the chair facing away from Laing and the waiter barely concealed his disdain as I slid into it myself and motioned her to take the other one. He rushed round to pull out the second chair and was rewarded with a toe-curling smile from Sammy and a long lingering look down the front of her dress.

I wondered if it would be enough to make him forget my breach of etiquette but he handed Sammy a menu as if he were passing her a love letter and pushed one at me as if he were serving me with a summons, so I guessed it would take more than Sammy's superb figure to wipe that one out. What the hell, tonight I wasn't going to be winning any prizes for good manners so I might as well start as I meant to go on.

"A double whisky, a malt, and you'd better make it a good one," I said in the sort of voice you'd use to tell an Alsatian to walk to heel. Then I stuck my head into the menu until he tapped his pencil on his notepad, coughed, and asked, "And for the lady?" with the accent heavily on "lady" as if offering Sammy his sympathy for being with a lout like me.

"Good Lord, she's got a tongue in her head, man. Ask her yourself."

Sammy kept looking at the table, her head down as if in prayer and her hands in her lap. "I'll have a white wine," she said, then looked up at the waiter through lowered lashes and moistened her lips and added "please". She turned her head to look at me and then looked past me over my left shoulder and smiled and I knew she'd seen Laing and that he'd seen her.

"Not bored already, are you?" I asked and her eyes snapped back to meet mine and she caught her breath.

"No, no, I'm fine."

"Well, what do you want to eat?"

"I'll have whatever you're having."

"God, you're such a doormat." The waiter returned with the drinks and I reached up and took my whisky off his tray while he was placing Sammy's white wine in front of her. I drank it in one swallow and handed it back. "Get me another." Sammy was looking at Laing again and nervously fingering her hair so that from where he was sitting he'd see she wasn't wearing a ring.

"How was work today?" she asked.

"Same as it always is, boring but well paid, and the last thing I want to talk about is how boring and well paid it is. I don't take you out to go over my business problems — that's what I pay an accountant for. I just want you to look pretty and smooth my feathers.

Sometimes I wonder how I've managed to put up with you for so long. And where did you get that dress?"

"A boutique in Chelsea, I thought you'd like it."

"You thought wrong. It doesn't suit you at all, it's not your colour. How many times have I told you not to wear black?"

My second drink arrived as she bit her bottom lip and said in a quiet voice: "I can't seem to do anything right today."

I slammed the empty glass down hard enough to shake the candles on the table.

"Perhaps you'd better just keep quiet then," I said and waved the waiter over, ordering for us both without consulting her and demanding another double whisky.

"And another white wine," I added.

"I'm fine, thank you," she whispered and there were tears in her eyes.

"You're not fine, now drink that up," I said. "You're more fun when you've had a few drinks. In bed and out of it." Now she was crying silently, hands playing with her serviette, screwing it up into a tight knot.

"I'm going to the toilet," I said and stood up unsteadily, pushing the chair back so violently that it fell over with a crash and the waiter scurried over to pick it up. "Don't fuss, man," I said and headed for the gents, managing to bump into two tables on the way. As I barged through the door I saw Laing get to his feet and move towards Sammy.

I stayed in the white-tiled room long enough for Sammy to spill her tale of woe to Laing, to tell him of a relationship that had gone sour but which she was too frightened to end, of the verbal and physical batterings I'd given her, of the times I had humiliated her and abused her. Then she would dab her reddening eyes and sniff and he'd put his hand on hers and tell her gently that everything was going to be all right and that if she really wanted to get rid of the bullying bastard he was just the man to do it, and she would flutter those long, curling eyelashes and say that she'd be so grateful, so very grateful, but to take care because she had seen me put two men in hospital because they'd taken too much of an interest in her. She would dry her eyes and smile bravely and tell him her name was Amanda, that she was a model and that she lived in Islington, and she would give him the address of the furnished two-bedroomed first-floor flat that we'd rented in the name of Amanda Pearson a week earlier.

I walked back to Sammy's table and stood looking down at her, hands on hips, glaring and demanding to know just what the hell was going on, spraying her with spittle as I spoke, every inch the drunken bore who deserved everything that was coming to him. Please God don't let him break anything, bones, teeth or nose.

"I think you'd better go," said Laing as he got to his feet, and it was the voice of a man used to getting his own way. He put a warning hand on my shoulder and two waiters hovered anxiously behind him, unwilling to interfere between a drunk and their favourite customer playing white knight.

"Keep out of this," I said without turning. To Sammy I said: "Get up, we're leaving."

"She's staying. With me. You're the one that's going," he said and the grip tightened. I took a deep breath and turned and pulled back my fist, and he hit me once about an inch above my solar plexus and my legs collapsed, the contents of my lungs exploded out of my mouth and I tasted bitter bile at the back of my throat, and then I was on my knees, hands clutched to my chest, coughing and choking. At least he hadn't hit me in the face, but even that was no consolation as I fought to breathe. I looked up at him and tried to speak and he stepped forward and thrust his knee into my face. I went backwards and the bile was replaced with the warm, salty taste of blood as my head hit the floor.

The two waiters stepped forward and picked me up and half led, half carried me to the manager's office where they wiped the blood from my mouth and told me that they wouldn't call the police this time, but I was never to darken their doorstep again and then they half carried, half pushed me out of the front door and down the steps to Berkeley Square.

"Jesus, boss, what happened?" asked McKinley, as I opened the car door and lowered myself painfully into the passenger seat.

"Just take me home, Get-Up. Slowly and carefully." I could just about breathe but it was an effort and my mouth and chin were on fire. Two of my front teeth felt loose, my lip was still bleeding and spots of blood fell onto my trousers until I held my handkerchief to my aching face.

"What about Miss Darvell?" he asked as he shoved the gear stick forward and hauled the steering wheel round. "Are you sure you don't want me to deal with this, boss?" he said before I could answer his first question. "It won't do your reputation any good letting somebody hit you and get away with it. Tell me who it was and let me sort them out for you."

"It's all right, Get-Up, honestly. Miss Darvell and I have just decided to part company for a while, that's all. Take me home. And if you see an all-night chemist on the way, stop off and get me some antiseptic. And some aspirin."

Then I closed my eyes and leaned back in the seat and stretched my legs forward. McKinley muttered under his breath as the car picked up speed. I'm not sure what he said but it sounded like "Jesus, she must pack a helluva punch."

"So Laing doesn't do much in the way of drugs now?" I asked, lying back in the armchair and putting my feet on the glass coffee table between the chrome ice bucket and the three-quarters empty bottle of malt that McKinley and I were working our way through.

It was one o'clock in the morning, two days after I'd introduced Laing to Sammy, and we'd spent the evening at the Eve Club in Regent Street. The lip was healing nicely. If I was lucky it wouldn't leave a scar. I'd been plying McKinley with drink for more than five hours, and now his eyes were bleary and his voice slurred and I was once again asking him about his past. It was a bit like mining for gold, you had to sort through tens of tons of worthless crushed rock to come up with an ounce of the yellow stuff.

"Don't forget I haven't seen him for seven years or so, boss, but from what I hear he still does a bit to keep his hand in, but he's up against the big boys now," McKinley said as he leant over for the bottle, shoulders straining through the dark blue suit I'd bought him two weeks earlier which was already soiled and stained with everything from spirits to engine oil and a few other substances I couldn't have identified even if I'd wanted to. He emptied the bottle into the glass, splashed in a handful of melting ice cubes and drank noisily as he wiped his wet hand on his trouser leg.

"Why did you never go back and work for him when you came out?" I asked. "You all went down quietly enough."

"Jesus, boss, what do you expect? If we'd grassed we'd have lost our kneecaps, our balls and anything else that hadn't been nailed to the floor. That's why we kept our mouths shut. I tried to see him my second day out but the message passed to me was that he didn't want anyone with a record on the payroll, so thanks but no thanks. All I got was a lousy five-hundred pound pay off — for seven years. Bastard." His glass was empty now and he looked at me expectantly, and I nodded towards the sideboard from where he liberated another bottle.

We drank in silence for a while, or at least McKinley drank while I remained almost horizontal and watched the brass light fitting in the centre of the plaster ceiling rose through half-closed eyes, making light patterns with my eyelashes as I listened to the sound of my own breathing.

"Do you think I'm stupid, boss?" he asked eventually.

"What?" I replied, opening my eyes and raising my head so I could see him slumped in the chair opposite mine and running his hand through his unkempt hair.

"I said, do you think I'm stupid?"

I leant back and looked at the ceiling again. "That's a tough one, Get-Up. I mean, if I were to ask you who Don Giovanni was, would you think that he was an Italian Godfather?"

His forehead creased in a frown but he saw by the look on my face that I wasn't taking him seriously and he didn't ask "Don who?" Whatever had been irritating his scalp had now crawled down to his beard which he scratched vigorously like a dog worrying its nether regions. "Don't take the piss, I'm serious, boss."

"I can see that, Get-Up. Come on, get it off your chest. What's worrying you?"

The irritation had migrated to his right ear and he was wiggling his index finger up and down and in and out furiously, screwing his eyes up as he concentrated and spilling whisky over his knees as his glass trembled.

If I'd been a psychologist I would probably have marked it down as acute displacement behaviour, but knowing McKinley it was more likely something with six legs and dirty feet.

I was sitting up now, holding my glass with both hands and trying to read this strange, big and possibly dangerous man mountain because any problem he had could quite easily and quickly become my headache.

"Well, it's like this," he said. "You've given me a job, and you pay me well, and you treat me with respect, though sometimes I don't understand what you're saying to me and sometimes I think you're taking the Michael, but generally you're OK and I like working for you."

"That's nice to know — if ever I need a reference I'll come to you. What is it you're after, a raise?" I knew it wasn't money he was after, it was an explanation, but I had to let him ask for it in his own sweet time.

"No, it's not that, boss. It's just that, well, it's as if . . ." He fell silent, staring at my shoelaces like Sammy's cat, deep in thought. Then, as if he'd finally made up his mind about something, he raised his eyes sharply. "It's all these questions you keep asking me. It's worse than being collared by the law. You keep pumping me about Ronnie Laing and his connections, how does he do this, how does he do that, who does he know, where does he live, where does he eat? Jesus, boss, I don't owe Laing no favours but I'd like to know what it is you're up to."

He'd stopped fidgeting with his hands but he chewed his lower lip as he waited for my answer.

"Fair enough, Get-Up, but there's nothing sinister happening, believe me. I used to do a fair bit of drugs dealing up in Glasgow, mainly cocaine — I've told you that already. I had contacts going all the way from the ice-cream vans that tour the housing schemes up to the guys who service the universities and I made a good living out of it, but eventually I ran into the same problem as your ex-boss. A gang of neds who used to

113

specialize in armed robbery decided to go into the drugs business in a big way at my expense. They didn't have my contacts but they found out where I was getting my supplies from and after a bit of persuasion those supplies dried up, and once I couldn't come up with the goods my customers moved on. That's why I moved to London."

This was starting to sound like something Hans Christian Andersen might have written on an off day, but from the way McKinley was nodding his head it looked as if he believed me. I refilled his glass with whisky and leant back in the chair.

"I need a new supply of coke, Get-Up, and when I discovered you used to work for Laing I figured he might be able to help. But from what you've been saying that's a non-starter."

"Too true," he said. "And anyway I'm yesterday's news as far as that bastard's concerned. He wouldn't do me any favours." He went quiet and looked at my shoelaces again. "I might be able to put you in touch with someone who could help, though."

I knew then how the Klondyke prospectors must have felt when they first found a small nugget of gold glinting in the dross, because at last I was going to get what I wanted from McKinley.

"I thought you'd be out of touch after seven years."

"Most of the old faces are still in the business, give or take the few who've moved on or been sent down. What is it you want, exactly?"

"You sound like a genie from a bottle, Get-Up. OK, I'll tell you what I want. I've got £250,000 in cash that

114

I want to turn into white powder. What I need is someone to arrange the deal for me, to fix up a time and a place where I can hand over the cash in exchange for the drugs. After what happened to me in Glasgow I want to keep as low a profile as possible, so whoever I get will have to have the right contacts and be the sort who'll keep his mouth shut about my involvement. I need a middle-man, not so close to the streets that he can't think bigger than a few grams, but not so big that he isn't hungry. Well genie, can you grant me this boon, or should I uncork another bottle?"

"I think I can help, boss," he said. "And, yes, I would like another drink." I poured him a refill before he continued. "One of the guys Laing used to arrange shipments through went down soon after me for a three-year stretch, Davie Read. When he came out he was in the same boat as me, Laing wouldn't give him the time of day, so he's been doing some freelance dealing. He's got the contacts but he doesn't have the money to set up anything big himself, he's strictly small time.

"I reckon he'd jump at the chance if you'd cut him in for a percentage. Do you want me to arrange a meet?"

"Sure, he sounds perfect. In fact he sounds too good to be true. Can you trust him?"

"I don't see why not, boss. I'll tell him you're the front man for some very heavy characters and that if he steps out of line you'll have both of his legs broken."

"You mean you'll appeal to the more sensitive side of his nature?" At that McKinley roared with laughter, he tossed his head back and I could have counted the fillings in the teeth he had left if I'd wanted to get a bit closer to his open mouth, but that had about as much attraction as inspecting a blocked drain.

"I've got a better cover story, Get-Up. This is what I want you to tell him," and I gave him a story on a par with Snow White and the Seven Dwarfs. Hi ho, hi ho, it's off to work we go.

Kyle's office was on the first floor of a refurbished building, in a narrow street a grapefruit's throw from Spitalfields Market. It was early evening and I waited near the carpark where Kyle's Mercedes was parked, sleek and shiny new and as green as the lettuce leaves blown up against the tyres by a light breeze.

The market had been closed for several hours and scavenging down and outs were sifting through the roadside rubbish, picking out bruised and rotting apples and potatoes and carefully placing them in old carrier bags or in the pockets of tired, worn overcoats.

Two rooks cawed and coughed and dived on a discarded banana, and pecked it apart until one of the last few delivery trucks roared round the corner and made them hop angrily on to the pavement. They were soon back in the road, pulling and eating, feathers as black and glossy as the leather briefcase I was carrying, which along with the Burberry and dark pinstripe suit branded me as one of the many office workers who'd moved into the area around Liverpool Street station as the overcrowded City pushed relentlessly east, upgrading buildings and filling them full of word processors, designer furniture and anti-static carpet tiles.

I was sitting on the low, red railing which surrounded the carpark, briefcase balanced on my knees, and from there I could see the door to Kyle's office, though I was too far away to see the small brass plate which read "Property and Financial Services".

On either side of the black panelled door, fixed to the wall about ten feet above the cobbled pavement, were two wicker cages, each containing a single songbird singing its heart out.

Maybe they were singing because they were happy, maybe because they wouldn't get fed if they didn't sing, maybe they were calling to each other and professing undying love, but I reckoned they were crying to be let out, to be allowed to fly free above the stonecleaned offices and reslated roofs and join the crows and down and outs foraging for food instead of singing for their bird seed supper.

The door opened, and the birds redoubled their efforts as Kyle stepped onto the pavement and started walking towards the car. I was already up and moving quickly, anxiously looking at my watch, a man in a hurry with a train to catch. I crossed the road ahead of him, looked at my watch again, thirty feet, twenty feet, and then I was falling, tripping over my feet and losing the case as I pitched forward, hands outstretched to break my fall.

I hit the ground at the same time as the briefcase caught Kyle below the knees, scuffing my gloves on the cobbles and feeling my trousers tear. As I cursed and swore and pulled myself to my feet Kyle picked up my briefcase by the handle, then held it by either end as he handed it back to me.

"Not hurt?" he asked and I said no, thanks for helping me and whose bloody idea was it to have a cobbled pavement in the first place? And then he was gone, on his way to the shiny green Mercedes leaving me with three perfect sets of fingerprints on the case, which I was careful not to smudge with my gloved hands and which was going straight into a polythene bag when I got back to the flat.

"I'd like to meet him," Sammy had said, and I knew without a shadow of a doubt that David would love to meet her. It was a nuisance to arrange, to explain to McKinley that I'd be out of circulation for a day, to fix up the Shuttle tickets and a hire car, to ring Shankland Hall and tell them I was taking David out.

It was a nuisance but it was worth it, worth it to see David hug Sammy and stroke her flowing hair, to see her talk to him and kiss him softly on the forehead. They clicked and I was overjoyed, she wasn't awkward with him, or pitying, she was just warm and tender, like a big sister. I loved her for it.

"The zoo," I told David when he asked where we were going. I drove while he and Sammy sat in the back and we played word games, calling out animals in alphabetical order. Sammy made an appalling attempt to cheat by claiming that asparagus and aubergine were types of mammals and got a gentle cuff from David.

The Highland Wildlife Park, near Kincraig in Inverness-shire, is about forty miles due north of

Pitlochry, and though I'd told David we were going to the zoo, it wasn't to see elephants, tigers and giraffes. All the animals there are native to Scotland, though many of them are long since extinct in the wild. Driving safari-park style along a wild and rugged road there are deer and cattle in something approaching their natural environment, and you can see brown bears, lynxes and Scottish wild cats close up. David and I were regular visitors, mainly I guess because he loved the Pets Corner where he could touch and hold and feed and play with animals who didn't care who or what he was, just that he was gentle and had food for them.

It was a chilly day despite a watery sun, so I made sure his old sheepskin jacket was buttoned up high over his thick red polo-neck sweater before we tramped around the enclosures. David was inexhaustible, running from cage to cage while Sammy and I walked after him, arms linked.

"What's your favourite animal?" I asked her.

"Easy," she said. "Polar bears."

"You'll have to explain that one."

"Purely visual, I suppose. Big and white and furry, friendly faces. They give the impression you could cuddle up next to them and be safe and warm and protected, but when they move you're left in no doubt about their immense strength and power, muscles rippling under the fur, paws big enough to rip a man's head off. Protective of their mates, gentle with their young, afraid of nothing. I love them. I'd take one home with me if I could."

"They're killers, you know?"

"I know that, and in a way that's part of the attraction. To be that close to something that could kill if it wanted to, and yet to be safe and comfortable. Do you think I need a father figure?"

"Sammy, that's the last thing I think you need," I said and she giggled.

"What's your favourite?" she asked.

"I knew as soon as the question left my lips that you'd ask it right back," I said, and slipped my arm around her waist. "I'll have to think."

Together we followed David towards the otter pool. It was just after three pm and it was feeding time. There are some questions that reveal a lot about a person. Sammy's answer had told me something about her, it had shown me a side of her I wouldn't otherwise have seen, and my answer would do the same, unless I lied. But I wouldn't lie, I decided.

"My favourite isn't here either," I said. "And I'm glad, I feel uneasy seeing any animal in captivity, but I feel most for the dolphins."

She was listening closely, head tilted, brushing the hair away from her eyes, watching my face. She didn't have to ask why because she knew I'd explain.

"They're so bright, so intelligent, so perfectly adapted to their environment. Have you ever seen them close up?"

"I went to a dolphinarium once, but it made me feel sad."

"I know. They do tricks, but at least they're not like sealions. Sealions are clowns, clapping, balancing balls

120

and walking on their flippers, doing tricks for food. Nature's buskers. I hate to see that."

A keeper was throwing small dead silvery fish to the otters with a minimum of fuss, and once the glossy animals had tired of chasing their food he tipped the contents of his red plastic bucket into the greenish water and walked away, leaving them to eat in peace, nervously eyeing each other as they chewed noisily like dossers in a soup kitchen.

"Dolphins are different," I continued. "They are much more intelligent. In the wild they're something else. Friendly, sociable, playful, gentle. They don't interfere with anyone else and they're completely non-aggressive, no claws, no sharp teeth, no spikes. But they'll kill to protect themselves, and they'll band together to fight off an enemy. God help the shark that tries to attack a dolphin."

We stood together, watching David watching the otters feed until they'd finished. Then he romped over and forced his way between us, holding our hands and bouncing up and down as we walked back to the car. He asked if we could come back and I said yes, of course and he said what about Sammy and I said yes, she'd come too and he said what about Shona and I had to think about that one.

She was waiting for us when we arrived back at Shankland Hall, leaning against her Rover, smiling the smile of the wounded.

"You might have said you'd be taking David out today," she said, looking Sammy up and down as we got out of the car. She stepped forward and kissed me on the cheek, and then hugged David before wiping saliva off his chin with a handkerchief. "Hiya, kid," she said to him and he laughed uncontrollably. The sister came out and David went inside with her, still laughing as he waved goodbye. This time there were no "don't go's", the parting was easier, and I think that was because Sammy had been there and he knew he had another friend.

The three of us drove to a small country pub three miles from the nursing home, taking the two cars which was a problem because I had to choose but it was no choice really, I had to go with Sammy. Strike that, I wanted to go with Sammy.

The pub was a weathered stone building amid a clump of grey houses, probably the only source of live entertainment for miles around, but it was virtually empty, just a few red-veined locals standing by the bar and downing whisky as if the licensing laws had never been relaxed north of the border.

An untidy tower of roughly-hewn logs burned in a large brick fireplace, filling the room with warmth and smoke. To the left was a small bench seat, in front of it a round knee-high table made from the same dark wood, with two comfortable old chairs on either side. Shona and Sammy each flopped down into one. That left the bench seat for me, and when I'd put the drinks on the table and sat down they were facing me like a pair of temple dogs.

"Well, this is nice," said Shona. "Cheers." It wasn't like her to be so bitchy but she was right, I should have let her know I was going to see David and I shouldn't have sprung Sammy on her like an unfavourable diagnosis.

"Did you enjoy yourselves?" she asked me, and I nodded and told her where we'd been.

"He's a lovely boy," said Sammy, and Shona smiled at her, the smile of a predator ready to pounce. I'd never have to ask Shona what her favourite animal was, it would have to be the tiger, sleek and beautiful, quick to purr and quick to kill. I'd seen her in action many times, and admired her for it, but this was different. This was Sammy, and Sammy was a friend on unfamiliar territory.

"Yes, he is," said Shona. "Have you been to Scotland before?"

"No, this is my first time," Sammy replied. "But I love it, the air is so fresh, the hills have a rugged beauty that you simply don't see down south, and the people are so friendly. I'll be back."

"I'm sure you will," said Shona. "I'm sure you will," she repeated, quietly and thoughtfully. I felt like a sick pigeon being fought over by a couple of alley cats, but I couldn't understand why their claws were out, they weren't a threat to each other and I wasn't playing favourites. Or maybe I was, perhaps that was the problem.

"Sammy's a friend of Tony's," I said, and Shona raised an eyebrow as if to say, "I just bet she is."

"Do you work together?" she asked.

"You mean Tony and I? Yes, sort of. I'm in public relations." Which was, of course, absolutely true but I still grinned and stopped worrying. She was a big girl

123

and could take care of herself. They fenced for a while but Sammy had the edge because I'd talked to her so often about Shona, and after half an hour or so the conversation eased and they discussed clothes and shops, diverting the rivalry into a friendly argument about the merits of their two cities, a dispute about cultures and not personalities. They parted as almost friends and I knew that next time they met they'd peck cheeks like old school chums but they'd never be close, never have heart-to-hearts or cry on each other's shoulders. I could live with that.

"You'll be back soon?" Shona asked me in the pub carpark and I said yes, a couple of weeks at the most, I promise, maybe sooner. We took the same road back to Edinburgh but Shona had her foot hard on the accelerator and she soon left us far behind.

A couple of days after Sammy and I got back from Scotland McKinley fixed up the meeting with Davie Read. To fit in with the cover story, we arranged an appointment at Salisbury House in Finsbury Circus, the London headquarters of the National Bank of Detroit. One of the biggest blocks in the area, its face of light brown sandstone and window boxes bursting with purple and white flowers looked down on four games of bowls being played by shirt-sleeved office workers on a tiny green in the centre of the Circus gardens.

I waited close to the polished granite steps leading up to the main entrance foyer until I saw McKinley and Read arrive in the Granada, the rear wheels catching the kerb as they turned into the Circus looking for an empty parking meter. I walked quickly up to the reception desk and asked to speak to Mr Kolacowosky and hoped to God they didn't actually have anyone of that name in the building. I kept one eye on the glass doors as the girl behind the desk looked through her internal telephone directory, shaking her head and saying yes, she had heard me say the name but how on earth did you spell it?

As McKinley and Read started up the steps I told her not to bother and that Mr Kolacowosky had obviously moved on to better things and I headed for the door. I met them halfway down and steered Read round, my arm on his shoulder, thanking him for coming and saying to Get-Up that, with the sensitive nature of the arrangements, it might be better if we spoke in the open air and not in my office where we never knew who might be next door with his ear pressed against a glass tumbler.

McKinley nodded and said he understood and Read said what a good idea, and all three of us were nodding like those little dogs you see in the back of resprayed Ford Cortinas with large fluffy dice hanging from the driver's mirror.

I herded them over the road to the Circus gardens like a collie with a couple of wayward sheep, encouraged them past the bicycles chained to the black railings, through the gateway and down the tarmac path which circled the bowling green.

It was two-thirty pm so most of the lunching office workers had gone back to their desks and computer terminals, but several of the wooden benches were still occupied by men in suits and women in smart summer dresses eating Marks and Spencer sandwiches, salads from Tupperware containers and doughnuts from brown paper bags as they stretched out their legs and enjoyed the waning warmth of the afternoon sun.

The air buzzed with the sound of traffic and the two-way radios of the motorcycle messengers. Through the trees came the sound of drilling and cutting and hammering from the repair and refurbishment that's always a part of the City background noise, standards and rents leapfrogging each other madly behind miles of dust-covered scaffolding.

Davie Read was about forty years old and a similar build to McKinley — as I walked between them I felt like a slice of corned beef in a roll. He was clean shaven and sweating slightly, either through nervousness or the heat, and in his large brown checked jacket and beige trousers he could have passed for a middle-ranking insurance salesman with a three-bedroomed semi in Ealing and a two-year-old Sierra in the drive. He wore a pair of gold-rimmed glasses and as we walked he pulled out a green handkerchief from his top pocket, mopped his wet forehead and blew his bulbous, slightly red nose. With his nose and girth he could have been a heavy drinker, but his breath smelt fresh so he was either a gin and tonic or vodka man or he was on his best behaviour. Whatever, he was all I had and McKinley said he could be trusted.

We passed four building workers lying shirtless on the grass, sunning themselves and looking up the skirts of anything aged between twelve and fifty that walked by.

"Get-Up's told you what I'm after?" I asked, as Read returned the damp handkerchief to his pocket, the sweat already reappearing on his mopped brow.

"Cocaine, a quarter of a million pounds' worth. That shouldn't be a problem, but he was a bit vague about why you wanted it — that's one hell of a lot of sniffing." The glasses slipped slightly down his nose and he looked over the top of them like an admonishing professor. Hurry up, boy, explain yourself, except if I did this professor would be off like a scalded rabbit. My feet tingled as a Tube train ran through the tunnel below us from Liverpool Street to Moorgate, and the back of my neck tingled because if he didn't believe me I could end up buried beneath the earth at a similar depth to the train.

"I need to make a lot of money, and fast," I said. "I represent a group of investors who borrowed heavily to invest in the commodity markets, coffee in particular. We were banking on a heavy frost this year but it never materialized and instead there was a bumper crop and prices fell like a stone. We weren't alone, a lot of people have got their fingers burnt, it took everybody by surprise. Unfortunately we're not in a position to pay back the money we borrowed and we've only got a few weeks to make good the loss.

"We've decided that the most effective use we could make of our remaining capital is to go back into the commodity market, but in a different way. If we import

£250,000 of cocaine we can realize it for close to two million pounds and recoup our losses."

I spoke slowly and clearly, like a marketing director revealing his strategy for the forthcoming financial year and hoping that nobody would spot any flaws. From where we were standing we could just see the top of the National Westminster Tower, rising a head and shoulders above the rest of the City office blocks. If you could find a very large lumberjack with an axe the size of a bus and persuade him to hack away at the base of the tower long and hard, and if he pushed it in our direction and it began to topple then the top two floors would crash down onto the three remaining games of bowls being played on the green. My mind was wandering, tension does that sometimes, and I brought myself back to reality. This was no time to be daydreaming. McKinley had already told Read the tale of woe, how a group of would-be City whizz kids had got their fingers burned gambling on the commodities market with other people's money and how those singed digits would be caught firmly in the till when the auditors came a-calling next month. And to make the cheese in the trap look even more tempting he'd told Read that I was so desperate that he'd be able to cut himself a slice of the action.

Read started to nibble. "How do you plan to get rid of it?" he asked.

Down boy, don't get too greedy. "That's my problem — you can leave the distribution to me. All I want from you is the stuff wholesale. I suppose I'm not telling you anything you don't already know if I point out that

128

coke is a rich man's drug. It's served up at all the best dinner parties instead of liqueurs, it's used widely in the City, everyone from advertising executives to merchant bankers is trying and enjoying it. And it isn't bought on street corners. The middle classes have their own distribution system and it's very well protected, believe me. It's not heroin, after all."

We walked on in silence, Read with his brow furrowed as if he had a difficult decision to make but he'd already decided to bite. The only thought in his mind now was how much of the cheese he could grab before the trap clamped shut.

"What's in it for me?" he asked, and he looked across at McKinley who was busy trying to scratch the middle of his back, shoving his left arm down his shirt collar and grunting. McKinley had already told him he could stick out for ten per cent of the gross if everything went smoothly, so when I offered him three thousand expenses up front and five per cent he sucked air in through his front teeth as if he was testing for cavities.

"Not enough," he said. I pressed him.

"I'm offering almost sixteen grand for setting up one deal. I put up all the cash, McKinley and I will collect the coke, you don't even have to be there. All you have to do is make a few phone calls."

He gave me the sort of look the wolf gave Little Red Riding Hood and he damn near started rubbing his hands together, pound signs rolling up behind the gold-rimmed glasses.

"Look, squire, if it's that easy you don't need me. And if it isn't that easy, and you can take it from me that it isn't, then I want more than a lousy five per cent."

"I could find somebody else."

"Sure you could, sure you could," he said. "Except we both know you're running out of time, don't we?"

I gave McKinley a withering glare for Read's benefit and fingered my watch. "I suppose I can go as high as ten per cent."

He positively beamed. "That's more like it. But I'm still going to want the three grand expenses."

I had the money ready and I handed it to him. "You're quite happy taking the rest of your fee in cocaine?"

"I wouldn't have it any other way," he laughed, because twenty-five thousand pounds in white powder would be worth ten times as much on the streets. He wouldn't be pushing it to estate agents and record company A and R men, he'd be selling it in little plastic packets diluted to a fraction of its original strength.

"I'd like to talk specifics," I said. "How do you plan to make the delivery?"

He took the handkerchief out of his pocket again, and snapped it open with a flourish as we started our second circuit of the garden.

"The people I have in mind usually bring it over from Ireland by sea, and I'll arrange to collect it, probably somewhere on the west coast of Scotland. I'll let you know where. But if you like I'll bring it right to your door. At no extra cost." He smiled, just sign on the dotted line, sir, you won't regret it.

130

"I want to be there when the stuff is handed over and when my cash is counted. And when you take your percentage."

"That's fine by me," he said. "I'll ring Get-Up with the arrangements."

"Don't leave it too long," I replied. "I'd like to get this over with as soon as possible." And that was that. Easier than ordering a three-piece suite from Harrods.

We turned back and walked out through the main entrance and threaded our way in and out of the Circus traffic. At the bottom of the steps to the bank I shook Read by the hand and said I looked forward to doing business with him. As he and McKinley returned to the Granada I went up the steps, through the double glass doors and back into the reception area. The girl's face fell as I gave her a cheery smile, put my palms down on the teak-veneered desk and asked her if, by any chance, Mr Kolacowosky had left a forwarding address?

Read got back to McKinley two days later, on the Wednesday. Yes, the deal was on, the cocaine would be brought over from Ireland in ten days' time on a fishing boat which would be anchored in the Firth of Lorn, a few miles off Minard Point on the west coast of Scotland. The delivery would be taken the rest of the way in a dinghy which would cut into Loch Feochan (McKinley pronounced it "Lock Fuckin") and land a couple of miles from a small village called Cleigh.

The drop would be at night and there was a complicated series of signal light sequences so that both sides could recognize each other, but McKinley and I wouldn't have to learn them because Read would be with us to make sure the handover went smoothly and to make equally certain that he got his cut. We arranged to meet at a hotel in Oban, about five miles from Loch Feochan, on the Saturday evening two hours before the drop.

Later that evening, with McKinley back in his hotel room, I made two telephone calls, one to Dinah telling him where and when I'd need him, the other to Iwanek for almost thirty minutes during which time his fee doubled. Yes he had the gun, yes he understood exactly what I wanted him to do, yes he would be in Oban to meet me, yes he was sure it would all go smoothly and yes he wanted his fee in cash. Always be careful of yes-men, my father had told me. Yes, dad, I remember.

The blue velvet curtains billowed gently into the room and through the open window I could hear the neighbourhood thrush telling me what a glorious evening it was, and how the one thing he really wanted in all the world was a lady thrush and how he'd be prepared to fight and die for her because he was the bravest and strongest bird around. Maybe I was taking a liberty with the lyrics but you couldn't fault the tune.

"She sounds happy," said Sammy as she moved onto her front, red hair falling over her face and spreading across the mascara-marked pillow.

"He," I said as I stroked the back of her neck. "The males always have the sweetest songs."

She lay by my side, face turned towards mine. With one arm above her pillow and the other underneath it, she looked as if she was embracing it the way she'd held me minutes before. I rolled on top of her, legs either side of hers, and kissed her cheek.

"Don't they just," she laughed, pressing herself against me and then lying still, her breathing quiet and even. I'd been meeting Sammy three or four times a week, usually in the afternoons, usually to check on how she was getting on with Laing and usually ending up in bed under the painting of the storm-tossed sea.

"It's time you had a holiday," I told her.

"By the 'you' I take it you mean me and not us," she giggled.

"And Laing. Somewhere abroad, somewhere sunny, somewhere French."

"How about Paris?" The one eye I could see glinted with mischief.

"How very astute of you. The tickets are in my jacket pocket — you'll be flying out a week on Friday from Heathrow, and you're booked into a four-star hotel in the centre of Paris."

"Who says Father Christmas always wears a red suit and a white beard?" she asked and then, don't ask me how she did it, I was flipped three feet across the bed and found myself lying flat on my back. Then she was on top of me and kissing me through a tangle of hair. I lifted her head and smiled.

"Will he go with you?" I said.

"Do zebras have stripey legs? Of course he will, and he'll have the time of his life. He'll have to make the usual excuses to his wife but he's used to that. And so is she. He'll get such a kick out of the fact that I'm paying, too. I take it I'm only getting a weekend, Santa?"

"Friday night and Saturday night, flying British Airways at half four and coming back late Sunday evening. What you do while you're over there is your own business. If you get my drift."

Her eyes flashed fire but her lips smiled as she grabbed my wrists, held them above my head and kissed me full on the mouth, gripping me tightly with her legs. "Come with me," she said. "Forget Laing and Kyle."

"Next time. I promise. And then it'll be pleasure, not business." And I meant it.

"Business can be a pleasure," she said, then kissed me again, hard enough to bruise my lips. "Tell me what to do."

And I told her about carparks, a Rolls-Royce with a personalized number plate and an American Express card, and then I made love to her again. Or she made love to me. Whatever.

Dinah fingered the studs in his ear as we waited for Laing and Sammy to arrive at the short term carpark at Heathrow Airport. It was a bright, sunny afternoon and we were both in shirtsleeves sitting in the front seats of a black Transit van with "Kleen Karparts" stencilled in white on the sides. We were tucked away in the far corner on the ground floor giving us a clear view of all the vehicles entering and leaving carpark 1A. Two spaces along was the Granada and I had the parking ticket for it in my chest shirt pocket.

134

Even with both windows wide open we were sweating, but that was probably nervousness and anxiety because we'd been parked for almost an hour. Twice Dinah had asked to go to the toilet. "No can do," I'd told him, "they could be here any moment," and now he was sulking.

"There they are now," I said, and nodded towards the entrance where Laing was leaning out of the driver's side of the Corniche for his ticket. He drove up to the first level and Dinah followed as I stepped over the seat into the back of the van and sat down next to a rattling blue metal toolbox. Dinah pulled up next to the parked Rolls and I peered over his shoulder. I was wearing sunglasses and a floppy white hat with "Arsenal" on the front and Laing had only seen me once but even so there was no point in taking any chances.

Sammy was stunning, hair tied back with a scarlet bow and wearing a beige boiler suit, a brown pullover knotted across her shoulders. Laing took two small suitcases out of the boot of the Rolls, slammed it shut and together they walked to the departure terminal, my stomach going cold as she slipped her arm through his and rested her head on his shoulder, then I mentally kicked myself because she was only playing a part. She was doing it for me. But that didn't make me feel any better.

"Nice bit of stuff," said Dinah. "Lucky bastard."

"Watch yourself, Dinah," I said. "Keep your mind on the job."

We gave them a full fifteen minutes, then I moved back into the passenger seat to keep watch as Dinah climbed down and stood alongside the driver's window of the Rolls.

I expected subtlety, a skeleton key or a complicated mechanical device that Dinah would wiggle and jiggle until he worked his way past the Corniche's sophisticated central locking system. Dinah was about as subtle as a brass knuckleduster. He took a sheet of sticky-backed plastic and covered the window with it, smoothing out the air bubbles with the back of his hand. From the back pocket of his black leather trousers he took a metal punch, looked right and left, gave me a curt nod and then banged it against the glass which cracked and shattered into a thousand cubes, most of them sticking to the plastic. He rolled it up and handed it to me through the window of the Transit van.

"Oh, nice one, Dinah. If I'd known it was that simple I'd have done it myself," I said, and dropped it into the back of the van.

"That was the easy part," he laughed. "It's the next bit you're paying me for. Keep your eyes peeled." He lay across the front seat of the Rolls, head under the dashboard, and it was a full ten minutes before the engine burst into life.

"Right, that's us," he said, wiping his hands on his blue T-shirt. He opened the back door of the Transit and took out a plastic brush and pan, sweeping up the glass cubes on the floor while I sat in the driving seat of the Rolls and ran my eyes over the controls.

"Follow me back to the garage, and for God's sake don't stall it," he said. We drove out of the multi-storey carpark and I handed over the Granada's ticket to get the Rolls through.

An hour later we were in the Karparts yard where Dinah fitted a new window — getting spares was obviously not a problem for him. He went to work with a couple of Rolls keys and a file and after two hours handed them to me with a flourish.

"Your car, sir," he said, and grinned. "When will you be back with it?"

"Sunday morning, early afternoon at the latest. Will you be here?"

"Ready and waiting," he said. "Ready for the car and waiting for my money. Take care with those keys, by the way. They're good but they're not perfect so don't force them. Be gentle."

He paused, then added: "What are you up to?"

"Best you don't know, Dinah." I slid into the plush blue leather seat and put the makeshift key in and turned it. The Rolls started first time and I winked at him. "See you Sunday," I said.

He walked over to the double gates, and while he was opening them I reached under the passenger seat and groped around until I found a small white envelope. Inside was Laing's American Express card and a note from Sammy, short and to the point. "Be careful. See you soon. S."

I drove through the gates waving to Dinah as I passed him, and collected my case from Earl's Court and McKinley from his hotel. Laing had bought the car only six months previously so McKinley hadn't seen it before.

"This yours, boss?" he asked.

"It's borrowed, Get-Up. And if you're very good I'll let you share the driving. Settle back, we've a long way to go."

The Rolls was a dream to drive and it swallowed up the miles to Glasgow like a ravenous schoolboy. I let McKinley take over the wheel after we passed Birmingham and told him I'd sit in the back and try to get some sleep. I'd left a clipboard and a sheaf of notepaper on the seat, and I placed Laing's American Express card under the bulldog clip and studied it while McKinley sat in the outside lane of the M6, foot down to the floor.

A dab of brake fluid would have removed the biro signature and I could have replaced it with "R. Laing" in my own handwriting, but I had plenty of time to practise so I thought I might as well do it the hard way. Most people don't examine signatures all that closely anyway, especially overworked receptionists. They just pick on a few obvious features, a tall loop on the "l", the way the "a" was almost circular and the lower part of the "g" curved back under the signature in a flamboyant underlining loop. If they match then the signature is OK.

I studied the way Laing signed his name and then I copied it over and over, using up sheet after sheet of paper, and by the time we got to Preston I could do a perfect imitation so long as I had the original in front of me.

It took me until we'd reached Carlisle and the M6 turned into the A74 before I could sign myself "R. Laing" without checking.

I took over the driving again after we'd stopped for a break at Gretna Green service station, and I'd dropped the sheets of counterfeit signatures into a rubbish bin after ripping them up into a hundred pieces while McKinley was in the toilet.

The road was busy and I played chicken with the speeding lorries on their way north, and tapped the wheel in frustration at the numerous roadworks and single file traffic jams. It's a bitch of a road. Whenever I had to go to London on business I always took the Shuttle, even in a Rolls it's a tiring journey, playing havoc with blood pressures and brakes.

The two of us spent the night at the Central Hotel in Glasgow, courtesy of Laing's Amex card, and first thing Saturday morning I picked up a BMW from an up-market car hire company in the shadow of the Daily Record building at Anderston Quay.

Before the blonde receptionist handed me the keys she rang up the credit card company to check it was valid but that wasn't a problem, Laing was in Paris (God, my heart ached when I thought of him with Sammy), and he wouldn't know it was missing. If he should realize it had gone astray then I'd arranged for Sammy to say that she thought she'd seen it on the floor of the Rolls.

I drove the BMW back to the city centre, McKinley following in the Rolls, and we took the A82 out of Glasgow and headed for Oban.

McKinley and I were booked into the Caledonian Hotel, an imposing brown stone building with slated turrets and white sash windows peering over Oban Bay towards the Isle of Mull.

We had adjoining rooms at the front of the hotel, and from my window I looked down on the battered fishing boats bumping gently into each other in the swell as seagulls glided and cried, every now and again dipping down and diving into the sea for a piece of rotting fish or hunks of bread thrown by tourists.

It was about five pm and we'd arranged to meet Read in the bar at seven, so I told McKinley I was going for a walk and headed along the harbour wall to the modern, cream-painted Park Hotel. It too had magnificent sea views and I could taste the salt on my lips as I walked through the reception doors and asked to speak to Simon Fraser. The pretty brunette in tartan jacket and skirt smiled and rang his room and told me to go up to one two three, and Iwanek had the door open to greet me as I stepped out of the lift.

He was in a single room at the back of the hotel, the colour TV was flickering in the corner with the sound off and on the small but neat bed was an unopened bottle of whisky and a small black leather suitcase.

In his hand was an empty tumbler, and he asked me if I fancied a drink and told me to help myself to a glass

140

from the bathroom. He poured me a decent measure and we clinked glasses.

"To crime," he said, and laughed. "And to not getting caught."

"Here's hoping we have a quiet night," I said and drank deeply. He sat on the edge of the bed and waved me over to a comfortable green easy chair in the corner of the room opposite the television.

"Take a seat," he said. "I take it everything is set?"

"No problems at all," I said, taking a large scale map of the area from my inside pocket and spreading it on the floor. I pointed midway down Loch Feochan.

"This is where the dinghy should be coming ashore at about eleven o'clock tonight. That's where I'll be with two other men. Our cars will be parked off the road, within sight of the shore. One of them will have a powerful torch to signal the boat and the handover should take place at the water's edge. It'll be dark, so as long as you keep away from the torch beam you should be able to get up close without being seen. There are no street lights that far away from civilization so leave your car on the road."

Iwanek moved back on the bed and leant against the wall. He was dressed like a polytechnic lecturer, brown corduroy jacket and trousers and a green sweater, a pair of scuffed desert boots and brown socks with black squares on them, but no polytechnic lecturer had eyes like his, and they studied me through half-closed lids like a sleepy lizard about to ensnare an unwary insect with its long and very sticky tongue.

"They'll be armed, I suppose?" He had the knack of making every question sound like a statement of fact.

"Almost certainly, but they won't be expecting trouble, they're dealing with somebody they know. And you'll have the advantage because they'll have the boat to worry about and you will be on dry land."

He brought out a packet of Silk Cut and lit one with an old gunmetal petrol lighter. He didn't offer me one which meant he'd been observant enough to notice that I didn't smoke or he just didn't care. He angled his head back and blew a smoke ring towards the pale green ceiling, but his eyes never left my face and he weighed me up through the wreaths of smoke.

"There'll be three of us, myself and two big guys. One is my bodyguard, the other is the man who set the deal up. I'll be carrying the briefcase with the money. For God's sake be careful, I don't want anyone killed."

"Not yet you don't," he said and laughed quietly, but it was only his mouth that smiled, there were no crease lines around the pale blue eyes and no spark of humour in them.

"Do either of your two friends know what you've got planned?" he asked.

"No," I said. "This is just between the two of us. So be careful. They're as likely to take a swing at you as the men in the boat are.

"I'll come back here to pick up the drugs and the money sometime within the following forty-eight hours. You just stay put and order whatever you want from room service. Then I give you the rest of your money and we part company for good."

He'd emptied his tumbler but made no move to refill it. I wasn't surprised because Iwanek was a pro and pros don't drink while they're working, not to excess anyway.

"Have you got the gun?" I asked, and he patted the suitcase next to him.

"A Fabarm Eight Shot Slugster, though you'd be hard put to recognize it now," he said. "Matt black anti-glare finish, three inch magnum, lightweight and fast operating." He didn't open the case but ran his fingers up and down the leather, smoothing it gently.

"The barrels are normally twenty-four and a half inches long but I've cut off more than half that and taken off the stock and the recoil pad and just left the walnut semi pistol grip. It'll fire eight shots and it's one of the sweetest pump actions around."

"Pity you won't get to fire it," I said and pushed myself out of the easy chair. "I'll leave the map with you."

Iwanek didn't get up, and he was still looking at the case and toying with the handle as I left the room, walked out of the hotel and turned along the harbour wall. It was starting to rain, drops splattering on the pavement, and I turned up the collar of my brown tweed jacket.

Before I reached the Caledonian I went into a small newsagent which was just about to close for the night and bought copies of all the national newspapers along with a *Glasgow Herald, Scotsman, Daily Record* and *Oban Times* and a packet of elastic bands.

143

The ruddy faced man behind the counter rang up the till and took my money. "You'll be doing a lot of reading, then?" he asked. "Or is it something in particular you're after?"

"What else is there to do in Oban on a wet Saturday night?" I asked. He followed me to the door and reached for the bolt as I stepped onto the pavement.

"Aye, you've a point there," he agreed and wished me a good night. I pushed the papers under my jacket and kept my head down as I walked back to the Caledonian. It was raining heavily now, and I started to run as water began to trickle down the back of my neck.

I borrowed a large pair of scissors from reception and spent the next half hour in my room cutting the papers into ten-pound note size pieces and bundling them together with elastic bands. On the top and bottom of each pile I put a real note, and by the time I'd finished I had sore fingers and what would hopefully pass for £250,000 in used tenners in a poor light. I packed them into the old brown leather attache case I'd brought with me and pushed it under the bed. Right on cue McKinley knocked on the door and said it was time to go down to the bar to meet Read.

We found him sitting on a high stool at the far end of the polished oak bar nursing a lager. He'd dressed for the occasion and looked every inch a Scottish landowner with his green tweed suit and heavy brown brogues.

On the back of his head was perched a shapeless hat of some unidentifiable material and I swear there was a fishing fly pinned to the brown band. I half expected him to tell us it was "a braw bricht moonlit nicht the noo," but he just smiled and asked us what we were having.

We took our drinks over to a table in the corner furthest from the bar, and McKinley attacked a bowl of peanuts while Read and I got down to business.

"You've got the money, squire?" he asked.

"Upstairs," I said. "Is everything still on?"

"It will be once I've made one phone call."

"It's a bit late for that, isn't it? Surely the boat will have left by now?"

"You've heard of ship-to-shore radios, haven't you? I call Ireland and they contact the boat. Then, and only then, will the dingy head for the loch. You're not dealing with amateurs, you know." He took his glasses off and began to polish them meticulously with a bright red handkerchief.

"I should hope not," I said. "Not for the sort of commission you're getting, anyway. I hope you're worth it."

"Take it from me, squire, I am. There's no way you could have arranged this without me, just remember that."

He removed his hat and placed it on the seat next to him and scratched the back of his head. That encouraged McKinley to delve into his beard again and pretty soon the two of them were scratching away like flea infested puppies.

"There isn't anything that could go wrong, is there?" I asked, and Read narrowed his eyes.

"Not getting cold feet, are we?" he asked. "It's too late to back out now. That would be about as smart as auditioning for the lead role in a snuff movie. Not to be recommended, squire. The sort of people we're dealing with won't stand for that, believe me."

"Hell, of course I'm not getting cold feet, you know just how badly I need this deal. It's just that a quarter of a million pounds is one hell of a lot of money and it's not cash I can afford to lose."

"No, I suppose it isn't." He turned and looked at McKinley. "Not on top of the money you've already lost," he added and laughed, shoulders jiggling up and down in time with his bellowing laughter.

McKinley smiled and helped himself to more salted peanuts. Read took a swallow from his glass and wiped his mouth with the back of his hand. For the first time I noticed how hairy it was, only the finger joints were clear of thick, black curly hair.

"They're using a fishing boat to cross the sea, and then the stuff'll be transferred to a small rubber dinghy with a large outboard motor. If it looks like they've been spotted they'll make a run for it, but there's as much chance of that as there is of Get-Up here passing the Institute of Advanced Motorists driving test." He laughed uproariously at his own joke, mouth wide open and a couple of gold fillings glinting somewhere at the back.

"But what about the dinghy? Surely that's vulnerable?"

"Let's get something straight, squire," he replied. "The coastline," he gestured with his drink, "out there isn't exactly crawling with customs men, you know.

Don't you read the papers? They're more understaffed than the Moscow branch of the CND. It's a chance in a million that they'll bump into anybody. If they do they'll run for it. And if they can't run for it they'll dump it over the side and go back for it later. Don't worry, it's easier than delivering milk."

"Will you be armed?" I asked.

"God, you are nervous. No, I won't be carrying a gun, but the men delivering almost certainly will be."

"I don't like the sound of that."

"Don't let it worry you. Remember, they're the ones who are taking all the risks. They'll be coming in with the drugs, you'll just be a guy on the lochside."

"With a quarter of a million pounds in his briefcase."

"Yes, there's always that, isn't there?" He laughed again. He hadn't been drinking much and it wasn't that funny so I guess he was more nervous than he was letting on, but I believed him when he said he wouldn't be armed. I also believed him when he said the delivery boys would be. Still, how good a shot could they be from a rubber boat tossing around in the loch? I would have touched wood but the table our drinks were on had never been near a tree. Anyway, the whole point of the operation was that I wasn't depending on luck. Luck is for amateurs.

"What's the time, now?" he asked, finishing his drink with a noisy slurp.

"Ten past seven," I replied.

"Time I was ringing Ireland. Can you lend me a ten-pence piece for the phone?" He roared at the look of surprise on my face and slapped me on the back.

"Come on, you can take a joke, can't you, squire?" He stood up, running his fingers along non-existent creases in his rumpled tweed trousers. "I'll see you back here at nine o'clock. Everything is going ahead exactly as I explained to Get-Up last week. Stop worrying. Just be ready at nine, we'll take both cars. What are you driving?"

"BMW. It's parked outside."

"Nice. Wrap up warm in case we're stuck outside for a couple of hours. See you." Then he was off out of the bar, picking up a huge green, yellow and red golfing umbrella from the cloakroom and tossing a coin into a white china saucer on the counter.

"He means well, boss," said McKinley, almost apologetically.

"I know, Get-Up, I know. You hungry?"

"I'm always hungry, boss, you know that."

"Go and get yourself something from the restaurant. I'm going for a walk."

I stood at the side of the hotel entrance and saw Read by the BMW, examining the tyres, looking through the window and checking the speedometer like a hesitant buyer on a used car lot. Any moment now a young chap in a sheepskin jacket would come along and tell him it had one lady owner and had been treated just like one of the family and did he have a trade-in, sir, or would he be interested in an HP deal? Read took a pen and notebook from his jacket pocket and wrote down the registration number and then began to walk away, glancing at the Rolls as he passed it.

148

He stopped and took a closer look at the registration number, then walked around to the back, running his hand along the white soft top and down the rear wing. He scratched his ear thoughtfully. Unlike McKinley he had kept in touch with Laing's drug scene and he was sure to know what car Laing was driving.

He began scribbling in his notebook again, and I knew his telephone call to Ireland wouldn't just be to arrange the delivery, that he'd mention the Rolls and suggest that maybe, just maybe, Laing was around or involved. It wouldn't be enough for them to abandon the delivery but alarm bells would start to ring. I waited until Read got into a brown Range-Rover and drove off before I walked out of the hotel.

I rang Iwanek from a call box along the harbour wall to say that Read wouldn't be armed, and to confirm that there had been no changes to the original plan.

"Don't worry," he said. "I'll be there." Suddenly everybody was telling me not to worry. That worried me. It had stopped raining but the wind was strong enough to whip up ripples in the pavement puddles as I wandered aimlessly towards the docks, shoulders hunched against the cold, fingers clenched tight in the pockets of my tweed jacket as I mentally ticked off the various stages of the plan.

I went over and over it in my mind and I couldn't find any faults. But they said the Titanic was unsinkable so I went over it again but it still seemed OK, and I relaxed a little and even started to whistle to myself but then I thought of McKinley and the whistle died on my lips.

If there was one weak link in the chain of events I'd set up then it was McKinley. He was like an affectionate Old English sheepdog, I trusted him completely and I only had to call and he'd come. He was faithful and loyal but I was using him, and if he ever found out he'd have every reason to turn on me, snapping and biting and going for my throat.

Several times I'd come close to telling him the truth, but I still wasn't sure how he would react or whether he'd use the information as a way of getting back on Laing's team. I trusted him, but not that much, and I couldn't take the risk. But that meant he would be at Loch Feochan tonight under the impression that he was taking part in a straightforward drugs buy, and when Iwanek turned up as the Lone Ranger he might take it into his head to go charging in like a head-strong rhino.

I couldn't tell him beforehand but maybe afterwards, after Iwanek had made off with the drugs and the money, maybe I'd tell McKinley the background, help him get away and start a new life. Then I thought of my parents and why I was doing this, and that what I really should do was to throw him to the dogs, another signpost pointing towards Laing.

McKinley was a bridge I would cross when I got to it. Until then I'd have to treat him like a mushroom — keep him in the dark and feed him bullshit. What the hell, he was a petty criminal and a violent one at that. I didn't owe him anything, he was being well paid, and if I started feeling sorry for him then it wouldn't be too long before I started wondering if Laing and Kyle deserved what was coming to them, and then I really might as well pack up and go home.

"Shit," I said out loud to the grey sea, and a wee Scottish wifey wrapped up in a dark wool coat and fur boots tut-tutted like a minister and gave me a filthy look. Hell, it wasn't the Sabbath. I sat on the harbour wall, feet dangling over the edge, and looked across the water towards mist-shrouded Mull.

A seagull swooped past, then curved around and landed on the wall next to me, feet clicking against the wet stones, wings flapping for balance. Head on one side he looked me over. A tourist with a bread roll pinched from the dinner table? A teatime piece of cake? Anything? Nothing? He gave me a look more disdainful than the wifey's and pitched beak first off the wall before pulling up into a graceful glide, wings outstretched but motionless. I was impressed but I still hadn't anything for him to eat so he was wasting his time.

Back at the Caledonian the black-suited undermanager handed me Laing's American Express card as I walked into reception, practically tugging his forelock. I guess they didn't see too many gold cards in Oban. I had signed the chit earlier and he'd held on to the card to call up and check Laing's credit rating.

"We'll fill the figures in when you check out, Mr Laing," he said, and I realized I was going to have to be careful going in and out of the hotel with McKinley. All it needed was for one of the staff to come haring after me calling "Mr Laing, Mr Laing, you've forgotten your bill," and I'd have some pretty heavy explaining to do.

151

McKinley had checked in under his own name and was paying in cash. Other than our meeting with Read in the bar we'd kept apart, so there was no reason for the staff to connect us and I'd have to make sure it stayed that way.

I saw McKinley through the glass partition leading to the restaurant, tucking into steak and chips and diving into extra portions of mushrooms, onion rings, peas, cauliflower and green beans scattered around the table, a large white napkin tucked into his shirt collar. His table manners were much the same as his driving, erratic, messy and a positive danger to anyone in the vicinity.

I left him to it and lay on the double bed in my room, gazing at the ceiling and feeling like a cigarette for the first time in twelve years.

I didn't sleep but the hour passed without my noticing and McKinley's knock on the door made me jump.

"Come in, Get-Up," I said, and he sidled into the room wearing a huge black duffel coat and green wellington boots like an overgrown Paddington Bear. Under the coat was a thick fisherman's sweater and grey wool trousers. He looked as if he'd just come out of a sauna, sweat pouring from his skin. I couldn't help but laugh and he smiled.

"It'll be better when I'm outside, boss. It's pissing down and the wind's getting up."

"Well, you can always shelter under Read's umbrella," I said, and he grinned wider and sat on the bed, wiping his forehead with the back of his hand. I went over to the bathroom to swill the bad taste from my mouth and splash cold water onto my tired eyes. I came out rubbing a towel over my wet face to find him playing with the bedside radio and television controls.

"Could you get Radio Four on yours, boss?" he asked. "Mine's on the blink."

"I'm not one for listening to the radio, Get-Up. I didn't realize you were."

"I used to listen to it a lot in prison. You get into the habit."

I stripped off my shirt and jeans and it was McKinley's turn to laugh as I pulled out a pair of thermal underwear from my suitcase. "Jesus, boss, Long Johns. My father used to wear those."

"Yeah, well they're coming back into fashion. Especially for men about town standing on the side of a sea loch late at night." Back on went the jeans and shirt, a woollen Pringle sweater from my golfing days and a pair of brown leather hiking boots. A Burberry scarf and the tweed jacket and I was ready, not exactly the best dressed man in Oban but there were no hard and fast sartorial rules about getting togged up for a drugs deal. Kneeling by the bed I reached for the briefcase and flipped it onto the chair by the door.

"I've never seen a quarter of a million pounds in one place, boss, do you mind if I take a look?"

"It'd only upset you, Get-Up. Come on, it's nine o'clock, we'd best get moving. Pop down and see if Read's there already. I'll see you outside." He closed the door behind him and I opened the case. It looked like £250,000 so long as you didn't pull out one of the

153

bundles and flick through it. If all went according to plan the case wouldn't even be opened at Loch Feochan, but if Iwanek was just a few minutes late and they got their hands on the money, or rather the cut up pieces of newspaper, then they were likely to shoot first and not bother asking questions.

The case had two locks and the key was in one of the leather pockets inside. I clicked the locks shut and left the key in the wastepaper basket. If we got to the stage where they wanted to look inside then it would give me a few extra minutes while I went through the motions of checking all the pockets in my clothing and asking McKinley if he had the key, and then if Iwanek still hadn't turned up maybe I'd get away with telling them the key must be in the car and if I was really lucky maybe I'd get to the BMW before they opened fire, and if the gods were smiling on me and no black cats crossed my path and if I hadn't broken any mirrors in the last seven years then maybe, just maybe, I'd get away without losing my kneecaps or worse. Now I really was starting to worry.

"He'll be there, he'll be there," I said to myself, and that worried me even more because I hadn't talked to myself since I was nine years old.

I locked the bedroom door and left the key at reception. Read and McKinley were standing by the BMW in the hotel carpark, sheltering under the colourful golfing umbrella. Read had added a green waterproof coat to his laird's outfit and he waved cheerily as I walked up.

"Ready for the off?" he asked, handing me a powerful electric torch. "You'll be needing that. There's a quarter moon tonight but it's cloudy enough to black it out every now and again. I'll be in the Range-Rover," he nodded towards the four-wheel drive vehicle next to the Rolls. "Don't get too close to me. These roads are bad enough at the best of times, on a wet night like this they can be treacherous."

He climbed into the Range-Rover as McKinley and I seated ourselves in the BMW. Tonight I would be driving and McKinley didn't argue. The briefcase lay on the back seat next to Read's torch, and the two banged together as I put the car into gear and followed Read out of the carpark.

"Don't forget your lights, boss," McKinley reminded me and I gave him a withering look.

"Just keep your eyes on Read," I told him. "I'll worry about the car." I left it a full two minutes before I switched the headlights on but he still grinned like an intoxicated Cheshire cat.

"Nobody likes a smart arse, Get-Up," I told him, but then my face cracked into a smile and I thumped his shoulder. "You take care tonight, hear?"

Read drove like a pensioner at the wheel of a Morris Minor, slowly, infuriatingly slowly, and carefully, decelerating before every bend, his brake lights on more often than off, and the BMW never got beyond third gear.

If it had been midday at the height of summer then we'd have had a convoy of impatient traffic behind us,

155

but we didn't see a single other car until we reached Cleigh and even then it was a farmer in a mud-splattered Land-Rover heading for Oban.

Once he stopped completely and the internal light came on as he opened the door and stepped into the road. He began running up and down in front of the Range-Rover, flapping his arms like a demented penguin. In and out of the long shadows he was casting along the tarmac road ran a handful of panicking pheasant chicks, speeding in circles and bumping into each other as they scurried and searched for their mother who was clucking anxiously on the grass verge.

Eventually the family was reunited and Read gave us the thumbs up in our headlights like a vaudeville star taking a bow on stage before getting back into the Rover and driving off again.

It took half an hour of Read's driving before we reached the tip of the loch and followed the A816 as it curved gently round to the right and along the southern shore towards the sea. We drove for about four miles until the loch narrowed and then widened again, then the Rover's hazard warning lights went on and it came to a dead stop beside a wooden five-bar gate. I pulled in behind as Read climbed out, opened the gate and drove through.

"Get out and shut the gate after I've driven through," I told McKinley and followed Read, bumping and bouncing down a narrow dirt track leading to the loch side. A small flock of black and white sheep, startled by the unusual nocturnal activity, broke into a run and disappeared out of sight behind a hillock, bleating with annoyance. Read switched off his lights and I followed his example, blinking until my eyes grew used to the shadowy gloom.

He walked over to the BMW with a large red plastic flashlight in his hand as McKinley ambled down the path, and I pressed the button to wind the window down. Read leant forward, elbows on the car door, eye to eye.

"We're early," he said. "Best we wait by the water, though. The distance they've come means that their timing is unlikely to be spot on. Bring the money with you, squire."

"I'd rather leave it here until I've seen the consignment."

For a moment Read's good-natured smile slipped and his eyes hardened, and I realized that behind the laird's clothing and the hat with a fly in it there was still a criminal, a man used to dealing in a world where the weak were quickly fleeced by the strong and where only the hard men survived.

"Bring it with you," he said again, and then he turned away as I got out of the BMW and leant into the back to pick up the case.

"OK, boss?" asked McKinley.

"Sure, Get-Up. I just forgot my manners," I said, because it did make sense, if the money was obviously not in sight when the delivery men arrived it would put them on the defensive. The fact that Read had seen Laing's Rolls was enough to put them on edge, and I wanted it all to be all sweetness and light until Iwanek appeared.

We stood together on the shore, scanning the wild waters of the loch through the gloom and listening for any sounds other than the bleating of sheep and the occasional hoot of a hunting owl.

McKinley noticed it first. "Listen," he said, and sure enough in the distance I could hear a low pitched growl like a far-off motorcycle which grew louder and louder and then suddenly stopped.

A light flashed from the middle of the loch, on, off, on, off.

Read pointed his flashlight and flicked it on and off, long, long, short, long, short, long, short, long, long. Out on the water the light replied, on, off, on, off, on, off. Another complicated series of dots and dashes from Read and then the outboard motor started up again as they headed for the shore.

I saw them first as a dark blur against the blackened water, a smudge heading for where we were standing, more conscious of the movement than its shape. As they drew closer I could make out three figures in an inflatable boat, one at the back with his hand on the tiller, two others in the prow, tossing with the motion of the waves. The engine cut out about twenty feet from the water's edge and the boat turned sharply side on, running silently parallel to the shore until it coasted to a stop.

One of the men at the front jumped out of the boat into the water and held it steady as the second climbed out carrying a green holdall, spotlighted in the beams of the two torches, twin circles of light that followed them as they splashed unsteadily to the shore.

They moved apart as they waded knee deep through the water and simultaneously reached inside their jackets and came out with pistols. My stomach tensed, apprehension rather than fear, Read had said they'd be armed but even so the sight of the guns brought home just how dangerous this was going to be. The one with the holdall stepped forward onto the beach while his partner stayed up to his ankles in the loch.

Read passed me his torch and held out his hand for the briefcase and I handed it to him under the watchful eyes of the gunmen. He walked towards the man with the holdall and held out his free hand for it. The man in the water dropped down into a crouch, both hands on the butt of his gun as the waves lapped against his legs. Iwanek, where are you?

Read took the holdall then the night exploded in a burst of light and noise and the man in the water flew backward, a gaping hole in his chest. There was a second explosion from somewhere behind me and Read pitched forward onto his face, the back of his green suit a mass of red, the briefcase still in one hand, the holdall in the other. His hat rolled off his head and the wind took it and whisked it away along the beach. Through the buzzing in my ears I heard the click clack of a third cartridge being thrust home as the gunman on the shore raised his pistol, but before he could fire there was another blast and he screamed and dropped the gun from his shattered hand. He flopped into the loch and threshed about in an imitation of swimming, dog-paddling his way back to the boat past the body of his colleague who was now floating face down.

I turned to see Iwanek, shotgun held across his chest, face streaked with black like a commando under a woollen balaclava helmet.

"Put your hands above your head," he hissed and pointed the gun at McKinley's groin. "Now."

We both raised our arms and Iwanek moved around us, picking up the briefcase and the bag with his left hand, the right keeping the shotgun level, covering us both. I wanted to say no, this isn't what's supposed to happen, you don't understand, nobody is supposed to get hurt, that's why you said you'd use a shotgun.

I wanted to say that there'd been a mistake, go back, start again, but Iwanek knew exactly what he was doing, there was no mistake. I'd hired a killer and now he was killing.

Over his shoulder I saw the swimmer helped aboard by the man in the boat, pulled over the side by the back of his trousers, legs flicking up and over. Then the boatman leant forward and picked up a gun, maybe it was a rifle or a shotgun, it was too far away to see clearly, but I saw him aim it and I flinched as Iwanek grinned and tightened his finger on the trigger. The boatman fired first, the bullet whined and kicked up a shower of stones by Iwanek's foot and he cursed. He dropped both bags and fired two shots in quick succession at the inflatable which was now about fifty feet from the shore.

Then he turned back to us and pointed the shotgun at McKinley and fired as I threw myself sideways into McKinley, sending him sprawling as the shot tore into

160

my left shoulder and arm, burning and biting into the flesh through the layers of clothing.

A burst of gunfire from the boat made Iwanek drop to the ground, arms and legs outstretched, then he rolled and was back on his feet, the shotgun still safe in his grasp. He gathered up the dropped bags and zig-zagged back to the road, keeping his head well down.

Through a cloud of pain I heard the outboard motor kick into life and subside as the boat headed back up the loch at full throttle, towards the sea. Then McKinley was looking down at me, asking me if I was OK, could I hear him?

The pain deepened and I felt myself slipping. I gripped his arm, hard, and he put his ear close to my mouth, beard rasping against my lips as I told him what he had to do and then his face blurred and spun and I passed out.

PART TWO

There was a fine mist in the room, the sort of drizzly veil that rolls down rivers on autumn days, blurring and blending the banks into a grey mass of misshapen lumps. River mists are cold and clammy and make the back of your neck crawl and arthritic joints ache, but this mist was warm and sticky like the inside of a sauna and the ceiling floated in and out of focus so I closed my eyes and concentrated on my breathing. I opened them again and the mist was finer and I could see a three-stranded brass light fitting, and the pink and white striped wallpaper seemed to jump into my vision and then Shona's face appeared, looking down at me side on which made my stomach queasy so I closed my eyes again and concentrated on not being sick.

The room felt hot and airless and my head rang with a cacophony of dull thuds and bumps, out of time with my breathing and my heart, and then I heard Shona say "he's coming to" and the next time I opened my eyes the mist had disappeared but so had the light because it was night and it was dark, but I could still hear the muffled bangs and thumps in my head, my throat felt raw and my right shoulder ached, and when I tried to sit up pure pain lanced through my arm and I lay back and closed my eyes and concentrated on not dying.

At some point during the night I woke up on my side with someone poking and prodding my shoulder and back, then I felt a sharp pain in my arm and I slept.

It was light again when my head finally cleared and I could open my eyes without feeling sick, or passing out or wishing I was dead. The first thing I saw was Shona, the second was the worried look on her face, then I felt her cool hand on my forehead.

"How do you feel?" she asked.

"Like I was dead," I tried to say, playing the wounded soldier, but my throat was so dry it sounded like a sea lion coughing. A glass of water appeared before me and I winced as she helped lift my head to drink. Sod the wounded soldier act, it hurt like hell.

"Thanks," I managed. "How am I doing?"

"The shot's all out, though some of it was very deep and you're going to be sore for a few weeks. A couple of inches to the right and it would have been a different story — you could have died."

The bedroom door opened behind her and Tony walked in and sat on the bed. She sat down next to him and said; "You should be in hospital. But after what your strange friend Get-Up told me I thought you'd want to keep this quiet. One of my father's friends is a surgeon at Glasgow's Royal Infirmary and he drove over to do the honours. He's well aware that it wasn't an accident but he won't say anything.

"He gave you an injection to make you sleep last night and he'll be back to check on you later this evening. You've been very lucky."

I knew that. "Where is Get-Up?" I asked.

"I don't know," she replied. "He dropped you off late on Saturday night, gave me a very cryptic breakdown of what had happened and then sped off in a Rolls-Royce saying he had to get to London."

At least he'd managed to drive the BMW to the hotel and pick up the Rolls. I didn't remember the switch but that was hardly surprising because I remembered nothing after being shot. "What time is it?" I asked.

"It's two-thirty, Monday afternoon. You've been asleep for more than thirty-six hours."

"Is he coming back? Did he say he'd be back? If he is, he should be here by now. Damn." Now I was talking to myself, had McKinley got the Rolls back to Heathrow in time? If so, where was he? Damn, damn.

"What is going on?" she asked, which was fair enough because up until now I'd been asking all the questions. Then Tony joined in. "Who is he? And who the hell shot you? Where has he gone?" Three questions from him fired one after the other like an over-zealous TV quizmaster without waiting for an answer. They both looked at me, concern mixed with anger in about equal amounts. They wouldn't exactly twist my injured arm to extract the information but if I didn't tell them I would badly damage two friendships, two friendships that were very, very precious to me.

"You aren't going to like this," I said, and tried to force a smile.

"Try us," said Shona, and she placed another pillow behind my head. "Just try us."

"What's that banging noise?" I asked. "It's been going on ever since I woke up."

"The Tattoo," said Shona. "They're putting up the seating and stuff, it'll go on pretty much non-stop for the next few weeks."

I remembered then that Shona's flat on the Mound over-looking Edinburgh was close to the Castle, home of the Edinburgh Tattoo, and every year about this time she and her neighbours had to put up with the preparations for the famous show. It was a small price to pay for the breathtaking views of the city, especially as the workmen now had to use specially-silenced tools, hammers and spanners all wrapped in cloth to cut the noise down to a minimum. I was just glad that the clinking and banging was coming from outside the window and not inside my head.

Tony stood up and walked around the bed, sitting opposite Shona so that I had to turn my head from side to side to see them both. That hurt so I looked between them while I talked. The fact that I didn't have to look at them helped. A little.

"Remember the two men that took over SCOT? Laing and Kyle?" They nodded. "They killed my parents, no ifs, buts or maybes. My father left a note explaining what had happened. I found it on the desk by his body. In it he said that Laing had phoned him, warned him not to put up a fight to keep SCOT and that if he did try to thwart the takeover he'd get hurt. That was the day before my mother died when the brakes of the Volvo failed."

Tony and Shona looked at each other in horror, and then back to me. I closed my eyes and Shona held my hand, tightly.

"Her death and the loss of his life's work were too much for him. He was depressed, lonely and afraid, and though it was his own hand on the trigger it was Laing and Kyle who killed him."

"You should have gone to the police," whispered Shona.

"I couldn't," I said, and opened my eyes. "There was no evidence, a letter from a man disturbed enough to kill himself wouldn't carry enough weight in court. There was no record of the phone call, and the brake fluid had leaked from the Volvo, or had been drained. It's not as if the brake lines had been cut. There was no evidence, nothing tangible."

"Then you should have come to me. I could have dealt with them," said Tony.

"How, Tony? What would you have done? Put out a contract on them? Just how long would it have been before it was traced back to you? Or to me? Neither of us are in the business of hiring assassins. And there were more practical considerations. I don't expect either of you to understand but I didn't want their deaths on my conscience, not directly. I couldn't kill them myself, even if I had the necessary skills. And I couldn't pay someone to do the job for me. I knew that if I did, it would always come back to haunt me and I'd wake up at night in a sweat with the sound of the gunshot echoing through my head and that one day I'd have to confess."

"So what did you do?" asked Tony.

"I sat down with David a couple of days after we buried Dad and worked out a way of getting someone else to do the job for me. I'd already made a few phone calls to London and got some background info on Laing and Kyle, and Laing's drugs connections seemed to be the obvious solution.

"I figured that all I'd have to do was to set up some sort of drugs deal and make it look as if Laing had double-crossed them. The sort of gangsters in that business would act first and ask questions later, so if I could set them up they'd tear him apart.

"Five steps were necessary. First I had to arrange to buy a large quantity of drugs. Then I had to get Laing out of the country. With him out of the way I'd get someone to steal the drugs, that was step three. Step four was to leave as many signs as possible pointing to Laing. Step five was to plant the drugs on Kyle, in the boot of his car.

"It was like setting up a line of dominoes, once the first one was pushed they'd all fall down, one after the other. The drugs dealers would hunt Laing down, and either they or the police would get to Kyle. And I'd be in the clear."

Tony and Shona looked at each other across the bed again, Tony shaking his head slowly while Shona squeezed my hand.

"It's a long way from a threadbare plan like that to pulling it off," said Tony. "How did you manage it?"

"I rented a flat in London and spoke to as many people who knew Laing as I could, carefully so as not to set off any alarms. I've an old schoolfriend who's now a crime reporter on one of the nationals and he told me the story of Get-Up McKinley, the guy who

170

dropped me here. He told me how he'd just come out of prison after serving time for an armed robbery that went wrong. He used to work for Laing. I traced McKinley and offered him a job as my minder. He jumped at it. Through him I arranged to buy quarter of a million pounds of cocaine. The deal was set up for Saturday night so I fixed up a weekend in Paris for Sammy and Laing."

"Sammy?" said Shona, turning towards Tony. "The girl you took to see David? You were using her, too?"

"Did she know what she was getting into?" asked Tony, ignoring Shona's question. "And what about Carol?"

"I told Sammy everything. We used a rented flat and an assumed name — there's no way anyone will be able to trace her. She's my friend now, Tony. I won't let anything happen to her. And Carol knows nothing, except that Sammy was helping me.

"I hired an ex-soldier to steal the drugs, told him when and where they'd be arriving. That was Iwanek, the man you caught following me. He wasn't supposed to hurt anyone, just to take the cocaine and run, handing it back to me later. But he obviously had plans of his own. He killed at least one of the drug couriers and the guy who'd fixed up the deal for us. Then he turned the gun on McKinley and I got shot."

"He took the drugs?" asked Tony. I nodded. "And the money?"

At that I smiled, thinking of Iwanek opening the briefcase and finding stacks of newspaper cuttings.

"No," I replied. "Just a couple of hundred pounds and a lot of waste paper."

"And how were you going to point the finger at Laing and Kyle?"

"McKinley was the first signpost, the fact that he was involved would trigger off Laing's name. To make it even more definite I borrowed Laing's Rolls-Royce and made sure that it was seen in Oban, close to where the drugs were due to arrive. And I paid for a hire car and the hotel bills with his American Express card.

"His trip to Paris was a complete secret because he didn't want his wife to find out. What can he say against all that evidence? He'd been pushed out of the drugs business and this was his way of getting his own back — the evidence is circumstantial but overwhelming. And it's not as if I had to convince twelve good men and true. Circumstantial evidence would be more than enough for the sort of people I've been dealing with."

"So that's why Get-Up drove off in such a hurry," said Shona.

"Sure, I asked him to put the Rolls back in the carpark at Heathrow, with the credit card under the passenger seat for Sammy to find. I just hope he did and that he didn't decide to keep the car and make a run for it. Laing will never know that his beloved car was up in Scotland, and he'll never see Sammy again.

"We left a hire car from Glasgow in Oban, and it won't take them long to find it and check that it was hired in his name and paid for with his Amex card. Laing won't know what's hit him when they catch up with him."

172

"They'll kill him," said Tony, and his voice was tinged with sadness as if a doctor had just told him I had a terminal illness. But it was sadness at what I'd done, not pity for Laing and Kyle.

"He killed my parents," I replied defensively. "Don't forget that."

"What about Kyle?" asked Shona. "What will happen to him?"

I was tired now and my throat was burning from the effort of talking but I had to finish it, I had to tell them everything, even though the fine mist had started to come back into the room and the banging in my head seemed to be getting louder and louder.

"I managed to get Kyle's fingerprints on a briefcase, and the idea was to put the drugs in it and plant the case in his car. It could have gone two ways then. Either I tipped off the police and he went to prison for a long time, or the suppliers would trace him through Laing. I didn't care much what happened. But that's all off now. No drugs, no plant. He's in the clear, for the moment. But if they catch up with Laing they might still get to Kyle." Despite everything that had happened the prospect still pleased me. I wanted them dead.

"If they're that dangerous you shouldn't have got involved with them," said Shona, concern showing in her eyes.

"You can't deal with filth like Laing and Kyle without getting your hands dirty," I said, and I was surprised at the venom in my voice and the way she recoiled from me. "It's all right, Shona, believe me."

173

She looked at me disbelievingly. "OK, I know this looks bad but it'll soon heal," I added.

Tears filled her eyes and she shook her head. "You just don't understand what you've done, do you?" she asked, but she ran out of the room before I could answer. I tried to raise my head, to call after her, but the pain in my shoulder made me wince and I lay back, gasping.

Tony sat silently by my side, and it was some minutes before he spoke again.

"You've been an absolute prat, you know that. You've let us all down, you've betrayed our trust. You haven't only been messing with the lives of a few London thugs, you realize that? You've put your friends and your family at risk through your stupidity. I expected more from you than that." He was looking through the window as he talked, down the Mound and across to Princes Street where afternoon shoppers mixed with office workers on late lunches. He walked over to the window and put his hands on the sill, resting his forehead against the glass. It steamed up from his breath as he sighed deeply, a depressing sigh that said as much as the verbal lashing he'd just given me. He stood upright and with his index finger drew a question mark in the condensed vapour, and as he pressed the dot under the curve he turned and folded his arms across his chest.

There was nothing I could say because he was right, and the fact that he had put it into words made it hurt all the more.

"What's done is done," he said, and now he was business-like, Tony the negotiator, the wheeler-dealer, the salesman who wouldn't take no for an answer. "Let's take this from the top. Is there any way you can be traced through this madman Iwanek?"

"None, I used a false name and I contacted him, not the other way round."

"Always?"

"Since the first time." He raised his eyebrows. "I answered an advert, he used a box number so I wrote to him and he telephoned me."

"Telephoned you where?"

"A flat I'd rented in Earl's Court — under a false name. The rent's paid until the end of the month and there's nothing in it that will identify me."

"Fingerprints?"

"I wiped it clean before I left for Oban. Thoroughly."

"What about the car thief?"

"False name again, and he never got in touch with me. I paid him in cash and he's no idea what I was up to. He didn't care so long as he got his money. I can't be traced through him."

"What about this guy, the one who fixed up the drugs deal?"

"Davie Read? He thought I was a London banker who'd been dipping into the firm's funds for a spot of gambling on the commodity market. Get-Up fed him the cover story and I used another false name. Anyway, Read's dead."

"Dead now, but he could have spoken to any number of people before you met him in Oban."

"There's nothing he could have told anyone. Besides, if he'd suspected anything he would have stopped the deal cold."

"True," he said and fell silent again, biting the inside of his cheek as he always did when deep in thought. He came over and sat on the right-hand side of the bed.

"How much does Get-Up know?"

"He doesn't know who I really am, or at least he didn't until he dropped me here. He thought he'd arranged a straightforward drugs buy, that I was a dealer who'd been elbowed out of Glasgow and was looking for an alternative supply. He thought he was doing me a favour."

"He thought you were going to hand over the money?" I nodded. "And he didn't know about Iwanek?" I shook my head. "And what the hell were you going to do afterwards?"

"Pay him off, tell him I was skint and that I was going back to Glasgow. I'd never have seen him again."

"And what do you think would have happened to him?"

I couldn't answer that, because we both knew the main reason for using McKinley was his connection with Laing and that the two of them would be in the frame together.

"You were sentencing him to death, you bastard," he shouted and thumped the pillow next to my head. "You callous, unthinking, cynical bastard. He probably saved your life, bringing you back here. He could have driven off and left you bleeding on the ground. And you were setting him up like a clay pipe at a shooting gallery."

176

I wanted to say that McKinley was just a foot soldier in the drugs war, that they probably wouldn't have hurt him, that they'd have gone for Laing first and probably got their cocaine back from Kyle and then they'd have called off the dogs, but I didn't believe it so I didn't say anything. I just nodded.

"You'll have to tell him everything now," he continued. "If he ever comes back. And if he doesn't, sport, we're all in trouble, you, me and Shona. He might not know who you are but he definitely knows Shona now and where she lives. You'll have to tell him everything and offer him a darn sight more than a payoff. He can't go back to London, you realize that?"

I nodded again. "I know." Read knew McKinley so the people who brought the drugs in would be looking for him. Besides Laing he was the one lead they had.

"The signpost you hoped would send them to Laing is now pointing right in your direction. Your only hope is to uproot it and bring it up here. Offer him a job, anything, but he has to stay close to you. It'll be a form of symbiosis, he'll need you to protect him, you'll need him to keep out of trouble. You'd better stick together like Siamese twins."

"I guess you're right, Tony. I'll speak to him when he gets back."

"If he gets back." He stood up and walked over to the window again.

"That leaves only one character in your sordid little drama."

"Sammy," I said.

"Sammy," he repeated thoughtfully, as if it was the first time he'd heard the name. He was chewing the inside of his cheek again and the arms were folded across his chest.

"I can't keep saying I'm sorry, Tony."

He ignored me. "How much does she know?" he asked. My heart soared then because his question meant that Sammy hadn't told Tony anything, she'd kept my secret to herself.

Because she loved me? Then I flushed as I remembered how I'd used her.

"Everything."

"Everything?"

"She knows who I am, who I really am, she knows what happened to my parents, she knows exactly what I planned to do and she was prepared to help me." I was proud of that, proud that she was my friend, my lover, and ashamed that I'd abused her trust.

"Then she's a lot dumber than I thought," he said. "Did you explain everything, she knew what she was getting into?"

I didn't have to answer that one because he could tell from my shamefaced expression that I hadn't. I hadn't told anyone the full story. I take that back, there was one person, David. "She's not in any danger, Tony. I promise."

"That's not a promise you can make, sport. What makes you think they won't track her down once Laing tells them where he was?"

"She didn't use her own name and I rented a separate flat for her. A short-term let, paid in advance.

She'd never met Laing before, and all she has to do is to lie low for a few weeks."

"Until he's killed? Is that what you mean?"

"Yes, if you like. There's precious little chance of Laing ever bumping into Sammy again, and once he's dead she'll be one hundred per cent in the clear. That still stands, Tony, whatever might have gone wrong she will be all right. I'll call her and tell her what's happened and that she's to take care, but it's hardly necessary. She knew that once she got back from Paris she was never to see him again. She knew what she was getting into."

"You'd better be right. You had no right to use people the way you did. I'm tempted to say that what has happened is all your own fault, but there's no point rubbing your nose in it. I just hope you've learned your lesson, that's all. Fight your own battles in future and don't play God."

Then he patted me on the shoulder and left me alone. Later Shona brought me a drink of water, her face tearstained and her eyes red from crying. She got on the bed, leant alongside me and hugged me and kissed me on the cheek, and then left the room without saying anything.

I slept fitfully, I dreamt of suitcases full of cocaine and shotguns exploding and dinghies full of men in black waving guns and shouting. They were chasing me and I was running through water, it dragged at my feet and held me back and the men in black were catching up with me, closer and closer, because they were running on top of the water, skating along the surface. I looked up, gasping for breath, pains in my chest, and I saw Sammy on the loch side and she was screaming, and then her face melted into Shona's and David was standing next to her, crying, and then the men in black had them, surrounded and held them. I kept on running in slow motion but I looked over my shoulder and they weren't chasing me any more, they were carrying Shona and David off into separate dinghies, and then the outboard motors kicked into life and I waded out into the water after them, waving my arms as they roared off into the darkness. Then I was alone and the freezing water was up to my neck, numbing my body, and then it was over my head and I lost consciousness.

I woke with a raging thirst. It was morning and the sun streamed in through the window where Shona was standing, her hands holding the cord which she'd pulled to open the curtains and thrown light onto my face.

She came over and helped me to sit up, pushing a pillow behind my back and fluffing up the duvet, fussing like a broody hen. "There's a mug of tea next to you," she said, smoothing the quilt professionally like a nurse with a difficult patient.

"Shona," I said, and waited until she'd stopped moving and stood by the bed, hands by her side.

"Yes?" she said in a low, quiet voice, looking through me with the lifeless eyes of a sleepwalker.

I wanted to say "sorry" again, to explain why I'd done what I did, to explain how special she was to me, how the only people I'd meant to hurt were Laing and Kyle, but I knew there was nothing I could say, that she'd always love me and be my friend but that it would take a long time before she'd trust and respect me again. Maybe she never would, maybe I'd blown it for good. Talking now would only sound like I was making excuses, the tail-wagging of a guilty dog.

"Thanks," I said, and she smiled and tossed her head.

"All part of the service," she said and left me on my own with my thoughts.

I dozed, drifting in and out of sleep until she came back with the telephone in her hand, one of those remote jobs that you can use in the car, the garden or the toilet.

"It's McKinley," she said. "For you."

"If he starts using bad language I'll call for help," I said and grinned. It felt like a snarl.

"Not funny," she said and turned on her heel and walked out of the room, and what the hell she was right, it wasn't funny.

"How are you getting on?" he asked and it sounded as if he meant it, but the voice lacked warmth.

"I'm fine," I replied. "The shoulder still hurts but I'm on the mend." If we had been in the same room we'd have been looking at each other warily, a couple of prizefighters who'd shaken hands and were ready to come out fighting. I couldn't tell from his silence how he felt.

"Did you get the car back?" I asked eventually.

"Let's get one thing straight, boss. You shouldn't have used me the way you did. You used me and you'd have thrown me to the wolves. I could have died, you know." The words were tumbling out, running into each other like rushhour commuters pouring off a packed bus.

"When the bastard pointed his shooter at me I honestly thought that I'd had it. If you hadn't pushed me to one side he'd have blown me apart. I'd frozen, I couldn't move." He dried up, an engine running out of steam.

He broke the silence after a few seconds, and this time his voice was bitter and angry.

"I'm not coming back. You'll never see me again. I can't trust you, not after what you did to me. I don't know what I'm going to do, but I'll do it on my own." The sentences came out in short, sharp bursts like bullets from a gun.

"Get-Up, listen to me. I can't take back what I did, but I can try to make it right, if you'll let me," I said, remembering Tony's words. Symbiosis. I needed this man.

"No," he said, with a finality that left me in no doubt that I would never see him again. But there was one thing I had to know before he cut the connection and disappeared from my life forever. Had he finished the job?

He continued. "If you hadn't saved my life I wouldn't even have phoned," he said and then ground to a halt, realizing what a daft thing he'd said, then blustering on regardless. "I would just have told Read's mates what you'd been up to. But you did, so the car's back where you wanted it. I rang Dancer like you said and he collected it from me. I said you'd send the rest of the money to him. Now we're even."

"Get-Up, listen to what I say. Keep away from Laing, right away. Keep your head down. And if you need any help you can come to me."

"No, I'm on my own now. You won't ever see me again."

"Good luck, Get-Up. I mean it."

"Go to hell." Click, and he was gone.

Later Tony came and sat on the bed and laid down the law. Shona was to move out of the flat, soonest. She'd go and stay with her parents. That way if McKinley went back on his word — I began to interrupt, to say that Get-Up wouldn't let me down, but Tony steamrollered over me — then nobody could get to her. Sammy was to be told to lie low, I certainly wasn't to go near her for a while, at least until we knew what had happened to Laing and Kyle. I was to keep out of the way, Tony would be my eyes and ears in London. Yes sir, no sir, three bags full sir. Tony made me feel small, small and vulnerable, but I accepted the sanctuary he offered, the safe cool sanctuary of the strong, and I remembered Sammy and the polar bear.

Shona and Tony wanted me to go somewhere warm, to lie in the sun for a couple of weeks, to come back suntanned and rested and ready to go back into harness. I agreed.

I telephoned Sammy and told her I'd be out of the country for a while.

"How was Paris?" I asked.

"Don't ask," she said.

"Good, I'm glad," I replied, and I was. My stomach had been churning at the thought that she might have enjoyed herself with him. She broke the silence by asking what had gone wrong and I told her, warning her to keep a low profile and to have no further contact with Laing.

"You don't have to worry on that score," she said, and I could picture her white teeth and easy smile as she brushed her long hair behind her ear. "How's Get-Up?" she asked.

"Vanished. I doubt we'll see him again."

"Where are you going?"

"I don't know yet, but I'll be in touch, I promise." I paused, unsure of how to pose the question. "Sammy?" I asked.

"I'm here."

"When I get back, will you come up to be with me in Edinburgh?" Hell, that didn't sound right.

"On the payroll, you mean?" she asked.

"You know what I mean."

"Yes, I know."

"Well?"

"Well what?"

"If I was with you, young lady, I'd put you over my knee and give you a good spanking."

"And if you were with me, I'd let you."

"Stop teasing, Sammy. Will you?"

"I think I might."

"Is that a yes?"

"It's a yes. But you knew that before you asked. Now away you go and enjoy your holiday — send me a card."

"I might."

"Rat. I love you," and that one caught me with my guard down, right under the chin, and it sent me reeling onto the ropes.

"Must go. See you soon," I said and fumbled the receiver back on the hook, cursing myself for becoming so awkward with her, and wondering how three words could so quickly turn me back into a gauche schoolboy. And I hadn't even told her that I loved her.

I rang her back. "I love you," I said.

"I know that, stupid," she said, and hung up.

The first package holiday Shona could arrange was a fortnight in Malta, and she flew with me to London and put me on the plane at Gatwick, partly out of concern but mainly to check that I actually went.

I asked her if she wanted to come with me but it wasn't on, because I'd done enough damage to the firm over the past few months and someone had to mind the shop.

Shona had booked me into a modern, comfortable hotel overlooking St Paul's Bay, just a couple of minutes' walk through its gardens and across the road to the seafront.

The resort had grown up around a picturesque fishing village on the north-east coast, and it reminded me a little of Oban with its work-worn boats bobbing in the sea.

I spent most of my time walking around the harbour, stopping off at the dozens of friendly bars and cafés, eating at the local restaurants, resting and exercising my shoulder. The stiffness was going and the scars healing, but it would still catch me unawares every now and again and the pain would make me wince.

I did all the touristy things, went on trips around the capital, Valletta, took a boat trip to the island of Gozo where I bought a lace shawl for Shona, and cruised around the Blue Grotto, but most of the time I just lay on a towel on one of the huge flat rocks by the sea and turned brown like a lamb chop under a grill.

At the start of the second week the young nephew of the hotel owner came running up and stood over me, blotting the sun from my burning face, bare chested and panting, his cut-off blue jeans several sizes too big and held up with a piece of grubby string knotted at the front.

"Telephone for you," he gasped. "Come quickly."

I gave him a handful of Maltese cents and patted his dark curly hair, jogged with him back to the hotel and took the call at the reception desk.

"Shona," I said, it couldn't have been anyone else, she was the only person who knew where I was. "What's wrong?"

The line was crackling and buzzing and it sounded as if she was talking with a mouthful of potato crisps, but I heard her say: "My God, what have you done? All hell's broken loose here." And then she explained what

186

had happened, repeating herself when the line got so bad that I couldn't make out what she was saying.

They'd found McKinley first, in a disused warehouse on the Isle of Dogs. He was naked and covered with cigarette burns and quite dead. The little finger of his right hand had been severed with bolt cutters or something, and he'd been kicked and beaten hard enough and long enough to break most of his ribs and his hip.

He'd been chained by the hands to a metal girder running sideways across the warehouse, and his wrists were chafed to the bone where he'd struggled and fought to free himself but there was nothing he could have done because his legs were also chained, to the rusting back axle of a long-scrapped truck and his ankles too were bloody and frayed.

At some point he'd been hit repeatedly with a long metal bar and there were weals across his back and stomach, but they were nothing compared with the patches of burnt flesh where lighted cigarettes had been pushed and gouged into the soft, vulnerable parts of his body.

It had taken him several hours to die, and he must have begged and pleaded for them to stop every second of every minute of every hour because he'd told them everything he knew and he hadn't done anything, he'd been used from the start, and please God why didn't they believe him?

There hadn't been a single thing he could have said to stop them.

Whoever had tortured and killed McKinley caught up with Iwanek two days later in Spain, where he'd rented a villa about half an hour's drive inland from Alicante airport.

It was a white-painted building around a cool courtyard that would normally sleep six people but Iwanek lived there on his own, high on a sun-bleached hill surrounded by groves of orange trees.

From the side of his private pool he could sit and watch planeloads of pale tourists arriving for their two weeks in nearby Benidorm and then departing with brown skins and suitcases full of sandy clothing and cheap presents.

He drank a lot, invited local girls and holidaymakers back to his villa and his bedroom and began to put out feelers, tentatively probing the market for the briefcase of white powder he'd hidden under one of the flagstones in the kitchen.

There were plenty of wealthy people in the villas around the east coast of Spain, many of them British villains on the run, and he reckoned they'd be keen to buy and he hoped to make contact with dealers in the Benidorm resort.

He thought he would be able to make six figures without trying, but that's not how it worked out, and the middle-aged woman who cycled up the hill to cook for him each evening found his body tied to the large oak bed in the main bedroom, spreadeagled like a stranded starfish on a white sandy beach, only the sheet she'd so carefully washed and ironed wasn't white anymore, it was stained with blood and sweat and shit, the flies buzzed around the burns all over his body and the mouth was wide open in a silent scream of agony. When she staggered to the kitchen to get to the phone, she nearly tripped over the stone floor which had been ripped up to get at the hidden drugs.

McKinley's death, macabre as it was, had at first merited only a few paragraphs in the London editions of the nationals, and the discovery of Read's body at Loch Feochan became a seven-day wonder of the "Police Probe Mystery Slaying" variety, but an enterprising reporter on one of the more sensational tabloid Sundays linked all three murders, cobbled together some spurious background on drugs smuggling between Spain and Britain and the paper splashed it.

The story spread north of the border, the *Herald* and the *Scotsman* both following it up and doing extended features on the influx of drugs along the Scottish coastline, and the *Daily Record* did a colour piece on the men who man the coastal cutters. The media's like that, feeding on itself ad infinitum, one reporter's throwaway line becoming another's page lead.

"What about Laing?" I asked.

"There's no sign of him. Tony thinks he's either been killed as well or gone to ground. Either way he says you'll probably never see him again. What are we going to do?"

"Don't worry," I said, trying to soothe her. "It's OK, that's the end of it. It's over."

"I can't hear you," she said through the crackling and buzzing. "Are you still there? Hello? Hello?"

"It's all right," I shouted, cupping my hand between the receiver and my mouth, trying to focus my voice and the reassurance in it. "It won't go any further. It can't. Nobody knows I was involved, Shona, and as far as anyone else is concerned the trail stops cold at Laing and Iwanek.

"From what you've said, it looks as if they've got the cocaine back and that's all they wanted. It's over, Shona."

"I'm frightened, I didn't realize it would end like this. Two people have been murdered, horribly murdered, and you're to blame. What have you done? Was it worth it? Are you proud of yourself?"

She was becoming hysterical now, hyperventilating and I was too far away to help, to hold her until the panic left her. "Do you want me to come straight back?" I asked. "I can probably get an earlier flight."

"No, stay where you are, you need the rest. I'll be all right, I just worked myself up into a panic, that's all. Be careful."

"There's no need to be careful, don't you understand?" I said. "It's over, finished. I'll be back in a week anyway. How's David?" I asked, trying to change the subject.

"He's fine, but we're both missing you. Take care."

"And you. And don't worry, it is finished. I promise. I'll see you soon."

Then she was gone, my link with home broken, but I couldn't stop smiling as I replaced the receiver because it was over, or at least it soon would be.

I walked down to the harbour and went along to one of the small bars with pretty white tables and blue and white striped umbrellas outside on the pavement. Inside it was cool and in semi-darkness, and I sat on a wooden stool at the corner of the bar furthest from the door and ordered a bottle of champagne. I filled a glass and raised it in front of me, towards the shaft of bright sunlight that sliced through the doorway, spearing the gloom and illuminating a black and white mongrel lying on the stone floor. The light had a religious look as it poured in, as if I was on hallowed ground, back in the church where I'd said goodbye to both my parents. I nodded towards the doorway.

"Rest easy, Dad, I got the bastards." I drank to him, and to my mother, then I drank for drinking's sake and then I ordered another bottle. Soon I was laughing out loud and drinking toasts to David, to Shona, to Sammy, to Tony, and to Ronnie Laing, missing believed tortured and killed. They'd catch up with him eventually, if they hadn't already. They wouldn't believe his protestations of innocence any more than they'd have trusted McKinley's version of events. Laing couldn't prove he'd been out of the country because passports aren't stamped for visits to France, a bonus of being in the EEC. Sammy had taken the receipt from the carpark at Heathrow along with anything else that could show Laing had been in France, and Amanda Pearson had long ceased to exist.

His car had been seen near the drugs snatch and the hotel bills in Oban and Glasgow had been paid for with his American Express card, along with a hire car that had been dumped in the hotel carpark. Guilty as charged and sentenced to die by torture, screaming, crying and begging them to stop.

Then I drank to Jim Iwanek, who'd died in agony on a bed in Spain, begging them to leave him alone and telling them everything he knew.

He'd told them where the cocaine was, and he'd told them who I was except that the name I'd given him was Alan Kyle, and before long Kyle would be dead and then the circle would be well and truly closed.

The second week passed quickly. I worked on the tan and spent the afternoons skindiving and I even went waterskiing, the shoulder giving me no problems at all. I managed to get the FT and the *Wall Street Journal* at a local shop, usually two days late and costing five times the cover price, but I read them from front to back as I lay on the rocks, water lapping at my feet.

I was looking forward to getting back to work, to the technicalities of handling a takeover or a share issue, the high-level discussions with board members and bankers, raising capital and restructuring contracts. I loved the job and for the foreseeable future I was going to give Scottish Corporate Advisors, and Sammy, my undivided attention.

The memory of Laing and Kyle would soon fade, an episode that I'd keep locked away in the dark recesses of my mind, along with McKinley's tortured corpse. It would return from time to time to haunt me, I knew that, and there would be times when I'd wake at night sweating and shaking after dreaming of burning cigarettes and scorched flesh, but in my heart of hearts I felt that my hands were clean and that it had been their own fault. It was behind me. It was over.

The plane touched down at Gatwick at eleven o'clock on a chilly autumn morning, the change in temperature a shock to my system after two weeks in Malta. I zipped up the linen bomber jacket that had been too warm to wear in the sun but which wasn't thick enough for Surrey with Christmas only a few months away.

I went straight through the Nothing to Declare customs hall, I had just one battered leather suitcase and a duty free carrier bag with two bottles of Glenfiddich, and I was eager to get back to Edinburgh where Shona had promised to put me up until I was ready to move back into Stonehaven. On the way to the taxi rank I bought an early edition of the *Standard* and I opened it as the driver pulled away from the terminal building.

Her picture was on page five under the forty-two point headline "Police Hunt Call-Girl Killer" and she was smiling. Her hair was longer than when I'd seen her rushing out of the door, and it wasn't as curly. It was an old photograph but the pouting lips and large almond eyes were the same. It was Carol.

The story said she'd been found naked in a bath full of water with her arms tied behind her back, and that she hadn't been raped but the police suspected it was a sex killing because of the cigarette burns on her breasts and thighs, and they were working their way through her client book which the *Standard* understood contained a host of top people including MPs, showbusiness and City names. Blood tests had shown that she'd taken a cocaine and heroin cocktail some time before she died and police were also investigating the drugs link.

Carol was dead and it was my fault and it was far from over because if they had found Carol they would find Sammy, and Sammy knew who I was because I'd told her everything and before they were through with her she'd tell them everything, too.

My mouth was dry and my hands were shaking and I felt like I was falling, a sick emptiness in the pit of my stomach and all I could hear in my head was Shona's voice saying "What have you done?" over and over again, and all I could see was Sammy's face and her eyes as she held me and told me it was going to be OK. The empty feeling became a cold hardness inside, and gradually my hands stopped trembling and I breathed deeply and locked her out of my mind and tried to work out what the hell I was going to do.

I rapped on the glass partition behind the cab driver's head and asked him to drive back to the airport, and he shrugged and hauled the cab round with a screech of tyres against the tarmac.

Back at the terminal I ran to the bank of payphones, rummaging through my pockets for change, sorting out the ten and fifty-pence coins.

I called Sammy first. There had been no mention of her in the *Standard* and there was an outside chance that she wasn't involved. Sure. And maybe pigs might fly. As it happened she wasn't in the flat and I did speak to a flying pig.

"She's in the bathroom, who shall I say is calling?" asked a male voice which was obviously more used to cautioning suspects than taking telephone messages.

"Just a friend," I said.

"Actually, she's busy at the moment. Give me your name and number and I'll have her call you back." At least he hadn't called me Sir.

"Good afternoon, inspector," I said, taking a pot shot at his rank, and slammed the phone down. Damn. Sammy was missing, and the chances were that she'd been there when Carol had been tortured. Tell us what you know, look what we're doing to your friend. Listen to her scream. Tell us everything about this man, Sammy. Where does he live? What does he do? Tell us about his family, Sammy. Oh my God, no. David. David?

I could feel the clammy fingers of panic clutching at my heart as I rang Shankland Hall, closing my eyes and praying until the sister came to the phone.

I fought to keep my voice steady as I asked: "Is David all right?"

"Yes of course," she said. "You've just missed him. Miss Darvell was here to collect him earlier this morning."

The sense of relief was overwhelming and I leant forward and rested my forehead against the cool plaster of the wall, allowing the tension to escape in a long drawn-out sigh. Sammy had got away, maybe she hadn't even been there when Carol was killed. And she'd gone up to Scotland to get David out of harm's way.

"They said you'd be ringing," continued the sister.

They? They? The panic was back now, a hundred times worse than before. I took a deep breath but my lungs still felt empty and hollow. It was as if my brain had been starved of oxygen, going under for the third time, drowning.

"Who was with Sammy?" I asked eventually.

"I rather assumed he was a friend of the family, or a relative of Miss Darvell. He seemed very close and took her by the arm several times." She paused and I could almost hear her thinking. "There's nothing wrong is there?" she asked.

"No, no, nothing's wrong," I managed. "I'm just back from a holiday and I'd forgotten that Sammy was taking David out. And the man will have been her brother. Did they say when they'd be back?"

I was sweating, the trembling had returned and I closed my eyes tightly. Please God let them be all right.

"No they didn't, I'm sorry. But it won't be tonight for certain, that I do know. They were going on a trip, I seem to remember Miss Darvell saying. She did say I was to give you a message, though. It was about work, I think. Let me see, I have it written down somewhere. Yes, here it is. She said you were to arrange the transfer of the funds and that she would call you at your home at seven o'clock with the details."

I thanked her and hung up but God knows how I kept the despair out of my voice, because now they had Sammy and David and I thought about the cigarette burns and this I couldn't bury in my subconscious. My eyes stung with tears because it was all going wrong and I'd lost control, and I could still hear Shona saying "What have you done? All hell's broken loose here."

I wanted to run, but there was nowhere to run to, and I wanted to hide but I couldn't because I was the only hope that Sammy and David had, without me they were dead and please God don't let them be dead already.

I was to arrange the transfer of the funds, Sammy had said, which meant that whether or not they'd got their hands on the drugs they wanted their money as well, all £250,000 of it.

I didn't have the cash, but if push came to shove I would be able to get hold of quarter of a million pounds by seven o'clock. It would mean pulling a few strings and twisting a few arms but I was in the money business so it wasn't a major problem. But I was under no illusions about the message Sammy had left. There was no way on earth that the men who had killed McKinley, Iwanek and Carol, and probably Laing and Kyle too, were going to swap a suitcase of money for Sammy and David and let us all ride off into the sunset.

The money was secondary, what they really wanted was revenge and a warning to others that there had to be honour among thieves. They wanted me dead and that meant killing Sammy and David, too. Please God don't let them be dead already.

I rang Tony's office. His secretary said he was in a meeting and wouldn't be available until late in the afternoon, but when I told her who I was she said that yes, Tony had been expecting my call and that if I would hold the line she'd go into his office and get him.

Tony was on the phone within seconds, and if I'd expected tea and sympathy then he soon put me right. This wasn't the friendly back-slapping Tony I knew, he was bitter and angry and for a moment I was glad he was on the end of the phone and not standing in front of me.

"You've seen the *Standard*?" he roared.

"I'm sorry, Tony, I'm really sorry. If I'd —"

"It's too late for sorry," he interrupted. "Christ, did you read how she died? And it's all your fault. You stupid, stupid bastard. Do you have any idea at all where this is going to end?"

"Tony, listen to me. We don't have time for this. Argue with me later, hit me if you want, ignore me, hate me, but first help me. I need your help now more than ever before. Just do this one thing for me." There was silence, and I closed my eyes and willed him not to hang up on me.

"Where are you?" he asked eventually.

"Gatwick Airport. I've just arrived back from Malta."

"Wait there. I'll be with you within the hour. And you've got some explaining to do."

"Don't hang up, Tony. I haven't finished yet. You have to do something for me."

I told him the two things I wanted and God bless him he didn't ask why, he just said yes, he could get them both and I was to wait where I was.

If he'd been my fairy godmother and granted me three wishes, and if I didn't have to go through a metal detector before catching the plane to Edinburgh then I'd have asked for a semi-automatic handgun as well, something small enough to hide in a coat pocket but big enough to kill at a distance. But Tony wasn't my fairy godmother and the only way to get up to Stonehaven in time was to fly, and anyway I couldn't risk using a gun that could be traced back to him. If Sammy had told them what she knew then Tony was in enough trouble already.

He arrived before twelve-thirty in his blue Lagonda and helped me load my suitcase into the boot without saying a word. It was only after we'd fastened our seat belts and my shoes had settled into the pale blue sheepskin carpeting that he turned to me, raising his eyebrows without a trace of a smile and asked: "Well?"

"Did you get what I asked for?"

He gestured with his thumb. "On the back seat."

I turned and looked over my shoulder and saw a green and yellow Harrods carrier bag. "Thanks," I said. "Were they easy to get?"

"I'm in the business, you know that. I had them both in stock. Where are we going?" Still no smile.

"I have to get to Edinburgh within the next few hours. The Heathrow to Edinburgh Shuttle is the best bet. Do you mind?"

"It doesn't look as if I've any choice, does it?" He started the car. "Tell me what's happening. And what do you want with the gear in the back?"

Tony was one of those drivers who got other motorists grinding their teeth and gripping their steering wheels, cursing and hitting their horns and brakes. I'd never seen him check his mirror before manoeuvring, his eyes were always on the car in front. He treated his Lagonda like a racing car, which in effect it was with its souped-up engine and specially modified steering and suspension. He weaved in and out of the traffic as we headed north towards Heathrow, hands light on the wheel and foot heavy on the accelerator, driving the way the manufacturers intended and the police frowned upon. It wasn't the most relaxing way of travelling and the atmosphere in the luxurious car was already tense.

"You know as much as I do, Tony. I told you last time I saw you, up in Edinburgh, what I'd planned, that I'd set up Laing and Kyle and got someone else to do my dirty work. I thought I'd got every angle covered but the whole bloody thing's gone wrong. Shona rang me in Malta to tell me that McKinley was killed last week, and it won't be long before they catch up with Kyle . . ."

He looked at me as he passed a Jaguar on the inside at eighty. "They already have done," he said. "He died three days before they got to Carol. I suppose the news didn't reach as far as Scotland. And Laing still hasn't surfaced."

So at least something had gone as planned, Kyle had been killed and Laing was dead or running scared. But there was no feeling of satisfaction, no warm glow of a job well done, just a gut-wrenching panic at yet another sign that the men I was up against would kill and keep on killing until everyone they thought was involved had been removed. It was a cold-blooded hunt which was a thousand times worse than the revenge I'd planned. This was business with no element of personal hatred. People were being killed solely as a warning to others, coolly, calmly and professionally. No hard feelings, business is business. They'd caught Sammy and David and I was next on the agenda.

"They have killed Kyle and I thought it would end there, I swear it. They caught up with Iwanek in Spain but that was his own fault. He'd barely arrived in Benidorm before he started trying to flog the stuff. It must have been like a bluebottle flying smack bang into the middle of a spider's web, setting off all sorts of trip wires."

"Trip wires stretching back to where?" he asked, and that was the £250,000 question and this time he deserved a straight answer because now he was in as much danger as I was. I took a deep breath to prepare myself because the shit was really going to hit the fan.

"Ireland," I said and turned to look at him. We didn't accelerate and he didn't slam hard on the brakes but the temperature in the air-conditioned Lagonda dropped at least ten degrees. It was a full thirty seconds before he spoke, and only after he'd softly rubbed the scar where the ridge of white skin merged into his moustache.

"Jesus Christ, what have you done?" he asked quietly, and it reminded me of Shona's words, except this time it was well and truly rhetorical because he knew exactly what I'd done. "I assumed it was a few London hoods you'd got involved with, that I could have dealt with. But the IR bloody A? You must have been mad. They'll never stop, you know that don't you? They'll keep on coming until we're all dead."

"It shouldn't have happened this way, the circle should have been closed once Laing and Kyle were killed," I said. "That should have ended it, Tony. I can't understand how Carol got involved."

"Carol got involved, you stupid, inconsiderate bastard, because you involved her. If you'd been straight with me from the start I'd never have let you within a million miles of her. She didn't deserve to die the way she did. Alone and screaming and blaming you and probably me too."

"It's too late for what might have been, Tony," I said. "We can't go back. God, I don't want to spout a load of clichés but what's done is done. If I could turn time back I would, believe me, but she's dead and McKinley's dead and I can't change that. I've got to look after myself, and Shona and David, and you've got to protect yourself. If Carol gave them your name then you're in as much danger as I am."

"You think I don't know that?" Tony replied. "That I hadn't worked that out for myself? I'm scared shitless, more frightened than I've ever been in my life. And you know how well protected I am."

I did, too. The Lagonda Tony was flinging around the A217 was enough to turn heads in its own right, but he'd spent another twenty thousand having numerous refinements installed. He'd got the car from a South

202

American dictator as part payment for an arms deal and it came complete with an ultra-sophisticated alarm system. A pigeon landing on the bonnet was enough to set off a howling siren and a personal radio bleeper which Tony always carried. Most of the money had gone on structural refinements, armouring the body panels and reinforcing the underside making it virtually bombproof, armour-plated glass replacing the original windows, a petrol tank that you could fire a bullet through without causing an explosion, if you could find a bullet large enough and with enough velocity to penetrate the armoured tank in the first place.

The tyres were practically invulnerable, you could drive them through fire or over broken glass without any problems, and a blow-out at ninety mph wouldn't even be noticed. The car had a common or garden radio telephone, but it was also equipped with a short-wave transmitter operating on a frequency used by diplomats and terrorist targets and constantly monitored by the Metropolitan Police.

At the touch of a button he could release five gallons of oil from the armoured boot which sounded like something only James Bond would need, but Tony swore he'd once had to use it and I believed him. There were other safety features he hadn't told me about, and as far as he was concerned it was money well spent.

His home was even more secure. It was a turn of the century five-bedroomed detached house on three floors in Notting Hill, standing alone in half an acre and surrounded by an eight-foot wall. From the outside it looked like a highly desirable residence, which it was, the sort of house you'd expect to be occupied by a Channel Four film producer. It was also a fortress, and inside Tony was safer than the Crown Jewels. Anything larger than a cat moving across the lawn would set lights flashing on a console within the house and in the police station a mile away. The front and back gardens were covered by closed circuit television cameras. Just like the Lagonda all the windows were of toughened glass, and the outside doors were reinforced with steel. Tony had no household insurance. He didn't need it.

Underground was a wine cellar which doubled as an inner sanctum, lined with concrete and entered through a three-inch thick steel door. Once locked it was airtight with a self-contained oxygen supply and virtually bomb-proof. There was a separate and well-protected telephone link with the local police station, and more than a few guests had remarked on the mauve telephone on the wall behind the chateau-bottled claret.

At home, in his office and in his car, Tony was safe, but we both knew that he was vulnerable when he moved between the three and we also knew that the sort of men we were dealing with now were fanatics with very long memories. If they decided that Tony was a target then it might be days, weeks, months, even years, but eventually they would come for him. Maybe while he was on holiday, playing squash, walking his Labrador, in his local pub, anytime, anywhere. No wonder he was frightened.

"But it's not myself I'm worried about, it's you, and those close to you," he said. "I got hold of Shona at the

204

office today so at least she's safe. But there's no sign of Sammy. Where is she?"

I'd been honest with him up to this point, but if I had any chance of getting Sammy and David out of this then I had to work alone. The last thing I wanted to do was to lie to Tony but I had no choice, if I could handle it myself and quickly then perhaps I could close the circle once and for all.

"She's safe, out of harm's way," I lied, as casually as possible. Another stain on my hypothetical painting.

"If that's the case, sport, what do you need those for?" and he glanced at the Harrods carrier bag.

"I'm going to take them on at their own game, Tony. And it's best you don't know the details. Either way you'll be OK. If I win then it'll be over, if I lose then perhaps they'll let it die with me. Whatever, I have to try. And you can't help me, nobody can. It's best you don't know."

"I might be able to help. I have friends. And don't forget that Laing could still be on the loose."

"God, Tony, I know that. If anyone could help it would be you, believe me. But I have to do this myself."

"A man's got to do what a man's got to do? Very macho. I'm your friend, let me help."

"I can't, Tony. I'm sorry."

He drove on in silence, burning up the miles along the M25 towards Heathrow at a steady ninety mph, flashing his headlights at anyone impertinent enough to stay in the outside lane and several times overtaking on the inside. "Where are you going?" he asked after a while.

"Stonehaven," I said. "There is one thing you can do for me."

"What's that?"

"You can order a hire car for me at Edinburgh Airport. Something big and powerful. I've got my Access card and a cheque book so there's no problem in paying but it'll save time if you book it for me."

"So Shona won't be there to collect you?"

"No. I'd rather she kept out of the way until this is over. And I'd feel safer if you did the same."

"Don't worry about me, sport. Just be careful. And if I can help, let me know. I'll be there like a shot."

"I know, Tony, I know. You've done more than enough already, more than I deserve. I won't ever forget this." I put my hand on his shoulder and squeezed gently but he didn't look at me and he didn't speak again until we arrived at Heathrow. He waved me goodbye and good luck as I walked into the terminal with the case in one hand and the carrier bag in the other. I'd left the duty free with Tony. I wouldn't be drinking for a while.

"The car will be waiting for you at the airport," he shouted after me, and it was when I arrived in Edinburgh two hours later. It was bitterly cold and the wind tugged at my hair as I loaded the luggage into the red Cavalier.

My watch said 2.55 and in just a little over four hours I'd know when and where this was going to end, one way or another. The Cavalier started first time, it had a full tank of petrol and it kicked me in the back as

I put the accelerator pedal to the floor and headed for Stonehaven.

I stopped off at a hardware store on the outskirts of Edinburgh, one of those tiny shops that have been in the same family for years, where they'll sell you fifty different types of nails, a brown paper bag of assorted screws and the sort of tools that Spear and Jackson no longer bother to make.

It smelt of wet string and candle wax and oil and the old man behind the counter in a stained brown overall called me Sir. I bought a hacksaw, a small wood saw and a strong carpenter's file. I couldn't see any packets of sandpaper but the old man asked what I wanted, dived under the polished wooden counter and came up with four single sheets of large grain paper.

"Anything else?" he asked eagerly, like an old Spaniel begging for a stick to be thrown.

"I don't suppose you've got any foam rubber, about so big and so thick?" I said, marking out the size with my hands.

"I think I have, in the back," he said, and scurried off. I wandered round the little shop, running my fingers through barrels of bulbs, a huge cardboard box full of assorted bundles of string, and racks and racks of screwdrivers, spanners, hammers and things for getting boy scouts out of horses' hooves. Before long he was back, a piece of yellow foam rubber clutched to his chest which he carefully rolled up, tied with string and placed in a carrier bag with the rest of the purchases.

I paid him and drove the rest of the way to Stonehaven trying to work out exactly what I had to do and the order in which it had to be done.

The day after my father's funeral the house had been closed, I had driven David to the nursing home and then gone straight to London in the Porsche. A lady from the village came in twice a week to air the rooms and dust the furniture, but other than that the house had been left alone, deserted. That's exactly how it looked as I drove up the drive and parked in front of the stone porch. It wasn't a home any more, it was a building waiting for a family. It had no heart, no soul. The leaves had started to fall from the sycamores that marked the boundary with the road and they swirled around my feet as I groped in my jacket for the keys.

It was early afternoon but the house seemed gloomy inside and it felt and smelt damp. I'd planned to bring David back to the house when this was all over, bring in a housekeeper to clean and cook for us, but now I was having second thoughts. Without our parents as a focus it was just a collection of stones and slates and wood and we'd be better off starting afresh.

I opened the door to the study and walked over to the green velvet curtains which had been drawn since the police forensic team had left. The room had been dusted once or twice, certainly not as thoroughly as the rest of the house, and though somebody had tried to wash the blood off the wallpaper there was still a speck or two there, and on the bookcase I could see a piece of lead shot looking no more sinister than the stuff anglers use to weigh down their lines. I found the key to the security cabinet in the bottom left-hand drawer of the desk.

From the outside the cabinet appeared to be a simple mahogany box, about five feet high and three feet wide with double opening doors. It could have held drinks or files but it was lined with steel and the lock was better than the one on the front door, and inside was a rack with spaces for a dozen shotguns including the one my father had used to kill himself.

The key turned easily and silently and I drew back the doors. The guns gleamed and light glinted off the engraved plates. There was a pair of Denton and Kennell Number Ones, walnut stocks and delicate engravings, and three Midland over and under shotguns my father used to give guests who fancied a little rough shooting. There was a Winchester over and under and a couple of Beretta Sporting Multichokes that he lent to more serious shots, but my father's pride and joy was a pair of Purdeys that he'd bought for nigh on £12,000 six years ago at a Sotheby's auction at Pulborough.

They used to belong to one of the best game shots of all time, the second Marquis of Rippon, who was reckoned to have blown apart something like half a million birds in his lifetime. They had a history and my father loved them.

He'd spent hours polishing and cleaning the pair, but it was only one of them that he'd used to blow his brains out and that was the one I took from the cabinet and tucked under my arm as I grabbed a handful of cartridges and relocked the doors. I picked up the carrier bag of tools and foam rubber, walked down the hall and unbolted the door leading to the back garden.

At the end of the garden next to the grey stone boundary wall was an old brick building that in years gone by had been a stable but which was now used as a tool shed, a place to store gardening equipment during the winter months and the place where we went to look for anything that had gone missing from the house. It was filthy and the wooden door was covered in cobwebs. It wasn't locked because there was nothing inside worth stealing, but it had the one thing I wanted which was a solid oak workbench with a huge steel vice, made like they don't make them any more.

The light switch wouldn't work or maybe the bulb had gone, but there was still enough light coming in through the cracked and dirty window panes to see by. I opened the vice as far as it would go, placed the shotgun between the heavy metal plates and clamped it as tightly as I could. The hacksaw cut easily, surprisingly easily, through the barrels, but I was still sweating by the time they clanked noisily onto the stone floor.

The stock was a lot harder. I tried to remember the shape of the gun Iwanek had used but he'd moved so quickly once the shooting had started that I'd barely caught a glimpse of it. I decided to try to cut it into the general shape of a pistol grip and I scratched into the walnut with a rusty six-inch nail I'd found on the bench, marking out the lines where I would use the wood saw. I had three of four goes but it still didn't look right. Eventually I attacked it with the saw, hoping that once I'd got started the shape would become obvious, like a sculptor chiselling away at a block of stone, allowing the material to define its own form rather than having one imposed on it.

It took half an hour of solid sawing to take off the bottom eight inches of the stock, the wood was hard and compact, more like metal than the product of a tree and I'd really worked up a sweat by the time I had finished. I used the hacksaw to cut the remaining bit of the stock into something approaching a grip but it was very uneven and wouldn't sit in my hand. The balance was completely gone and it was going to need both hands and a lot of concentration to fire accurately, but I planned to follow Iwanek's advice and get in close so maybe that wasn't too important.

It was starting to cloud over and I could hardly see what I was doing inside the shed so I picked up what was left of the shotgun and the sandpaper and went back to the study.

I sat in my father's captain's chair in front of the desk and rubbed and sanded the grip until it was smooth and slid into my hand and my finger could reach the trigger without straining. I loaded two cartridges into the breech and went into the garden again carrying a thick blanket from one of the spare bedrooms, down the crazy paving path to the stable building.

It wasn't overlooked; behind the boundary wall was a field of yellow oil-seed rape and in this part of the country a shotgun going off at dusk wouldn't worry anybody, local farmers were forever taking potshots at rooks and rabbits. The stable wall furthest away from the house was bare brick with no windows or doors, and I hung the blanket over it by tying two of the corners to the old rusting guttering.

I stood about twelve feet away and let go with both barrels, one at a time, the shot ripping through the blanket, shredding and tearing it and kicking up puffs of brick dust from the wall. At that distance the shot spread out in a seven-foot wide circle, much wider than a standard shotgun but that's why the barrels are normally so long, to focus the energy and the destructive power. Shorten the barrel and the range is drastically reduced, but close up that didn't matter and judging by the state of the blanket there wouldn't be much left of the target from twelve feet away.

The gun had kicked in my hands and pulled to the left when the first barrel exploded, but when I fired the second I was ready for it and steered the gun round, held it steady and firm and hit the already tattered blanket dead centre.

Back in the study I cleaned and polished the Purdey, much as my father used to, carefully, lovingly, but above all efficiently. When I had finished I tried to fit it into my brown, metal-framed leather briefcase, a present from Shona, but it was too narrow and the lid wouldn't close.

Then I remembered my father's old briefcase, a black plastic one, scuffed and grubby with a thick plastic handle with indentations for the fingers. The reason he'd always used it was that it was a good five inches deep and held twice as much paperwork as any other case he'd ever had.

I found it in the cloakroom under the stairs and by its weight it was obviously full of papers. It was locked with two gilt combination locks at either end, the gilt finish long since worn away. The numbers were my father's birthday, 611, and my mother's, 129, and I tipped out the papers onto the floor, took the empty case through into the study and heaved it onto the desk. The gun fitted diagonally, plenty of space above and below and at least an inch and a half to spare at either end.

I took the shotgun out and untied the rolled up piece of foam rubber which was about half as big again as the case but about the right thickness. All I needed was a pair of scissors or a sharp knife to cut a hole for the gun, and I found the former in one of the drawers under the kitchen sink and I hacked and cut the foam rubber so that it fitted tightly around the gun with a couple of gaps where my fingers could grip the barrel and the butt and pull it out smoothly.

It was six-thirty pm and I spent a full thirty minutes practising walking with the case, swinging it onto the desk in one fluid motion, then flicking the locks open, lifting the lid and bringing the gun out.

I did it again and again, until the actions felt right and I could get the shotgun into my hands while looking perfectly calm and relaxed, until I could do the whole operation blindfold, doing it all by touch while my eyes looked straight ahead. I did it with my eyes closed, I recited poetry with a fixed grin on my face and eventually it came naturally, one moment I was placing the case on the desk, the next the gun was in my hands,

cocked and ready to fire. Bang, bang, you're dead.
Maybe.

The call came at seven, exactly as promised, and it was
a girl. At first I thought it was Sammy, and half a
sentence had passed before what she was saying
registered and I realized the voice was slightly softer
and younger than Sammy's and that it came with a
warm, Irish brogue.

It was a voice J. Walter Thompson could have used to
sell Guinness, Irish whiskey, or holidays in tinkers'
caravans, a voice that was mellow and sweet, that you
felt was ready to break into an infectious laugh and
tease you and scold you.

"... but I suppose there was no way you wouldn't be
there, now was there? You have the money with you?"
There was a slight intake of breath as she asked the
question, a startled gasp as if she'd just been kissed
unexpectedly on the cheek.

"I have it here," I said. "I want to speak to Sammy."

"Well now, you'll just have to be wanting, for a while
at least. They're quite safe, and they'll stay that way as
long as you do as you're told, and you are going to do
as you're told, aren't you?" A pause. "Aren't you?"

"Yes. Don't hurt them. Please."

"Do you have a pen and paper? I'll say this once, and
only once. Drive from Edinburgh, across the Forth
Bridge to Perth and from there take the A9 to
Pitlochry, exactly as if you were going to Shankland
Hall to see your darling brother.

"This time, though, you'll continue along the A9 for another forty-five miles or so until you reach Kingussie. Then you'll leave the A9 and take the B9152 to Kincraig, on the northern shore of Loch Inch.

"Go through Kincraig and drive for exactly 2.4 miles from the last streetlight in the town. Then you'll see a signpost on the right for Inshriach Distillery, down a single track road. The distillery has been shut down so we won't be disturbed.

"Follow the track to the end, you'll pass a terrace of cottages on the right, and then you'll come to the carpark in front of the distillery building. It's E-shaped and on the left you'll see a large black door. Immediately to the right of it are metal steps leading to another door on the first floor. You'll be met there.

"Now, I want to make one thing clear to you. You will be watched, and if we should for one minute think you are trying to double-cross us again your lady friend and your brother will be dead. If you don't come alone they're dead. If you don't have the money with you they're dead. The drive will take you four hours if you're lucky, four and a half if you're not. If you are not here by midnight then they're dead. And once they are dead we'll come for you. I suggest you hurry."

Then the line was dead, and the message was all the more chilling coming from such a provocatively sexy voice. In the bookcase behind the desk was a leather-bound atlas and I turned the pages until I came across a large-scale map of the Scottish Highlands. The distillery would be close to the River Spey and by the look of the map it was in the middle of nowhere which

215

is why they had chosen it. To the west was Loch Ness and south west was Loch Ericht. To the east were the Cairngorm Mountains and the whole area around the distillery seemed to be thickly wooded so there'd be no problems if they had to make a run for it. But at least it would be dark when I arrived, and tonight the weather forecast was cloudy and there wouldn't be much in the way of a moon.

Four hours sounded about right for the drive so I sat for a while, head in my hands and elbows on either side of the atlas, thinking harder than I had ever thought before because this time it was my life that depended on the decisions I made now. My life and Sammy's and David's.

Fight your own battles, Tony had said. How? With a gun I'd fired twice? Against professional killers? My conscience was in cold storage now because I had already accepted that this time it was going to be my finger on the trigger. The luxury of getting somebody else to do the killing, of removing myself mentally and physically from the end result, was something I couldn't afford now.

As I studied the map and tried to put together a workable plan I felt no guilt for what had happened or for what was about to happen. That would come later, and I'd try to deal with it then. For the moment the part of my brain that solved problems and worked out strategies was insulated from the part that decided morality and apportioned blame. Friends and enemies were just pieces on a chessboard, taking part in a game I had to win.

There were three points in my favour. They were professionals dealing with an amateur, which meant there would be an element of surprise on my side. They wouldn't expect me to be armed, but I would have a shotgun and I was prepared to use it. And it would be dark. They were my strong suits and however I played it I'd have to maximize those advantages.

In the kitchen I found a pile of large, black plastic bags and a ball of thick string. In the stable building I dug out an old inflatable dinghy in which my father had taken me fishing before the pain in his back became too much to bear. It had been deflated and carefully packed into a green nylon bag with rope handles, and I loaded that onto the back seat of the car along with a foot pump and two plastic oars.

All I needed now was something heavy, and under a trellis table I discovered four long rusty chains made up of half-inch diameter steel links. Each was about fifteen feet long and I could only lift them one at a time into the boot and the car sagged on its back axle. A helicopter buzzed over the distant fields like an angry wasp as I slammed the boot lid shut.

Back in the house I raced up the stairs three at a time and rushed through my wardrobe, picking out the darkest pullover and trousers I could find, and choosing a pair of dark brown walking shoes. In the cloakroom I grabbed a green Barbour jacket and hurtled through the front door as a tall figure in a fawn raincoat came around the side of the house. I fumbled for the locks on the briefcase, cursing loudly, as the man broke into a run, coat flapping against his legs as his feet crunched into the gravel.

"Whoa, sport, it's me," shouted Tony, and for the first time I heard the high-pitched whirring whine of a grounded helicopter as the blades came to rest. I'd been so caught up with my own thoughts that I hadn't noticed it land in the field behind Stonehaven.

"Thanks for dropping in, Tony," I said, trying to clear my head. He still wasn't smiling, and neither was I. What the hell did he want? I thought, but I already knew the answer. I didn't offer to shake his hand, this wasn't a social visit.

"Who's the chauffeur?" I asked.

"A friend. A good friend and somebody who's done me a great many favours in the past. I didn't like having to ask him again. And be careful what you say, you're skating on very thin ice at the moment. His name is Joel Riker. He learnt to fly in Vietnam, Hueys, H-23 Hilliers and Chinooks, but now he can fly anything with a rotor blade. That's a Sikorsky we picked up at Edinburgh. I'd cut out the cracks about him being a chauffeur, too. A year before the war ended he was flying a gunship near Pleiku in South Vietnam when he was shot down. The gunner was killed and Joel and his co-pilot were on their own for six days. They had to fight their way through thirty miles of Viet Cong infested jungle before they were picked up. Between them they killed sixteen VC, most of them with their knives."

Over Tony's shoulder I could see Riker climbing down from the white helicopter and walking towards

218

us, head bowed under the slowly-turning blades. He was tall, thin and wiry, three inches of wrist sticking out of the sleeves of a tatty old sheepskin flying jacket, a gaunt face topped with a shock of prematurely grey hair.

"How do you know they weren't exaggerating?" I asked. "These Yanks are all the same."

"They came back with sixteen sets of ears," said Tony quietly, and there wasn't a lot I could say after that.

I shook Riker's outstretched hand, his grip was soft and gentle, the handshake of a dowager duchess. His voice, too, was effeminate, a nasal, slightly out of breath purr. He sounded a bit like Bambi.

"What's the game plan?" he asked Tony.

"Give me a chance, Joel. I haven't even found out what the rules are yet. Come on, inside."

"Tony, I don't have time. I have to go. Now."

"You're not going anywhere, sport. Inside."

The two of them bundled me back through the front door, along the hall and into the study.

"Sit," said Tony, and as I opened my mouth to speak he placed a finger across my lips. "Be silent."

Riker leant against the desk, legs crossed at the ankles, arms folded across his chest as Tony paced slowly up and down in front of me, thoughtfully chewing the inside of his cheek.

"I rang up Shona from London and got the number of David's nursing home. So I know he's missing. And Sammy's disappeared, too. And you raced up here like a dog with its tail on fire. I want to know where they are and what you plan to do. Come on, Rover, give."

I gave. I had no choice, I didn't have the time to mess Tony about, and even if I ran out on him all they would have to do was to follow in the helicopter. I gave. Where, when and how. The lot. When I had finished Tony looked at Riker and raised his eyebrows.

"It could work," said Riker, answering Tony's unspoken question.

"There's no alternative," I said. "I have to go in alone. They'll be watching me."

"I agree," Riker said to Tony. "If we had enough time and manpower, then we'd stand a chance of storming the place, but as it is . . ." He dropped his hands to his sides, palms out. "I think we should let him do it."

"OK," nodded Tony. "You're the expert." He turned to me, rocking gently back on his heels. "We're coming with you."

"No," I said, and stood up. "I have to go alone. Haven't you been listening?"

"You will be going alone," he said patiently. "We'll take the high road."

"They'll hear you coming for miles in that thing."

"Give me credit, sport. Have you got a map of the area?"

I pointed towards the atlas on the desk behind Riker. Tony picked it up and stood with the pilot as he ran his finger across the page.

Riker spoke quietly. "It'll be dark so we won't be seen, but the noise will carry for at least two miles, possibly three even if I come in low. Let's say three and a half to be on the safe side. Here." He jabbed at the map. "Then we move through the woods on foot. That

220

could take two hours, say two and a half at most if we don't get lost. We can do it. But we'll have to leave soon. Like now."

"Me too," I said, but they weren't listening to me.

"Fuel?" asked Tony.

"Enough."

"Anything else?"

"Artillery," said Riker, and I realized that they had also flown up from London and passed through the metal detectors. I unlocked the gun cabinet and pulled open the doors like a magician producing a rabbit from a hat.

"Gentlemen," I said. "Choose your weapons."

Riker took the Winchester and Tony chose one of the Berettas. I handed out cartridges and felt better, I felt part of it.

"OK?" Tony asked Riker.

"Sure. Let's do it."

"Now listen to me, sport," Tony said to me, laying his hand on my shoulder. "Do exactly what you planned to do. We won't make a move until you go inside and we hear shooting. Just forget we're around."

"We have to go," Riker interrupted, checking his watch.

"Right," said Tony, looking at me long and hard. "One more thing. Laing still hasn't surfaced, which could mean he's dead, or on the run, or that he's behind the killings. Be careful."

Then they turned and I followed them into the evening gloom and watched as they walked down the side of the house, vaulted cleanly over the dry stone wall and waded through the yellow flowers to the helicopter. I locked the front door and pocketed the keys.

It was 7.45 p.m. when I slid into the driving seat of the Cavalier, next to the attache case and the Harrods carrier bag, and pulled out of the drive and pointed the car towards the Forth Bridge as the helicopter clattered into the air.

About ten months before all this had started, before I'd even heard of Kyle and Laing, I had helped one of the few remaining independent whisky firms in Scotland raise cash through a rights issue, and I'd been their guest at a weekend "fact-finding exercise" visiting distilleries in and around Moray and sampling large quantities of the amber fluid.

The tours of the distilleries had been very much like a school trip, lectures by serious-faced men with ruddy complexions and tweed jackets who had been in the industry all their working lives and for whom whisky really was Uisge Beatha, the water of life.

I remembered very little about the individual distilleries because they all looked basically the same, but a few facts had stuck in my mind like midges to flypaper.

Each year, Scotch whisky earns more than £700 million in markets all around the world. A bottle of Scotch is drunk every tenth of a second in the United States, a bottle a second in Venezuela, a bottle every seven seconds in Norway and a bottle every twenty seconds in the Philippines or Malaya or somewhere, and it all comes from about 130 distilleries in Scotland, each making a whisky with its own distinctive taste. Perhaps the weekend whisky binge hadn't been a complete waste of time, after all. It was only when I began to pull the facts out of my memory that I appreciated just how much I had learnt about the industry.

Most of the whisky they make goes for blending, producing brands like Bell's or Famous Grouse, but some are just bottled as single whiskies, malt or grain. Blends account for about ninety-eight per cent of sales and it can take up to fifty individual malt and grain whiskies to make one blend.

At each distillery someone in the party had asked: "But what gives Scotch its flavour? Where does the taste come from?" The question would always be greeted with a knowing smile and a load of Highland waffle about that being one of the great mysteries of distilling, and if everyone knew the secret then the Japanese would be able to produce the real thing instead of the paint stripper they mixed with imported malt to make something that a true Scot wouldn't dream of allowing past his lips.

The most honest answer we had been given came from the export director of the host company, a tall, thin greying man with a bushy handlebar moustache who wore the kilt for the whole trip but who was never out of a dark pinstripe suit when in the firm's Edinburgh head office. The simple answer, he said, is that we just don't know.

One of the folk laws surrounding Malaysia's national drink is that it's the old stills that produce the spirit's flavour and bouquet, and that when new stills are needed the old ones are faithfully copied, knocks, bashes, dents and all. There seems to be an element of truth in that, all the tweed jackets agreed, but research scientists with PhDs can drink the stuff all night and still not decide why that is. Or why cheaper whiskies result in harsher hangovers than a good single malt.

What they can tell you is that whisky, when it has been distilled, is a mixture of ethanol and a host of other minor constituents, essential oils from the malted barley and other cereals and chemicals from the peat, which do depend on the type of still, its shape and even the way it's operated.

Going over in my mind the way whisky is made triggered off memories of the four or five distilleries we'd visited and I tried to picture their layout. All were sited near streams or rivers or pools and most were well away from towns and cities. That meant the men and women who worked there were supplied with cottages, usually in terraces close to the distillery with pretty gardens front and back.

The girl on the phone said the distillery had been abandoned, so the cottages would be empty. Mothballed distilleries are pretty common in Scotland now as gin, vodka and white rum become more popular, and their design and isolation means the buildings aren't good for anything other than whisky production. The big whisky firms just close them down and move the

224

workers out, sometimes keeping a token staff on a care and maintenance basis.

One of the distilleries we went to had its own malting room where the barley was screened and soaked in huge tanks of water called steeps, before being poured into revolving mechanical maltings about three times the height of a man where the barley germinates and the starch turns into sugar.

Then it's dried in a peat-fired kiln, the air thick with smoke, before being ground up to form grist. Most distilleries miss out this stage, though, preferring to have the malt delivered from a central malting firm — it's more economical and means they always have a regular supply. If Inshriach had one, the chances were it would be on the ground floor or in a separate building.

The handover of the cash was going to take place on the first floor which meant it would be in one of three places, the mashing room, the fermentation room or the stillhouse.

The floors in all three would be of thick wire mesh running the whole length of the building with steel staircases climbing up and down to link the various levels.

The mashing room is where the grist is mixed with hot water in large metal barrels with gleaming domed copper lids about twenty feet across. Much of the mash tuns is below floor level with about six to eight feet sticking through, and inspection hatches set into the lids along with temperature sensors. The wort, the thick sugary liquid, is drawn off from the tuns and the crud that's left is sold for cattle food. "Which is why the

Highland coo always has a wee smile on its face," we were told on four separate occasions. The whisky might vary from distillery to distillery but the jokes remain the same.

The wort is cooled and pumped into even bigger vessels, fermentation vats, this time made of wood and holding up to 45,000 litres. Yeast is thrown in and this converts the sugar into crude alcohol.

The fermentation rooms always smelled like breweries, the air heavy and sweet as the wort bubbled and frothed. "One chap fell in and took four hours to drown. He wouldn't have lasted so long if he hadn't had to get out and go to the toilet twice." That one we heard three times.

Again, the bulk of the fermentation vats is below floor level. About twelve feet in diameter, they would come up to a man's stomach, and unlike the mash tuns the lids are flat and made of wooden sections which can be removed one by one.

There could be as many as a dozen vats in the fermentation room. A good place to hide, and to fight.

Somewhere close to the fermentation vats would be the stills, tall copper cones, rounded and bulbous at the bottom like an onion and stretching up to five, six, maybe seven times the height of a man, thinning out until just a few feet thick and then bending over so that the evaporating alcohol pours off and down towards the spirit safe, where the still-man can check the quality and proof of the whisky without being able to touch it.

There would be at least two stills, probably more, larger wash stills for the first distillation and smaller

226

spirit stills for the second time around. The spirit that's eventually sold in shops and pubs and bars is the middle cut of the second distillation, but even that is barely drinkable until it's been allowed to mature for several years under lock and key and the watchful eye of HM Customs and Excise.

The casks would be stored in long, narrow, bonded warehouses, probably wooden with pitched roofs and likely to be found at the side of the distillery. If the distillery was in mothballs then chances were the warehouses would be empty too, except for the smell of maturing spirit and whisky-soaked wood, but they'd be kept secure and without windows so that's where David and Sammy could be kept out of the way. Maybe.

Thinking of the two of them added a good fifteen mph to the speed of the Cavalier, but I didn't ease back because Tony and Riker had delayed me and the roads were good as I passed through Perth and headed for Pitlochry.

It was starting to rain and I switched on the windscreen wipers and turned up the heater, then turned it down again as I realized I couldn't be cold because my palms on the steering wheel were sweating.

It was dark by the time I reached Kingussie following the route Sammy, David and I had taken to visit the Highland Wildlife Park. God, it seemed a lifetime ago. I turned into the B9152, driving to Kincraig parallel to the shore of Loch Inch. The Cavalier headlights carved out tunnels of light through the blackness, the road speckled with raindrops, the windscreen wipers whirring quietly. The effect was almost hypnotic and twice I braked too late and too hard when an insomniac sheep wandered in front of the car.

The inhabitants of Kincraig were all indoors out of the rain when I passed through the town, and it had been more than an hour since I'd seen another car on the road. I felt like the last man alive, the only occupant of a dead world, a ghost planet. When I crossed the last streetlight, plunging into the dark and leaving the glow of the town behind me, I pressed the trip counter on the speedometer and watched it count off the tenth-mile segments as the road twisted and turned through the hillside.

I saw the signpost just before it clicked up 2.4. It leant to the right, the wood was cracked and gnarled and the lettering was obscured by green moss, but I could just make out the "Insh" of "Inshriach" and I pulled the wheel round sharply to the right and drove into the woods.

The track was just wide enough for one vehicle with passing places every hundred yards or so. It was rutted and potholed and the car bucked and swayed as it bounced from hole to hole.

The soaking tree trunks glistened under the headlights, branches whipping to and fro in the wind. The windscreen wipers began to clog up with fallen leaves, and the car skidded as I followed the track to the right and guided the car uneasily alongside a line of stone terraced cottages, gardens overgrown behind white picket fences, windows blank like the eyes of a blind man, washing lines bare, rainwater cascading over blocked gutters. On the downstairs window sill of the middle house sat a brown and white cat, its eyes glowing brightly, tail twitching as it turned to watch the Cavalier go past.

The track opened up into a large tarmac carpark in front of the distillery itself, a two-storey whitewashed building, E-shaped with the three prongs of the E pointing towards the cottages. On the left of the building was a white Ford Sierra and I parked by the side of it, three yards away from the black door the girl had described. I switched the lights off and allowed my eyes time to get used to the watery moonlight which faded and flickered as rain clouds passed overhead, then stepped out of the warmth of the car with the briefcase.

My footsteps echoed around the courtyard as I climbed the metal steps. At the top I wiped my soaking hands on the Barbour jacket and seized the brass door handle.

The door opened easily and silently and I crossed the threshold into the mashing room, moonlight reflecting off the copper-topped tuns.

Down the left-hand side of the whitewashed stone wall were a series of small, circular windows, five times the width of a ship's portholes. Through them I could see clouds passing over the dulled stars in the night sky and then the moon was blotted out and I was in complete darkness.

At the far end of the room was an oddly-squeezed goal-post of light, and as my eyes became accustomed to the dark I could see it was a closed door with light shining through from whatever lay beyond. Then the moon reappeared from behind a cloud like a scolded child putting its head around a door and I moved across the room, the thick wire mesh floor rattling under my feet with each step, briefcase handle gripped firmly in my right hand, left hand forward to open the red-painted wooden door in front of me.

I felt like a latecomer to a party as the door opened and I stepped into the light, blinking. All conversation, if there had been any, stopped and everyone was looking at me as if I'd arrived at a black tie reception dressed in a blazer and slacks. But this wasn't a party and there was no smiling host to step forward and cover my embarrassment and offer to introduce me to everybody.

The light came from a battery-powered lantern which was hanging from one of the steel girders that criss-crossed the high roof above the fermentation vessels. There were no windows in the fermentation room and the lamp suggested that all power had been cut off to the mothballed distillery.

I could see four people in the room, spread among a dozen wooden circular tubs which came up to just above stomach height, ranged in three lines of four, two lines close to the walls and the third running down the middle. With the red door behind me I was standing in a corridor between the central line of four vats and the right-hand batch.

At the end of the room and to the left were David and Sammy, David sitting with his back to one of the vats with his legs pulled up against his chest, Sammy

230

standing by his side, ruffling his hair. David beamed as he saw me and tried to get up, but Sammy crouched down beside him and whispered into his ear. He settled back down but watched me carefully with wide eyes. I smiled and waved with my free hand.

"It's all right, David, you'll soon be home," I said loudly, still walking, now passing the first vat, the hand holding the briefcase clamped tightly shut, eyes taking in as much as I could.

The girl was standing six feet to the right of David and Sammy, in the space between the left and centre lines of vats. She was about five feet two with close-cropped red hair and an elfin face with a crop of freckles around her pert nose. In thigh-length boots and green jerkin she could have passed for Peter Pan, but she was wearing a green waterproof anorak zipped up to the neck and blue jeans and in her right hand hanging by her side was a large black handgun.

She took a cigarette from her lips with her left hand, dropped it to the ground and moved to stamp it out, but it fell through the wire mesh in a shower of sparks to the room below. "Well now, just in time," she said, glancing at her wristwatch. "And with the money, too." Hers was the voice on the phone.

She smiled and turned to her partner, tall, thin with a mane of black curly hair and a long, hooked nose. He was standing at the end of the corridor I was walking along, but slightly to the right so that the lower part of his body was obscured by the last wooden vat in the right-hand line.

He was wearing a similar anorak, but his was open to the waist showing a white crew-necked pullover underneath and he had on grey herringbone trousers instead of jeans. They both wore blue and grey training shoes and could have passed for students hitching around Europe, if they'd had a couple of rucksacks and if they hadn't both been carrying guns.

His was black and seemed bigger than hers and from sixty feet away it looked like a revolver, but the lamp was tied with a piece of wire to the girder which crossed the room directly over their heads so it shone straight down on them, and it was hard to judge exactly what they had in their hands other than to see quite clearly that his was pointing at my stomach.

The door clicked shut behind me and I whirled round in a panic because I'd left it open. Ronnie Laing was there, leaning against the wall, arm across the door, a lazy smile on his suntanned face, every strand of his blond hair in place, blue eyes watching my every move with cold amusement.

He wasn't carrying a gun, with two professional killers on tap he didn't need one. He rubbed his long tapered hands together, smoothing them like a concert pianist about to play to a packed Albert Hall. The smile grew wider.

"So glad you could make it," he said softly, the spider to the fly. "I was almost hoping you wouldn't come and I'd be able to play with Sammy." The eyes behind the green-framed glasses blazed with evil intent and I knew full well that unless I came out on top he would get to play with her and that she'd die screaming while he stood over her, smiling his lazy smile.

I was surrounded, but two had guns and one didn't so it was no contest. Laing would have to wait.

I turned my back on him and began walking again. I swung the case slowly backwards and forwards in time with my feet and started talking, not concerned with the words or the sense, just trying to keep their minds off the case and what it contained and my mind off what was going to happen and what could happen if it all went wrong. Mouth in overdrive, brain on auto-pilot, I was back in my father's study in front of his desk, reciting poetry.

"The money's all here," I said, and I was surprised at how steady my voice was. My throat was dry and my tongue felt twice its normal size and I couldn't swallow. "Just keep calm," I said. "There's no need for anybody to get hurt."

The girl smiled at that and she moved to the right, away from David and Sammy, and stood behind the penultimate vat in the middle line about six paces away from her partner who moved to his right and stood in the corridor facing me.

She raised her gun in both hands and pointed it at my chest and my skin crawled as I saw that she was still smiling, eyes flashing like a flirtatious teenager.

Now I'd passed the second vessel and the third was only three steps away, left, right, left and then I was swinging the briefcase up in a relaxed, fluid motion across my body and onto the wooden lid of the vat in front of me.

The man's gun was pointing down towards the floor and I hadn't seen him take off the safety catch but that didn't mean anything because the chances were it was already cocked and ready to fire. They'd both moved forward and their faces were in shadow, the lamp shining behind them giving them halos around their hair like two wayward angels.

The case came down on the lid with a dull reverberating thud and I saw Sammy jump. She stayed low beside David and put her arms protectively around his shoulder, hugging him to her. Our eyes met and instinctively I realized that she knew exactly what was going to happen next. She half smiled, a brief flash of her perfect teeth, and she nervously reached up to brush a strand of loose hair away from her face. As my hands moved towards the case she shifted her body, putting herself between David and the two killers, watching me over her shoulder, muscles tensed, a cat ready to spring.

I could feel Laing's eyes boring into my back and I fought the urge to turn and look at him. If I did I knew for sure that I'd be lost. The man and the girl were moving again, she walked round to the right and into the corridor next to him, he then shuffled across to give her room and the bottom half of his body was once more hidden by the last vat in the right-hand line.

I wanted to scream at them, to tell them to stand where they were. Stay calm. Stay cool.

"I suppose you'll want to count it but I'd be grateful if you'd get a move on because I want to get David home as soon as possible," I said, as my hands moved to operate the locks on the case. I'd already set the combinations and the locks flew open as I pushed the gilt buttons either side, the two clicks sounding like one.

The girl's gun was still aimed at my chest, the man's down at the ground. They turned to smile at each other as I raised the lid.

"You've no idea the problems I had getting the money together at such short notice," I said. "I almost didn't make it. And you didn't give me nearly enough time to drive up from Edinburgh, the roads can be vile at this time of night . . ."

I was talking too much but it didn't matter any more because the shotgun was in my hands and I stepped away from the open case. In one movement Sammy pushed David sideways onto the wire mesh floor and threw herself on top of him, using herself as a shield, a tigress protecting her young. But David wasn't her offspring, he was my brother, and she was still risking her life to keep him out of harm's way. Whatever happened I promised myself I'd never let Sammy down again, no way would I ever disregard the loyalty she'd shown, a loyalty I knew I didn't deserve. I held onto that one thought, blocking all else from my mind.

The girl turned first, her eyes opened wide and her mouth formed a perfect circle of surprise as she fought to unscramble the messages from her retina.

The man saw the look of confusion on her face and he stepped forward towards her and then began to turn. Her gun was pointing at my groin but she made no move to pull the trigger, and she frowned in confusion like a little girl trying to remember her nine times table and then I fired.

The shot ripped through her anorak and jeans the way it had shredded the blanket tied against the outbuilding back at Stonehaven, and the green and blue of her clothing was stained with red as she lurched backwards and slammed into the wooden vat behind her, mouth still open, face untouched because I'd aimed low. Behind me I heard Laing curse and scrabble for the door handle. I ignored him, he wasn't armed.

The gun dropped from the girl's fingers and rattled onto the metal floor and she groaned and pitched forward with her hands clutching her bloodstained stomach.

I turned the shotgun towards her partner but I knew I wouldn't make it because his gun was already levelled at my chest and the finger was tightening on the trigger and I still had to move through ninety degrees to stand a chance of hitting him, so I angled it upwards instead and fired at the lamp above his head.

The two bangs were simultaneous and the lamp went out. I heard it shatter and the pieces slam against the roof as the bullet from his gun caught me in the chest, lifted me off my feet and threw me backwards down the corridor. I hit the floor shoulders first and then my head crashed back and I felt it open and bleed, but the pain was nowhere as bad as the crippling numbness in my chest. The door behind me opened and closed as Laing fled the scene, footsteps clattering and echoing.

I could breathe only in short, halting gasps, like an engine starved of petrol, shuddering and juddering. My

236

ribs felt as if they'd been hit with a sledgehammer and at least two were cracked or broken, but I was lucky that he'd gone for the chest and not tried a head shot or hit me in the legs because then the lightweight bulletproof vest that Tony had given me at Heathrow wouldn't have saved my life, and I'd be lying bleeding to death on the floor like the girl and not inching backwards to rest against one of the empty oak vats and groping around to find the shotgun in the blackness.

David started screaming and then his piercing yell was muffled as Sammy put her hand over his mouth and comforted him. "Are you all right?" she called. "My God, are you all right?" But I couldn't answer, I was still recovering my breath and, anyway, to have replied would have given away my position — horizontal, hurt and, for the moment at least, helpless. Sammy didn't call out again, though I could hear her whispering softly to David.

Somewhere in front of me the man moved, slowly and carefully because he was as blind as I was in the pitch-dark room, but he was fit and healthy while I was lying winded on the floor and feeling as if an elephant had sat on my chest. And he had a gun in his hand.

He had seen where I'd fallen so all he had to do was to inch forward in the dark until he found me and then it would be over. I managed to pull myself sideways, dragging myself to one side and out of his way but stopped when he heard me moving, and then there was a flash and a bang about fifteen feet from me and a bullet tore a chunk out of the vat to my right so he knew I wasn't dead, but at the very least he must have thought I was in a bad way because he'd seen the first bullet slam into my chest.

A second shot hit the floor and the bullet screeched off the metal and ricocheted into the blackness. Then there was only silence and I tried to steady my breathing because in my ears it sounded like a steam engine puffing and blowing, and I could hear my heart pounding but there was nothing I could do about that.

I screwed up my eyes and then opened them wide but it made no difference, the darkness was absolute, no light at all in the room. Then my eyes started to play tricks and I saw greenish circles and spots of red which twisted and rolled, and white whirlpools swirling above my head as my information-starved brain produced its own signals to make up for the lack of stimulation from the optic nerves.

He moved again and this time he was creeping sideways, to my right, but I wasn't used to relying solely on my ears so I couldn't tell if he was ten feet away or twenty as the perspiration dripped down the back of my arms like blood from an open wound.

I reached into the pocket of the Barbour jacket and pulled out Tony's second going away present. They smelled of rubber as I pulled them over my eyes and pressed the ridged button on the right-hand side. The light intensifiers flickered once and then I could see again, the goggles picking out details of the room and its contents in a greenish-grey hue.

They came from a consignment Tony was in the process of selling to a West African state. Manufactured by Ferranti, powered by a small nickel-cadmium

238

battery, they were the perfect issue for infantry fighting at night.

Worn like a pair of ski goggles, they didn't have to be fixed to a rifle like the Nato night sight, and they allowed soldiers to move easily in the darkness with their hands free to shoot and fight.

From where I was sitting I couldn't see Sammy or David but the man was there, about fifteen feet away to the right, facing in my direction and creeping stealthily towards me, right arm holding his gun at waist height and his left waving in front of his chest.

He was pushing one foot forward, slowly, feeling along the metal floor so that as soon as he touched my body he'd know where to pump in the bullets. He stopped moving his left foot, transferred his weight over and then began moving his right. Two feet ahead of him was my shotgun and he was heading straight for it.

Reaching for it was out of the question, I could barely breathe never mind crawl to the gun before his probing feet found it, and once I had started moving he'd have a good idea where I was, and it wouldn't take more than a few random shots in my direction to hit me and this time I might not be so lucky.

My ribs felt on fire as I took a lungful of air and spoke. "You're standing two feet to the right of a vat, your right foot is forward and you're holding your left hand out in front of your body. Unless you drop your gun I'm going to blow your balls off."

Immediately the words left my mouth I rolled over twice, wincing with the pain as I got out of his line of fire.

He stopped dead in his tracks and in the grey-green image intensifiers he looked like a zombie with his arms outstretched, his mouth open so that he could breathe shallowly with the minimum of noise and his eyes wide and staring, trying to pick out any details in the dark and wondering how it was that I could see him when he couldn't make out his own hand in front of his face.

He pointed the gun at where I'd been lying and then what I had said sunk in and he dived to his left, thudding into the vat and falling to the floor where he scampered off in a panic on all fours towards the wall.

He disappeared from view but I heard another dull thud as he collided with something in his rush to get away. I managed to crawl to the shotgun on hands and knees, the metal mesh biting into my skin. I knelt with the gun between my thighs as I fumbled for a couple of fresh cartridges from my pocket, and as I slotted them into the breech I saw the man again, this time standing upright in the far corner of the fermentation room, face towards the wall with his arms outstretched, palms touching the whitewashed bricks. He was moving quickly crabwise, legs moving together and then apart, like a rock climber traversing a cliff face. He was heading for a door at the end of the corridor I was in, the twin of the entrance I'd come through from the mashing room.

He reached for the handle with searching fingers as I brought up the shotgun, still kneeling, but he tore open the door just before I pulled the trigger and moonlight flooded in and the goggles went opaque. I fired anyway, but when I ripped off the goggles the door was open and a cloud of white powder was billowing down from the pockmarked wall above it.

I staggered to my feet and lumbered to the door, the goggles bouncing around my neck, bending double because of the pain but also to keep myself as small a target as possible. I peered around the door frame and saw a row of four stills, copper gleaming in the moonlight. At the far end of the stillhouse long, thin windows stretched from the ceiling to the floor below as if in a church, and they rattled eerily as the wind outside buffeted and pushed and threw squalls of rain against them.

A shot cracked through the air, whistled past my ear and into the roof behind me and I pulled back my head. Footsteps clanged as he ran down metal steps to the ground floor and then it was quiet again.

Still bent double I went over to Sammy and David, crouched together on the floor, David crying and Sammy holding him in her arms, whispering gently into his ear, kissing away the tears. I knelt beside them and stroked the base of David's neck.

"Stay here," I whispered. "Whatever happens, stay here."

Sammy seemed too shocked to speak and she just nodded dumbly and carried on petting David. Neither of them was dressed for a night in an unheated Highland distillery. David was wearing old brown cord trousers and an American baseball jacket I'd brought back as a present from a business trip to Baltimore last year. Sammy wore a light-weight blue linen trouser suit, and they were both shivering.

I took off my jacket and put it round her shoulders, but it didn't stop her trembling because it was fear and anger that were making her muscles shake and spasm, not the cold.

The girl's gun was lying three feet in front of her and the butt was dotted with blood. She was moaning softly, almost purring like a contented cat. There was a dripping sound, plop, plop, plop, like water from a tap, but it wasn't water it was blood running through the metal grille and onto the concrete floor below.

I didn't feel sorry for her and I didn't move to help her, because she'd been the only one smoking and that meant it had been her who tortured Carol and it had been her that Carol had begged to stop. But she hadn't stopped and Carol had died in her bath, burnt and bleeding.

I picked up the gun, wiped off the congealed blood and handed it to Sammy, who looked at it as if I'd given her a dead mouse. I checked the safety catch was off and that there was a bullet in the chamber as the gun trembled in her elegant hand. It looked out of place, like an air raid shelter in a pretty country garden. Would she use it? Probably not, but it made me feel a little easier knowing it was there.

"I'm going to shut the door again and then I'm going outside," I said to her. "No matter what happens, stay here. It'll be pitch dark so don't move around. Do you understand?"

She nodded and hugged David tightly, her eyes wide and afraid and fixed on the girl's body.

242

"Listen to me, Sammy," I said, and she looked up and forced a half smile.

"If that door opens when I'm gone, fire the gun." I pointed to the doorway leading to the stillhouse. "It won't be me, I'll come back the way I leave, through the door at the end," and I gestured towards the door where I had walked in only minutes before, swinging the briefcase and telling everybody to keep calm.

"And make sure it's me. Laing's still around. Do you understand?"

"Yes," she answered, her voice dull and flat, but at least she was looking at me when she said it and not through me. I kissed her on the forehead, and as I ducked back to the door I heard her say "Take care."

I fired the shotgun's second barrel through the doorway then slammed the door shut, plunging the room into darkness once more. After pulling the goggles back over my eyes I ran to the opposite end of the fermentation room, the way Laing had gone, through the door and to the top of the stairs at the entrance to the mashing room, footsteps ringing on the metal floor.

The clouds were thicker now and they completely covered the moon so I kept the goggles on as I took the stairs two at a time, reloading as I went.

I was so busy looking out for Laing that I lost my footing on the wet metal at the bottom and pitched forward, going down on one knee and cursing, but the noise wasn't a problem because I wanted them both to know I was coming.

The courtyard was deserted save for the two cars, no sign of Laing or of Tony or Riker. Maybe they'd had mechanical trouble, or maybe it was just taking longer than they had planned to get through the dense forest. Whatever the reason for them not showing up, I was alone. It was to be one against two but one of them was a professional and well used to killing and I was an amateur, fighting because I was hurt and angry and in a corner. Place your bets, gentlemen. Evens the hired killer from Ireland, thirty-three to one the corporate financier from Edinburgh.

"Where are you, Tony, now that I need you?" I asked of no-one in particular. But the plan from the start had been to end this myself and it was too late to call time now.

At least if I did fail then there was still a chance that Tony and Riker would arrive to clear up the mess and save Sammy and David, the cavalry arriving in the final reel, in time to save the day but too late to rescue the hero.

The door at the base of the staircase was locked so I moved back and fired at the wood just below the lock. It splintered and cracked and some of the shot ricocheted off the brass fittings, but the door sagged on its hinges and the second explosion knocked it back completely, throwing it through the doorway and onto the concrete beyond.

My ears roared with the echo of the shots as I went back up the steps, quietly, on tiptoe, but moving quickly, free hand on the rail so that this time I wouldn't trip and give my position away.

244

I waited until I reached the top before reloading, and then stepped inside the mashing room and silently closed the door. I tiptoed between the stainless steel mashing vessels, grey-green in the goggles, and stood in the middle of the room, shallow breathing, completely still, shotgun pointing down.

I started counting in my head, slowly ticking off the seconds, more to calm my breathing and racing pulse than to keep track of time.

The floor below was clearly visible in the image intensifiers, the metal grille acting as a veil, and after a short while I could forget it was there, moving my head from side to side to keep the whole of the concrete area in vision.

A block of weak moonlight fell on the floor in front of the shattered oak door and my heart stopped as something moved, but it was coming from the wrong direction and it was furry with four legs, the brown and white cat come to investigate the noise and see if there were any rats or mice poking around for stray malt pellets.

It stood stock still in the moonlit square, tail twitching as it sniffed the peaty air, and then it gently lifted its head upwards and stared straight at me through the grille. Fifty-five, fifty-six, fifty-seven, and then there was the rasp of a shoe against concrete and the cat turned and ran in one movement, back into the night.

He was down in a crouch, about thirty feet from the fallen door where I would be silhouetted against the moonlight and he'd get a clear shot. He licked his lower lip, and if he'd had a tail he would have twitched it. Ninety-three, ninety-four and he was moving again, still crouched, into the centre of the room below.

It must have been a storage area at some time but now it was bare and he was as unprotected as a beetle on a Formica kitchen top. He took the gun in both hands, steadied his feet shoulder-width apart and held the weapon out in front of him like a cop in an American TV movie.

He was five feet to my right and I didn't want to risk firing the shotgun at an angle, but if I moved he was bound to hear me so I stayed where I was and counted, one hundred and ten, one hundred and eleven.

Something clattered in the courtyard outside, probably the cat but he thought it was me and he tensed, moved two steps to the left to get a clearer view and then he was right underneath my feet.

I pressed the open barrels of the Purdey against the metal grille and fired, the gun kicking in my hands as the shot funnelled through the gaps. The floor rattled and shook and the top of his head disappeared in a shower of crimson, a scarlet rain that blew across the concrete.

He stayed upright, the gun still levelled at the doorway, one hundred and twenty-five, one hundred and twenty-six, and then the arms started to rise upward, pointing to the ceiling above his bloodsoaked head which turned up to reveal a pulpy mess where the face had been, strips of flesh hanging down over the chin and the lips, what was left of them, drawn back in a grimace of a smile. His eyes, untouched by the shot,

246

were white circles in the red and they looked into mine as the arms moved higher, one hundred and thirty-three, one hundred and thirty-four, and they went right over his bloody head and he fell back onto the concrete like a sack of malt tumbling from a conveyor belt, a lifeless thud followed by a ringing echo as the gun rolled along the floor.

One hundred and fifty-nine, one hundred and sixty, I couldn't stop counting, my brain fixed on the numbers so that it wouldn't have to dwell on the man twelve feet below me, eyes wide open and staring as his legs and arms twitched, nervous spasms because there wasn't enough brain intact for conscious movements.

He had stopped moving by the time I reached one hundred and eighty, only three minutes since I'd waited for him to investigate the wrecked door. I went back down the steps and stood over the body, kicking it gently, just in case, but it wasn't necessary. I didn't have to hold a mirror against his mouth or check for a pulse because the sightless eyes showed that he was dead.

I knelt by the corpse and went through the pockets of the anorak, loose change, a cigarette lighter (so maybe he was a smoker too and maybe he was the one who'd used the lighted cigarettes), a box of cartridges and the keys to the Sierra. There was no wallet, no driving licence, no identification, but that was to be expected. They were professionals, and professionals don't wear labels.

As I took the keys I heard a footfall in the doorway behind me and I swivelled around still in a crouch, ready to fire the shotgun with one hand which would have snapped my wrist like a damp Twiglet if the hammers hadn't clunked down on two empty chambers.

"What a fucking pity," said Laing, and this time he did have a gun in his hand. "What a fucking pity," he repeated.

I stayed down, hunched low but ready to dive to one side, left or right, like a goalkeeper preparing himself for a penalty. One chance, sudden death. Please God let him shoot me in the chest.

"They were going to kill me," he said. "They'd already killed Alan and that bastard of a mercenary you used to double-cross them, and then they came after me." He shook his head slowly from side to side. "You almost made it. You were that close." He held up his left hand, index finger and thumb an inch apart.

"Do you want to know why they didn't kill me?" he asked. I nodded. Keep him talking, pray that Tony and Riker would get here.

"A postcard," he said, grinning boyishly. "A fucking postcard that I'd sent to Alan, care of his office. All it said was 'Having a time here. Wish you were lovely', but it was posted in Paris and the date showed when I was there. That postcard and that stupid joke saved my life. But it was too late to save Alan. They found it in his office after they killed him."

He was toying with the revolver, slowly scratching the barrel along his cheek. I tensed, ready to leap.

"I like the idea of the bulletproof vest," he said. "But it won't work again. The next one goes right through your fucking head."

248

I relaxed, sagging down onto the concrete floor, cradling the useless shotgun, beaten.

"Sammy told me why you did it, you know. She told me everything before we killed Carol. They let me help, they wanted me to help, to involve me, I suppose. But I'm going to have Sammy to myself. Completely and utterly to myself. Shall I tell you what I'm going to do to her?" And he did, carefully and precisely, missing out none of the details, while tears of rage, of shame, of frustration, of pure helplessness, welled up in my eyes because there was nothing, absolutely nothing I could do now. I'd lost the edge. I'd lost control. I'd lost.

"You must have really loved your old man to go through all this," he said thoughtfully. "I didn't exactly shed a tear when my dad shuffled off this mortal coil. Mind you, he didn't top himself."

"I'm going to kill you," I whispered.

"You're not, you know," he said, and levelled the gun at my head. "I'm afraid it's going to be the other way around. Give my regards to your parents."

Time stopped. You know how it is when they show the film of the assassination of President Kennedy, the black and white grainy frames played in slow motion, his head whipping forward and backward and then forward again, so you can't tell how many shots there were, or where they came from, whether the only shots came from Oswald in the Dallas book warehouse or if there was someone else to the side or behind the motorcade, firing at the same time. You can't tell, no matter how many times you see the film, and no matter how often I reran Laing's death in my head I still couldn't get it right, I couldn't work out if his head erupted first or if his chest turned red and wet, whether there were two shots or three, whether he fell forward towards me or just crumpled in a heap. I didn't even hear the shots. He was dead, that was all that mattered, and I was splattered with his blood.

Then I heard Bambi say "Easy, son," and I saw Riker and Tony in silhouette, guns at the ready.

"Jesus, where have you been?" I asked, struggling to my feet and breaking the shotgun, ejecting the spent cartridges.

Riker stepped over Laing, walked past me and then looked down at the body of the man I'd shot. He surveyed the metal grille above our heads. "Nice shot," he said approvingly. "Very nice."

For some reason his approval made me swell with pride, praise from a pro, so I bit back the remark I was going to make about it being no wonder America had lost the war in Vietnam if that was an example of their time-keeping. I was starting to get cocky, and it was overconfidence that killed the cat as my grandmother used to tell me. Sweet old lady, but she could never get her proverbs straight. If the cat fits, wear it, was another of hers. It was years before I found out what that one meant. My mind was wandering, I suppose shock and panic does that, so I fought to steady my thoughts, concentrate on the job.

"What kept you?" I asked Tony, and he shrugged. I noticed then that his raincoat was dirty and torn and that his trousers and shoes were covered in mud. His face was criss-crossed with scratches, several still bleeding. It couldn't have been a picnic clawing their way through thick woods at night.

"Forget it," I said. "I'm just glad you're here." Riker, too, looked abashed as he joined us in the doorway.

"What's the position?" he asked, shouldering his shotgun.

"I've killed two of them," I said. "The other's upstairs." For some reason I added "She's a girl" but there was no reaction. "Sammy's upstairs with David. Could you get them away, now? Not back to Stonehaven, to Shona's parents, maybe. Stonehaven's in a bit of a mess," I finished lamely.

"Sure," said Tony. "What are you going to do?"

"I'll clear up here and join you later."

"We'll help," said Riker.

"No, it's my mess. I'll clean it up. There's no point in all of us taking any more risks. I want to see this through to the end. And it won't be over until the bodies are buried." I handed him the keys to the Sierra. "Where's the helicopter?" I asked.

"In a clearing about three miles away," said Riker.

"That's a point," interrupted Tony. "What are we going to do about the chopper?"

"Leave it where it is tonight," said Riker. "There's no way I'm going through those woods again. I'll come back to Edinburgh with you and then pick it up tomorrow. Assuming I can find it." He smiled. "Hey, what would I tell the guys we hired it from? 'Sorry guys, I've lost your Sikorsky somewhere in the Highlands.' Do you think we'll lose the deposit?"

Tony slapped him on the back and together we walked up the steps to the first floor. When we got to the door of the fermentation room I held up my hand, motioning them to wait.

I banged on the door hard and shouted, "It's me, Sammy. It's OK. I'm coming in." But I needn't have bothered because when I knelt beside the two of them the gun was lying by her side and both her arms were around David.

Riker and I walked David through the mashing room and down the steps after Tony and Sammy, and together we eased him into the rear of the Sierra. There was an old tartan blanket in the back and Riker tucked it around David, for warmth and for comfort.

"He'll be OK," he said. "By the look of him he's been drugged, Librium or Valium, something to keep him calm and sedated. I don't think he'll remember much of what's happened." He sat next to him and closed the door.

"They made him take some white tablets soon after we picked him up at Shankland Hall," Sammy said as she got into the front passenger seat.

"What about you?" I asked as I bent down to get level with her.

"They didn't give me anything, but it might have been better if they had. I've seen a lot of things tonight that I'd sooner forget."

"Did Laing hurt you?"

"No, but I saw what he did to Carol and he took great delight in telling me what he planned to do." She started to cry, softly.

252

"I'm sorry."

"Hey lover, it's not your fault, I don't blame you." She reached out and gently punched me under the chin. "The man had to do what the man had to do," she said, echoing Tony's words. She smiled. My heart fell every time she gave me one of her forced smiles, and this was one of them.

"Bullshit," I said.

She leant forward and kissed me on the lips, her long red hair brushing against my cheek. "I understand," she said. "That's why I wanted to help." Then she smiled and this time my heart didn't fall.

She reached for my right hand and played with my fingers. "I don't think the girl's dead, she was still moaning," she said. She shuddered and then slipped the Barbour off her shoulders. "Here, you'll catch cold," and dropped it over my arm before closing the door.

I walked over to David's side of the car as Tony switched on the engine and flooded the courtyard with light.

I wiped his tearstained moon face with my handkerchief through the open window until I realized I was smearing him with blood. He didn't notice and tried to touch my cheek. He looked like a Red Indian covered with warpaint.

"All for one?" he said in a halting voice.

"And one for all," I finished, and ruffled his untidy, greasy hair. "You're going home with Sammy and Tony. They're going to take you to see Shona. Be good." Tears started to brim in his eyes so I quickly added: "I won't be long, I promise. I've just got a few things to do here. I'll see you soon."

Riker leant across and wound the window up and I stood back and waved them off. As the sound of the Sierra faded into the distance my eyes grew used to the darkness once more, and with the quarter moon reappearing from behind a cloud and the stars starting to twinkle in the sky again, I didn't need the goggles to find my way back up the stairs to the first floor.

The girl had stopped moaning, but as I rolled her onto her back the eyes flickered open and her tongue gently moistened her lips through small white teeth.

Enough light came in through the open door to illuminate her torn apart chest and legs. Rivulets of blood were collecting in the folds of the tattered nylon anorak, she was bleeding from so many places that there was nothing I could do to stem the flow. Plop, plop, plop.

"I'm cold," she whispered. I put the jacket around her and gently stroked her hair.

"I'm so cold," she said in a voice that was scarcely more than a whimper. I knelt next to her and took her hand.

"Can you hear me?" I asked, and squeezed. It was the hand of a small, frightened child and it went with the voice. Her eyes opened again, halfway at first and then fully, a slight smile on her lips.

"Of course I can hear you, boy," she said, and shivered as if someone had walked over her grave.

"What's your name, love?" I asked.

"Maggie." Her eyes closed again.

254

"Listen to me, Maggie. Listen carefully. You're dying, Maggie, and there's not a thing I can do about it. You've lost a lot of blood and there's no way I can get an ambulance out here, we're hours from anywhere even if I could get to a phone. I can't move you. Do you understand? There's nothing I can do."

Her grip tightened, and then relaxed. "And what's the good news, doctor?" she whispered.

Her chest had stopped rising and falling but she wasn't dead, not yet.

"Can you hear me still?" I said, lips close to her ear, and she squeezed again. "There's something I have to know, Maggie. Does anyone else know about me? Did the two of you report back to Ireland or were you working alone? I have to know."

Her eyes opened again, the pupils wide and black in a circle of pale green. "James," she said. "Where's James? Where's James?"

"He's dead, Maggie. I'm sorry. Listen to me, Maggie, please. Does anyone else know about me? Is anyone else going to be coming after me?"

She began shivering again, tremors running right along her body. I put my free hand on her forehead and she was cool to the touch.

"Maggie, I must know. Not just for me but for my family, too. And my friends. Are we safe?"

"You're safe," she whispered at last. "You're safe, boy. We were to get in touch only when the job was finished." She coughed and blood trickled down one side of her pretty mouth, bright red against the whiteness of her skin.

"Oh, James," she moaned softly. "James." Then her grip tightened, so hard that her nails bit into my flesh. "Don't leave me, not yet," she said urgently. "Stay with me. Please stay with me." I was back at Shankland Hall saying goodbye to David, frightened of being left on his own, needing to be with someone who loved him.

"It's OK, Maggie. I'm not going anywhere," I said gently. She lay quietly until another spasm of coughing wracked her body and she sighed, a long moan that came from somewhere deep within her.

She lay still with her eyes closed and I thought she was dead. When she spoke again, even though it was just a faint purr, she startled me. "You'll be hearing my confession?" she asked, and I held her in my arms, listening and forgiving until she died.

I lifted her easily and carried her down to the Cavalier, laying her down on the tarmac as I opened the boot and wrapped her in two of the black plastic bags, sealing them with tape, winding it around and around like a child doing up a Christmas present.

She was easier to handle when completely covered. I didn't have to look at the tousled red hair, the pert nose or the blood on her lips, she became just a parcel to be disposed of, not a pretty young girl that I'd killed with a shotgun. Out of sight, out of mind.

Laing was surprisingly light and I tossed him into the boot with Maggie, sheathed in plastic. James was heavier but I was still able to carry him draped over one shoulder after I'd put the bags round him. I lowered him onto the front seat, clipped the belt across him and closed the passenger door before going back for the shotgun, lying where I'd left it, next to a pool of his blood.

The water would have been cut off as well as the electricity, so I just left the blood to soak into the concrete. Besides, there was no way I could repair the damaged door or collect all the spent cartridges and bullets from around the distillery so I'd have to leave it, another mystery to lie unsolved on the files of the Highland police. That and the Loch Ness monster.

I put the goggles on and thoroughly checked all the rooms, looking for anything I might have left that could point to my having been there. Not that I thought I had dropped something incriminating because I'd left all identification back at the house. It was my conscience getting to work already, niggling and probing like a tongue worrying a loose filling. You won't get away with it, you've done wrong and you'll get caught, you'll pay for this. My father telling me that it didn't matter what I'd done so long as I told the truth.

I gave the area around the car a going over, too. It was all clear but it didn't make me worry any less. I was about to slip on the Barbour jacket I'd taken from Maggie's body until I noticed the blood on the lining, so I threw it into the boot with the shotgun on top of the two bodies. God help me if I was stopped by the police tonight, three bodies, a sawn-off shotgun and a bloodstained jacket. Calling that circumstantial would be on a par with claiming that Hitler had a bit of a temper.

I pulled away from the distillery, lights raking the terraced cottages as I headed for the tunnel of trees.

The cat was back on its perch, head turning to watch me drive away, as the plastic wrapped body strapped into the passenger seat bobbed back and forth each time the car hit a pothole.

I thought of driving with the lights off and using the image intensifiers but decided against it. With the headlights switched on any oncoming traffic would be dazzled and unable to see inside the Cavalier, but at this time of night the roads would almost certainly be deserted anyway.

The car felt leaden, weighed down as it was by four occupants and the inflatable dingy, and I kept it at a steady forty-five mph as I followed the A9 over the River Spey and back towards Pitlochry. I left the main road after passing the village of Etteridge and drove along a little-used track to Dalwhinnie, close to the northern tip of Loch Ericht, sticking to the route I'd planned earlier in the evening in my father's study after Maggie's phone call.

Shown on the map as a thin line linking the A9 with the A889, it was a short cut across the bleak Glen Truim, barely wide enough for two vehicles in places, wires strung between EEC-funded fence posts to keep sheep from wandering in front of what little traffic there was.

When I reached the sleepy granite village of Dalwhinnie I turned the Cavalier right onto an even narrower track which wound along the northern shore of the loch through the thickly-wooded Loch Ericht forest. On the map it appeared as a dotted line which petered out after Benalder Lodge, but I'd no intention of going that far.

Two miles down the track I stopped the car and switched off the engine, listening to it crackle and clunk as it cooled in the frosty night air. The tree tops whipped to and fro as the wind tried to pluck them from the black, gritty soil, and I shivered as I opened the car door but I still couldn't bring myself to wear the jacket.

There was no convenient gate as there had been at Loch Feochan when McKinley and I had driven down to the shore with Read, but the track was less than fifty feet from the water's edge so I reckoned I'd be able to carry everything without too much trouble.

I took Laing first. He seemed to have got heavier and I had to manhandle him out of the boot and drag him through the fence and half roll, half pull him over the rough grass and heather. James was next and I dragged him, too. Maggie I carried, carefully, tenderly, head against my chest as if I were taking her over the threshold, and I put her down gently where the water lapped on the ribbon of stony beach.

The chains and inflatable boat I dropped over the wire fence and then I drove the car half a mile back down the track towards Dalwhinnie, just to be on the safe side, in case a passing poacher got curious or a courting couple decided to drive along for a lovemaking session in the woods. Both were unlikely in the extreme, logically I knew that, but the maggots of unease and guilt were already gnawing away at my mind and the inner voice that was my conscience was telling me that I wouldn't get away with it, that somebody would catch me, somehow, somewhere.

I walked back in the darkness, jacket in one hand and shotgun in the other. My heart missed a couple of beats when I thought I'd gone too far but then I saw a hump in the grass by the fence. It was the boat in its bag, and I stepped through the wires and pulled it, and the chains, down to the lochside.

Clouds passed over the moon but they were thin and wispy, no heavier than a veil across a bride's face, so I didn't need the goggles as I unpacked the canvas bag, tipped out the deflated boat and unwrapped it on the beach. I connected up the plastic foot pump and it took four or five minutes to inflate the boat, my legs ached and I was breathing heavily by the time it lay on the stones, rocking in the wind. The plastic oars were each in two halves and I screwed them together and pushed them through the rowlocks.

I pulled the boat half into the water and weighed it down with one of the lengths of chain while I hauled the parcel that was Laing along the beach and heaved it in, knocking one of the oars out as the inflatable distorted and bent with the added weight. I pushed it into deeper water and climbed in, my legs soaking from the struggle.

I rowed slowly but powerfully through the choppy water until I was about a hundred yards from the shore. Making certain the oars were secure, I tied the chain around the body and rolled it over the side. It cut cleanly through the water and disappeared without a sound leaving the inflatable bouncing up and down, freed of its heavy load. A few seconds later a small stream of bubbles trickled to the surface and then they too were gone.

The journey back to the shore was easier than the hard slog out, but the wind pushed me to one side and rather than exhaust myself pulling against it I went along with it, beached the boat some fifty yards further along from my setting off point and carried it back to where Maggie and James lay side by side.

By now the adrenaline was flowing and the pain in my ribs had been replaced by a dull ache so I dragged James to the boat with little difficulty.

The black plastic around his feet tore on the rocky beach as his shoes scraped along the ground, and as I pulled him through the shallow water one fell off and I had to go back for it. I pitched him into the boat and then ran back for the chain that would hold him on the bottom of the loch until he rotted.

Water flooded into the inflatable as I pulled myself in and lay for a few moments gasping for breath, my head resting on his stomach, before I rowed out into the middle of the loch for the second time and pushed him overboard.

Back on the shore, I carried Maggie in my arms and placed her in the boat as it bucked and rolled in the water like a floundering porpoise. The chain, and the shotgun I'd used to kill her, I put by her side.

I thought of her confession as I rowed out into the loch for the third and final time, of the things she'd done in her short life, the people she'd killed and the way she'd killed them.

She had killed for money, she'd killed for her beliefs and she'd killed for information. There had been no regrets during her confession, just a baring of her tarnished soul before she went to meet her Maker. She'd died without apologizing and with the name James on her lips.

I sat with her as the boat drifted in the wind, oars at rest. I wanted to tell her I was sorry, that I would turn time back if I could, that I was sorry that she'd died, sorry I'd killed her, that revenge wasn't sweet, it was poisonous and bitter, a taste not to be savoured and enjoyed but to be spat out in disgust.

I needed to tell her what I'd done, to bare my soul the way she had to me before she died. So I spoke to Maggie for the best part of an hour as we tossed in the loch, in a quiet voice that she couldn't have heard even if she'd been alive, the wind taking my words and dispersing them over the water like dead leaves scattering down from autumn trees. I didn't feel any better, I didn't feel any easier. I'd confessed, but confessions to the dead don't count.

After wrapping the chain around her and tying the bloodstained jacket to her legs I tried to drop her over the side as close to James as possible, but there were no reference points to guide me and it was impossible to judge distances in the dark. Still, I tried. It was important, to me if not to them.

With a grunt I rolled her over into the loch, but unlike James and Laing she floated, spinning slowly in the dark water until I prodded and pushed with one of the oars and the air trapped in the bags belched out and she sank slowly beneath the waves.

As the black shrouded parcel went under I remembered her pale green eyes, her pert nose and her mischievous smile. Then I blotted her out of my mind though I knew she would surface eventually, like a corpse rising from a hastily-dug shallow grave.

Now I was alone in the boat except for the sawn-off shotgun. I picked it up by the shortened barrels and caressed it, the metal ice-cold but the polished wood smooth and warm to the touch.

"I'm sorry, Dad," I said. "It wasn't worth it."

I threw it high and far, and as it spun through the air the breech opened and the gun formed a "v" like an unwieldly boomerang. It bounced along the water with a splash of spray and then was gone.

My brain registered movement at the periphery of my vision and I turned to watch a hunting owl swoop down and land in a clump of heather, wings outstretched and talons open.

Then, with a flurry and a flapping it was up again, climbing into the night sky and crossing the moon as it flew silently over my head towards the far side of the loch. In its claws a brown fieldmouse twitched once and was still. I gripped the oars tightly and pulled for the shore.

Also available in ISIS Large Print:

The Chinaman

Stephen Leather

In the top rank of thriller writers   **Jack Higgins**

The Chinaman understood death.

Jungle-skilled, silent and lethal, he had killed for the Viet Cong and then for the Americans. He had watched helplessly whilst his two eldest daughters had been raped and killed by Thai pirates. But all that was behind him. Quiet, hard-working and unassuming, he was building up his South London take-away business. Until the day his wife and youngest daughter were murdered by an IRA bomb in a Knightsbridge department store. Then, simply but persistently, he began to ask the authorities who were the men responsible; what was being done — and was turned away, fobbed off, treated as a nuisance. Which was when the Chinaman, denied justice, decided on revenge . . . and went back to war.

ISBN 978-0-7531-7792-1 (hb)
ISBN 978-0-7531-7793-8 (pb)

Hungry Ghost

Stephen Leather

Geoff Howells, a government-trained killing machine, is brought out of retirement and sent to Hong Kong. His brief: to assassinate Chinese Mafia leader, Simon Ng. Howells devises a dangerous and complicated plan to reach his intended victim — only to find himself the next target . . .

Patrick Dugan, a Hong Kong policeman, has been held back in his career because of his connections — his sister is married to Simon Ng. But when Ng's daughter is kidnapped and Ng himself disappears, Dugan gets caught up in a series of violent events and an international spying intrigue that has run out of control . . .

ISBN 978-0-7531-7790-7 (hb)
ISBN 978-0-7531-7791-4 (pb)